Never Go Home Again

Also by **SHANNON HOLMES**

B-More Careful

Bad Girlz

Shannon **HOLMES**

Never Go Home Again

ATRIA BOOKS
New York London Toronto Sydney

1230 Avenue of the Americas
New York, NY 10020

This book is a work of fiction. Names, characters, places, and incidents are products of the author's imagination or are used fictitiously. Any resemblance to actual events or locales or persons, living or dead, is entirely coincidental.

For information address Atria Books, 1230 Avenue of the Americas, New York, NY 10020

ISBN: 0-7434-8783-4

First Atria Books hardcover edition December 2004

3 5 7 9 10 8 6 4 2

ATRIA BOOKS is a trademark of Simon & Schuster, Inc.

Manufactured in the United States of America

For information regarding special discounts for bulk purchases, please contact Simon & Schuster Special Sales at 1-800-456-6798 or business@simonandschuster.com

Never Go Home Again

Word from the Author

My novels show life and death as they play out on the streets of urban America. But it was never (nor will it ever be) my intention to have my novels become guidebooks on lawlessness. If I chose to, I could be more detailed about the ways and means for the crimes I describe. But I pick and choose what I want to say and am deliberate in how vague I am about how things get done. I simply paint my characters into a corner with words and show how they react. Besides, I've turned too many people on to "hustles" in the past when I was doing dirt. Now that I've been blessed to become a successfully published author and my words are received by the masses, I have been given the power to communicate with the people, to have my voice heard and influence people's thoughts and opinions (sometimes even move them in ways that I've never before imagined). With that said, I feel a greater sense of responsibility, not only to myself, but to God and my readers. Many people pursue writing as a career, but few are chosen. I was blessed with a gift to chronicle the street life, what I've seen, done, heard, and learned. I truly feel that I didn't choose the publishing game, the game chose me.

While I was in prison, often I prayed to God, but I never once prayed for money, fame, or power. I prayed for success! In whatever form God deemed me worthy of. For me, success meant getting out of the drug game and once again being around my family. For me, success meant not having to look over my shoulder in fear of the law or some up-and-coming young thug. God granted me that, helping me find myself while I was incarcerated. He showed me just what my greater talent was and blessed me to become an author. I never once asked for it!

Writing came to me at the loneliest time of my life, while I was in prison, during those long, repetitive days and cold nights locked in a cell. At times it gave me a direction when my mind wandered aimlessly. It gave me hope for the future.

I came into this publishing game with blind expectations, with arms open to embrace whatever happened, and to embrace my fellow authors—until I saw how they really were. With the exception of a select few, they're not as cute or friendly as they appear to be on the back of their book covers. I got into this game misunderstanding how things were supposed to play out. I thought everyone, for example, was supposed to love me. After all, here I was, this kid from the streets who was committing genocide by selling crack to my own people, and now I had gotten myself together and changed what I was doing from destructive to constructive. I thought the responses to that would be positive. But what often came was negativity. Envious eyes cast their gaze upon me. Jealousy reared its evil head. I learned that the literary world is no different than, for example, the music industry. Both are filled with cutthroat people. I discovered something else: when a million people love you, a couple hundred thousand will hate you. Most times for no good reason at all.

People in the literary world have said, "He didn't pay his dues," "He's an overnight success," etc. Well, I beg to differ. I've worked hard for what I got in this business. I spend countless hours alone crafting my novels. I don't know of any author who's ever been shot at for selling books. I lived the life I tell about. I've lost many things, such as my innocence, and more than that, time, things I can never regain. And to me I'm not a flash in the pan.

A good friend of mine once said, "Shannon, you waited all your life to become a writer." I didn't take his comment too well at first, because the majority of my life I didn't know what I wanted to become. Neither did I know who I was or what I was doing. "No, I didn't wait all my life to become an author!" I said. He replied, "That's not what I meant. I mean you used all your life experiences, your lifestyle, to become what you are today, a good author." Looking at it from that perspective, I agreed with him.

The experience and quality that I bring to my writing can't be bought, faked, or learned in school. It's called realness or authenticity. In other words, readers know I know what I know. I ain't faking it till I make it. I was in the streets seven days a week and three hundred sixty-five days a year. I'm not proud of it either, but I sold drugs in more cities and towns than most people have relatives. My eyes have witnessed a lot of what happens around sex, money, murder, and poverty. And now I'm just like the rap group the LOX: I'm Living Off Xperience.

Through my novels, I invite the readers to journey with me into the streets. Come see what I've seen; go where I went, in your mind, from the safety of your living room, bedroom, or office. If you have never been to Baltimore, Philadelphia, or whatever other urban community I choose to write about, let me take you there. Let me show the gritty and grimy undercarriage of society. The side that some in the working class don't acknowledge or aren't aware of. With my writing I try to dissuade those who are easily influenced by negativity, who believe all that glitters is gold. The day I stop presenting the "flip side of the game" is the day I ask God to not let me write another word. So know there is a method to my madness. And that I'm in the position I'm in for a reason.

In conclusion, I'd like to thank my fans, the book-buying public, who appreciate my efforts, and even those who don't.

And to my peers in the literary world: Whatever the rhyme or reason, it's not that serious. You are not going to heaven just 'cause you wrote a book. Writing is just your job, and hopefully a passion; something (if you are fortunate enough) that pays the bills. You should be grateful to have a job that you love. I know I am. I've said this before and I'll say it again a million more times: "Success doesn't make you anything, it exposes you to you. Who are you? And what are you?" These are the questions you need to look in the mirror and ask yourself. Ain't nothing special about me, so I know ain't nothing special about you. (You do not walk on water or cure lepers.)

If you want to know why or why I am who I am in this genre called hip-hop fiction, just remember this, in the immortal words of rapper artist 50 Cent: "It's not my plan, it's God's plan!"

The kid is truly blessed. Too blessed to be stressed!

IN THE SYSTEM

Chapter 1

Damn! Corey quietly cursed himself as he sat on the hard wooden holding-cell benches, awaiting his fate. As he stared off into space, his mind was in another world. Or at least he wished he were. Presently, he was confined to a trash-littered bull pen beneath the Bronx Supreme Court that strongly reeked of urine from an unflushed toilet in the back corner. Combine that with the musky mixture of body odor that still lingered from the countless prisoners that had passed through the bowels of the justice system this day and the stench was damn near unbearable.

Just a few short hours ago, this very bull pen had been bursting at the seams with blacks and Hispanics. Some were going to arraignments and preliminary hearings, while others were here for more serious matters, such as sentencing and bail-reduction hearings. Their crimes varied from shoplifting to murder. Corey watched closely with his face pressed between the thick steel bars as the court officers marched defendant after defendant into courtrooms, like cattle being led to the slaughterhouse. Silently he wished each and every man good luck, knowing that whatever their fortune or misfortune was, it could easily be his, when it was his turn to face the judge.

His hopes soared like an eagle whenever a man caught a break or got released. Then they'd plunge faster than the stock market whenever a man received what Corey perceived as a travesty of justice from the court. He was on a never-ending emotional roller-coaster ride.

Naive to the ways of the system, Corey would learn the hard way, over time, that it would take more than just luck or well-wishing for a minority to get a fair shake in any courtroom in America. Contrary to popular belief, the system of justice isn't blind; it sees very well the color of a man's skin. As morning slowly turned to afternoon, one by one the majority of the prisoners returned to the bull pen with all hopes of freedom dashed. Each man returned to the holding cell with his own personal horror story.

"Mmmaann, *them crackers is playin' hardball in dat courtroom!*" one black man said. "I came here for a bail reduction and dem bastards raised my bail. They gave me a ransom. Dat bitch-ass D.A. Miller told the judge that I was a habitual offender, a menace to society. Then they started talkin' 'bout dat three strikes shit . . ." His high-pitched voice bounced off the cell walls. This was center stage and he was holding court. He had the undivided attention of every prisoner in the cell. Every man wanted to know just exactly what he was up against.

The skinny black man continued, "All I did was pick a few

pockets and snatch a few chains on the train. I'm a smoker. I ain't kill nobody."

After Corey and a few other serious criminals heard the man's reason for his crime spree, they lost what little respect they had for him. He was just another crackhead—someone who was looked down upon in the criminal realm. At the bottom of the street food chain, he was nothing but a customer, a consumer—chasing a high—whereas Corey was a drug dealer—chasing a dollar. People like this man were messing the drug game up. A crackhead like him had gotten Corey into his current predicament.

"Hope y'all got paid lawyers, cuz dem faggot-ass public defenders ain't worth shit!" the man said with anger in his voice. "Mine just sat there looking stupid while the D.A. assinated my character." Then as quickly as he started running his mouth, volunteering information, he stopped and started begging. "Ay, yo, papi, lemme getta short on dat cigarette," he appealed to the old Hispanic man he was talking to, who never said a word, just handed him the cigarette butt that had been passed around and smoked by practically every man in the bull pen. But that didn't stop the man from wrapping his own lips around it. He wanted a pull on the cancer stick bad. He wanted to fill his lungs with some nicotine, to calm his nerves now that he realized he was going back to jail.

When other prisoners, from different cells, were shuttled past, those in the bull pen hollered loudly to find out how they had fared. "Yo, money, how you make out?" someone yelled out. Escorted by two sizable court officers, the man had a dejected look as he said, "Dat muthafucka Judge

Brown jus knocked me out da box. He gave me twenty-five ta life."

"Be strong, baby boy!" the man suggested. "Hold ya head. Go up north, hit the law library hard. And you'll be back in court on appeal."

Corey's heart began to pound against his chest at the mere mention of that kind of time. Judge Lawrence B. Brown was his judge too—Corey's judge, jury, and executioner. Under the youthful offender act, Corey had initially accepted a plea bargain for five years probation on the advice of his public defender. But he caught another drug charge while out on bail, and that blew the deal that he'd agreed to. He was now at the mercy of the court. And the court didn't have any mercy.

Trouble was nothing new for Corey. All through his turbulent adolescent years, he was running afoul of the law. Now at sixteen, all the dirt he'd done had finally caught up with him. He had succeeded in getting into major trouble. His sudden departure from home, subsequent arrests, and imminent jail time that hung over his head signaled his arrival into the big time. According to New York State law, he was an adult, though he was still very much a child. Nonetheless, he would be held accountable for his actions. He was moving closer and closer toward the self-destruction that his parents had predicted for him, if he kept doing what he was doing, living the street life.

Having already posted bond for one direct sale to an undercover cop, a few months later he was arrested on a humble possession with intent. His cab had been pulled over by police for a minor traffic violation and the vehicle searched. The police found four ounces of crack cocaine on him. The first arrest had been a blatant setup, retribution for some foolish act Corey had committed in the streets. He had lost his temper and made a stupid move that had caused his world to come crashing in. But when his man caught up with that crackhead Kelly, she'd regret the day she ever laid eyes on him. But today was Corey's Judgment Day. Hers would come soon enough, only it would be in the court of law. Her trial would be held in the streets.

After a late-afternoon court recess, all that remained on the docket was the sentencing of Corey and two other co-defendants in the next cell. All the other occupants of these various holding cells had been transported back to the Bronx House of Corrections, Rikers Island, or whatever other institution they'd been imprisoned at. The lucky ones were released on their own recognizance, ROR bail. Corey's stomach growled. He was hungry as hell but he was unable to eat. Something about going to court ruined his appetite. Plus, the state-issued carton of milk and slab of cheese between two stale pieces of bread, masquerading as a sandwich, that was provided for his lunch wasn't appealing. Something else was making him feel queasy, though. Maybe his body sensed what his mind couldn't comprehend, that something was wrong inside the halls of justice. Corey scanned the graffiti covering the walls, reading every legible message to help pass the time, trying to decipher them for some hidden meaning.

"Plead guilty!" someone had written.

"Rather be judged by twelve than carried by six."

Another sign read, "Next time hold court in the streets!"

Vulgar messages addressed to Judge Brown caused Corey to chuckle to himself. "Judge Brown can suck my big black dick. You racist son of a bitch!" "Judge Brown is givin' niggas 4ever and a day."

These degrading statements from the present and not so distant past were testimonials of the judge's abuse of power. These harsh sentiments were drawn with matches, ink pens, or whatever other instruments that would record them, by some of the many minority men who had stood before the judge. Their words of warning were recorded on the ceilings and every wall for posterity. For those who were about to enter the belly of the beast, it gave you fair warning to beware.

"Yo, shorty!" a deep-voiced man in the next cell called out, interrupting Corey's train of thought. "Yo, shorty!" he called again before Corey could respond.

"Yo, whut up?" Corey replied.

"Ay, yo, you got any stogies over there? A nigga need something ta smoke, bad!"

"Naw, money," Corey quickly answered. "I don't smoke." Corey fell silent again.

Next door, the two codefendants began talking in hushed tones. ". . . fuck that! I ain't goin' out like that," one man promised. "We gonna give 'em a reason ta give us all dat time. Know what I'm sayin'?"

"Word!" the other man strongly agreed. "Let's do this—"

Suddenly, the loud squeaky sound of the door that led to the courtroom ended the conversation. The footsteps of the court officers could be heard getting closer and closer. Soon they were upon them; walking past Corey's cell, they stopped in front of the next. As they passed, Corey's heart skipped a beat. For a second he thought, *This is it.* He was scared to death of that white man dressed in a black robe. The fear that he was experiencing was unlike any he'd ever known in his life.

"Damon Moore, Tashaun Griffin, the judge will see you now," the black court officer announced as he inserted the gigantic key into the lock, opening up the cell. Looking to avoid any potential problems, the court officer handled these two with kid gloves, careful not to rile them up. One glimpse at these two hulks and you'd know why.

At six foot three and six foot six respectively, each man weighed close to 250 pounds; they were huge. Just by the looks of their thickly muscled physiques that rippled through their T-shirts, one would have thought they were born with dumbbells in their hands. But in truth, these were two hardened criminals, who'd done time in some of the toughest jails in New York State. While incarcerated upstate, they ate and worked out like madmen, developing their physiques into that which would rival a professional bodybuilder's. Now this two-man crime wave was about to receive its punishment: two twenty-five-to-life sentences for their parts in a botched armed robbery turned double homicide—of a Jewish jeweler and his son, at their jewelry store on Fordham Road in the Bronx.

These codefendants were never going to walk the streets of New York City again. They were being sentenced to rot and die in jail. With an extensive record like theirs, neither would ever make parole, so they'd concocted a plan to strike a blow at the system, to go down in criminal folklore for decades to come.

"Step out of the cell and place both your hands behind your back," the court officer commanded.

Passively, the two giants obeyed the orders of their captors, not wanting to give any hint of their next move. Just fastening the handcuffs around their big wrists was a problem for the officers. But, once they were cuffed, they were led away to the courtroom. As they passed Corey's cell, one man nodded his head in his direction, as if to say, "What's up?" Corey nodded his head in response.

All eyes were on them as they entered the half-empty courtroom. A hush fell over the court employees and the small group of spectators present. The victims' family was seated in the front row, directly behind the prosecutor. The weeping widow and the jeweler's elderly father anxiously awaited justice.

Through his horn-rimmed spectacles, and from the safety of his ivory tower, the Honorable Judge Lawrence B. Brown looked down at these two monsters and called them to the bench. He eyeballed these two black codefendants, who had had the audacity to kill a white man, and his pale white face began to turn beet red with rage. Judge Brown, a racist, worked with a hang-'em-high attitude. But now instead of using rope to hang the black man, he used a more conventional method: he slowly strangled the life out of them with time. He used the judicial system better than any Klu Klux

Klansmen used his rope. This was just another tool, a legal form of lynching. It was okay to him when a nigger killed another nigger. When minorities committed genocide against their own race, they were doing the world a favor, in his mind. But the minute one of these black bastards, as he saw them, crossed the line and took the life of a white man, he was vexed.

Judge Brown was an undercover racist only because he couldn't be out in the open in this day and age. The rules of society had changed. He missed the good old days when you could call a nigger, a nigger. And, he was upset when New York State had abolished the death penalty. He had personally sentenced more blacks and Hispanics to the hard time than he cared to remember.

Rumors still swirled, like ghosts, around the courthouse whenever any minority came before him for trial or sentencing. He always threw the book at him, imposing the hardest sentences he could.

"Look out the window," he commanded one felon. "Count out loud the number of pigeons there are on the ledge." Having taken his own tally, he already had a rough estimate. Give or take the few that flew away or landed.

The man did as he was told. "One, two, three . . . eight," the man counted.

"That's how much time I hereby sentence you to, eight to sixteen years in a state correctional institution," the judge cold-bloodedly replied.

Dumbfounded, the man screamed, "Eight muthafuckin' years fa whut? I'm a fuckin' shoplifter, notta killer! I only stole to feed my family." That was all he managed to say before being dragged away by the court officers.

Another black convicted felon was told to do the same thing. He got slick and said, "There ain't no pigeon out there."

Not to be outdone, the judge had another trick up his sleeve. He wasn't about to let him get off the hook that easily. "Don't you see that small plot of soil where that tree is?" the judge asked.

Falling for the trick, the man answered, "Ain't no tree out there!"

The judge retorted, "There will be one when you get out! I here by sentence you to ten to twenty years."

"Your Honor, I can't do all dat time!" the despondent man told the judge.

"Well, give me what you can," the judge sarcastically remarked, making a mockery of the man.

That was a different time, a different era. Standing before him now were two more black men whom he planned to send to prison till their dying days.

Following courtroom procedure, the two codefendants were uncuffed before their sentence was pronounced. As they were freed from their restraints, they scanned the courtroom, sizing up the puny, undermanned staff of court officers, strategically positioned around the courtroom. And though they were outnumbered and outgunned, it didn't even matter. They were bold enough or stupid enough to believe their plan would work. A few feet away, at the prosecutor's table, the Bronx district attorney, J. Phillip Tyler, had a satisfied look. He had quickly secured a conviction for the state. This was an open-and-shut case. The jury had deliberated for less than an hour before returning a guilty verdict. This high-profile case would advance his career for sure. Not to mention all the brownie points it would earn him within the powerful Jewish community.

"Do either of you have anything to say before the court pronounces sentence on you?" the judge bellowed. This was his favorite part of sentencing. This was his chance to publicly humiliate the defendants.

"Yes, may I address the court?" Moore asked.

"Go right ahead," the judge replied.

Moore growled, "Fuck all y'all racist mutherfuckas!"

The two public defenders who represented each man looked at them in shock. Then they began to move away from the two stone-cold killers, fearing for their safety.

Griffin turned and spat at the victim's wife, "Fuck you, bitch!"

The court officers converged in a desperate attempt to subdue Griffin and Moore, who began knocking the officers out with powerful blows from their fists, shedding them like fleas.

The courtroom exploded in pure pandemonium; spectators began running for their lives. Judge Brown began to pound his gavel. "Order in the court! Order in the court!" he yelled repeatedly at the top of his lungs.

After demolishing every unarmed court officer within arm's reach, Moore spat out two sharp single-edge razors that were cleverly hidden underneath his tongue. Then he charged the prosecutor.

Everyone was caught off guard; help was slow in coming. It was Friday, the end of a long workweek and workday. Getting home to his or her family was on everyone's mind. After dealing with an overcrowded court docket all day, no one ever expected this. Following his partner's lead, Griffin flipped over the defense table and made a beeline for the bench. The court stenographer scurried to get out of the way as the giant rapidly approached.

This was a nightmare. The district attorney stood in disbelief. Horrified, he'd watched in slow motion as the razors had suddenly appeared, his mouth agape from pure terror.

Weakly, he threw up his right arm in self-defense to try to ward off the razor attack and succeeded in avoiding one potentially fatal slash, taking the blow on his forearm instead of his neck. But the D.A. wasn't strong enough or quick enough to dodge the second strike. This one found its mark: the most vital and vulnerable part of his body, the carotid artery. Blood began to gush out of the side of his neck, like water from an open fire hydrant, drenching him and his assailant. Despite the blood, Moore kept on pounding and slicing him, pummeling him to the floor—even after it was evident that he was dead.

Meanwhile, Griffin was scaling the witness stand in an all-out attempt to reach the judge. Using reflexes he hadn't seen in years, Judge Brown bolted out of his chair to the side door that led to the safety of his chambers and his gun. He slammed the door shut behind him. As Griffin advanced in his direction, court officers not immediately involved in the melee sprang into action. With guns drawn, they took aim at

Griffin. A hail of bullets stopped him in his tracks. The shots rang out with an earsplitting noise that drowned out all the cries and screams for help.

After killing his codefendant, the court officers turned their guns on the bloodthirsty Moore. His life was cut short by four bullets to the head and chest.

They died as they had lived, going all out together, taking the law into their own hands.

Chapter 2

In a remote prison in upstate New York, Corey sat inside a classroom where he worked as a teacher's aide, staring out a window lost in thought. He recalled all the madness he had witnessed or heard about since entering the penal system—years ago at the tender age of sixteen, such as the murderous rampage that had taken place on his sentencing day.

Despite the direction in which he gazed, his eyes weren't focused on the tall steel fence, the endless rows of concertina razor wire, or the armed prison guards in the watchtowers that were the last line of defense between him and his freedom. Corey's mind was on going home. He wanted his freedom so bad he could taste it. But it seemed as if the closer he moved toward his ultimate goal, the farther away home seemed and the longer his days became. He went back to marking off days on a calendar—something he hadn't done in years.

Time seemed to have slowed to a snail's pace as his anticipation and anxiety were steadily building. One of Corey's old heads, Tate, had warned him about days like this. "Just keep doin' what ya been doin'," he advised. "Don't break up ya bid now. It's too late in the game to start somethin' new."

As Corey's thoughts ran wild, Mr. Fisher, the elderly white schoolteacher, quietly walked up on him. Corey didn't hear him coming and didn't know he was there until Mr. Fisher placed his bony, liver-spotted white hand on Corey's broad shoulders. "Hey, son, whatcha doing? Daydreamin'?"

Startled, Corey tried hard not to show it. He simply turned toward Mr. Fisher and grinned. Mr. Fisher was one of the most genuinely nice people he'd ever met in or out of prison. He was white, but there wasn't a prejudiced bone in his body. He treated a man like a man, regardless of the color of his skin, and he bent over backward for Corey. After having seen Corey doodling, Mr. Fisher was convinced that he had talent and had encouraged him to practice and cultivate his gift of drawing. He helped to get art supplies into the prison for Corey.

Over time Corey drew big beautiful portraits and made homemade cards for the inmates' wives, girlfriends, kids, and other family members. Art became his hustle—a profitable one at that. His locker stayed full of cartons of cigarettes, bags of chips, cakes, and other commissary goodies. Anything a prisoner wanted or needed to live comfortably, he had. Caring people like Mr. Fisher within the Department of Corrections reaffirmed Corey's belief that not all white people were racists or devils. After Judge Brown had thrown the book at Corey, and after the years he had spent dealing with these hillbilly COs, he wasn't so sure.

"Yeah, Mr. Fisher," Corey replied, "I was out there on da streetz fa a minute. You know how it iz when somebody get short, right?"

After all those years of working for the Department of Corrections, being incarcerated eight hours a day, Mr. Fisher was down with all the jailhouse slang. He even incorporated some of it into his vocabulary. So he knew exactly what Corey was talking about. But one word was taboo for him or any other white person to use, and that was *nigger.* Mr. Fisher not only didn't use the word, but didn't take too kindly to that word being used in his presence. He thought black people were strange for using it. Their ancestors had fought long and hard, boycotting and picketing, just to get whites to treat them fairly, like equals and human beings. He couldn't imagine why the younger generation so casually tossed the N-word around as if it were nothing. He knew that they often used it as an affectionate greeting but didn't understand why. Dr. Martin Luther King and Malcolm X would probably roll over in their graves if they could hear the way these young blacks talked today. Corey was conscious enough not to use the N-word in the presence of Mr. Fisher or any other white person.

"Getting short, huh, Corey?" Mr. Fisher asked. "You know I'll be glad to see you go home. From the first day I laid eyes on you, I said to myself this kid doesn't belong here. With certain people it's obvious why they're in jail. But you, you were different. It was something about the way you carried yourself, your mannerisms. I could tell you had some good home training. You weren't the bad guy that your institutional record made you out to be. Maybe you just had a little difficulty adjusting to imprisonment. And rightfully so, this is an unnatural environment for any man. We weren't put on this earth to be caged like animals. See, Corey, you just made some bad decisions along the way, exercised some poor judgment, in here and out there. You took the shortcut to the American dream. Yup! You tried to get rich selling drugs."

Often Mr. Fisher and Corey had lengthy discussions that went well beyond the bounds of inmate and administration. They talked about everything from politics and religion to race, in ways that made Corey think and take a long, hard look at what life outside of the street life was like.

"Corey, for heaven's sake, whatever you do, don't go out there and try to sell drugs again," Mr. Fisher said. "Don't go out there and make the same mistake twice. The state, local, and federal governments are building more jails, hiring more cops, which all equals up to more prisoners and longer prison terms. The correction system is one of the fastest-growing industries in America. It's sad but true. I tell you, it costs them plenty to lock you up, but they'd rather lock you up than send you to college. No matter that it's cheaper. Listen, Corey, you've got talent and potential, don't waste it. They say the worst thing in the world is wasted potential. Man, those portraits you draw are unbelievable. You could make a good living as a commercial or graphic artist. You could, I'm telling you. Corey, you're still young, you could do a lot of positive things with your life. You just have to put your mind to it. Be patient, do everything with patience. "But . . ." The old man fell silent midsentence.

"But whut?" Corey inquired.

"You can never go home again."

Their eyes locked, with each man holding a trancelike gaze. Mr. Fisher cracked a smile and let out a chuckle. He patted Corey on the back and walked away.

Corey watched him as he hobbled back down the aisle to his desk. Mr. Fisher's sudden departure was as baffling as his last statement. *Never go home again.* The words rang in Corey's ears. *What does he mean by that?* Corey thought. He could have followed him and pressed him to explain. With Mr. Fisher, sometimes his questions, answers, and statements could be twofold. He made wild statements like that at times so Corey could use his brain and draw his own conclusions. A part of him wanted to ask Mr. Fisher for an explanation. But pride kept Corey's mouth shut. *Never go home again, my ass!* he thought. *I'm about to bounce. I got four more soul trains and a wake-up. Four more weeks in this miserable muthafucker!*

* * *

Later that night, alone in his cell, Corey pulled out his photo album and went down memory lane. This was a ritual for him, something he did from time to time, to break up the monotony of prison life. Something he did to stay in touch with his old self. To keep his mind focused on home. If home is where the heart is, then Corey's was definitely on the streets. His photographs helped reincarnate the bodies and souls of his deceased comrades. This is how Corey kept their memories alive. Thinking about what once was and what could have been. And could now never be. Deep in thought, Corey blocked out all the hollering and screaming that went on every night on the tier during lockdown. Corey got into a frame of mind that put him back on the street—a New York State of mind—a million miles away from this madhouse. Slowly, he turned the cellophane-covered pages, staring at the glossy five-by-sevens, eight-by-tens, and Polaroid pictures of his loved ones. There were his mother and father hugged-up on the living room couch. Corey looked like a carbon copy of his mother. Bronze complexion, with thick, black, silky eyebrows. He behaved like his father, having inherited his temper, as well as his height and walnut-colored eyes.

There were photos of his older brothers, Chris and Courtney, and his two older sisters, Paula and Felicia, plus his numerous nieces and nephews, who were getting bigger and bigger with each picture. Some of them didn't know him yet; they were born after his incarceration.

Corey's cell was smaller than your average apartment bathroom. He was told when and what he could eat. His every movement was restricted and monitored. He had adapted to this way of life in time. And now time seemed to have quickly passed and gone on for his family and his block without him. He'd been gone four years and some odd months. He looked at pictures of his crew taken on the block and in a local club, called the Stardust Ballroom. These memories—good and bad—were etched in his brain.

One face stood out: his nemesis, Lord. *Look at this fuckin' sucker,* Corey said to himself. There was bad blood between them, stemming from several incidents in their childhoods.

Now the word Corey was getting from the streets was that Lord was the man on the block. Corey couldn't believe it. Lord hadn't even been hustling when Corey was home. The block and the game had to be all messed up if cats like that were in power.

He realized that a great majority of his childhood friends were either dead or locked up; only a select few from back in the day were still on the street. And still in the game. How they'd managed to avoid death or prison was beyond him.

Taking a mental roll call, Corey tallied up the dead: Flip, Greg, Les, Bee, Eddie, John-John, and Tony, and the list went on. All their lives had come to a violent end at a young age when they had so much more living to do. The reasons for their untimely demises were all drug-related—drug raids and sweeps, and a rash of shootings and homicides. Worst of all, he lost his best friend, Omar.

Corey blinked back tears as he looked at a photo of him he had had blown up. He couldn't believe his man was gone. Murdered, but by whom? And for what? Nobody seemed to know anything. "Nine outta ten times, drugs kill drug users. And drug dealers kill other drug dealers," old head Doc always said. Corey couldn't help but wonder whether his presence would have made a difference. Would his man have been taken out if he had been on the streets with him? Or would he have been taken out with him?

The bond that Corey and Omar shared was special. One that not even death could break. Even while Corey was incarcerated, Omar was one of the few cats from the block who held him down. Omar made sure that Corey didn't want for nothing. "O" sent him large money orders regularly. Over the months, the money orders began to accumulate, so much so that Corey decided to open up a bank account, in a small bank in a sleepy upstate town. So he could draw interest off his money.

O had come up in the drug game, without Corey, and he still hadn't forgotten about his man. That was just one of the reasons Corey would never forget about him. O would share his last with him. He was the same person broke or paid. Friends like him only come along once in a lifetime. And in time, Corey promised to avenge his death; somebody had to die. They'd made a pact and Corey's word was his bond. As a tribute, Corey had "Omar R.I.P." tattooed on his chest. This was a constant reminder, to keep it real to the end. Corey wondered why those other cats on the block hadn't found out who the triggerman was and handled it. Maybe they didn't love him the way Corey loved him. Or maybe the cowards didn't wanna get involved. Whatever the case may have been, it left some ill will in his heart toward the block. Taking on a me-against-the-world attitude, Corey refused to write or respond to any letters from anyone else from the block. What was once a close-knit group, a family, with everybody looking out for each other, was no more. Now everybody on the block had his own agenda to tend to—drugs, money, and guns. If you weren't rolling with them, then you were against them. You would be dealt with like a stranger.

The more he thought about the whole situation, the angrier he got. His hand stopped on another familiar face. One that brought excruciating pain to his heart too—just in a different form—his ex-girlfriend, Monique. She was gorgeous, light-skinned with long, black hair and sexy, slanted oriental-like eyes. Monique was Corey's first love, the love of his young life. Who would have thought she would have betrayed him as she had? Not him. He didn't lose her to another man though; he lost her to his imprisonment. The separation of time was too great an obstacle for their young love to overcome.

But, they'd shared so many dreams and plans for the future, Corey couldn't see himself with anybody else. Over time, through lack of communication, the very thing he'd feared would happen had happened. She had gotten pregnant with the next man's baby, while Corey was locked down.

Her pregnancy was a bitter pill for him to swallow. The news came right around the time Corey was coming to terms with knowing that she would find affection and sex with someone else. That was to be expected. In his heart he knew, if the shoe were on the other foot, he'd do the same.

Had Corey truly analyzed the situation, he would have realized that the dirt she did to him didn't even compare to all the wrong he'd done to her. What neither of them bothered to take into account was time lost. The wild card in this love affair was the uncontrollable emotion. Time waits for no man, dead or alive, incarcerated or free; time marches on. Time makes liars out of some of the most honest people, and the heart has no reason that reason can explain. It exposes you to you.

Corey couldn't help but think that the baby she had given

birth to should have been their baby. Wasn't that the plan? At that moment his feelings for Monique were like a double-edged sword, cutting both ways. On the one hand he still loved her, but on the other he chose to hate her. He hated the betrayal. That was the street mentality in him. His animosity toward Monique, though, came and went. Because no matter how much he drilled bad thoughts about her into his head, they never stayed in his heart. Secretly, Corey still harbored thoughts of getting back together with Monique. Her baby's father hit and run, making her a single parent. So in the name of love he was contemplating accepting the responsibility of helping her raise her baby.

From the long conversation they had had months after the baby was born, he knew that reconciliation was possible. Monique had expressed remorse over the mistake she had made. She could get over it, but could he?

Never say never was his motto. Keep all your options open, Corey told himself. Then he took a deep breath and continued counting the days, hours, and minutes till he could see her again.

* * *

On the last page of his photo album were his two prison father figures, Tate and Doc, whom he affectionately referred to as his old heads. They were his yin and yang. They proved to him that there was some bad in everything good, and some good in everything bad. He'd befriended them in prison, but he kicked it with Doc and Tate as if he'd known them from the street.

Tate was a jailhouse lawyer and scholar, and Doc was a street gangster and philosopher. The wisdom that he received from each of them was priceless. Their thoughts and opinions help shape Corey's own ideology, and he had nothing but love for them both. The only way he could possibly repay either of them was to go home and do good—even though that meant two completely different things to them.

Tate wanted Corey to go straight. Tate's idea of doing good was getting out of the game, getting a job, and settling down. Doc's idea was to go home and get paid. Go home a bigger, stronger, smarter criminal. Make the system pay for all the time you'd spent on lockdown. Both Doc and Tate were constantly in Corey's ear, trying to sway him in two separate directions. In each one's presence, he said what that one wanted to hear. But in his heart, Corey knew that he would follow his own mind.

He closed the photo album and tucked it underneath his thin state mattress. Hours had gone by and all the ruckus had stopped, the tier was dead quiet. It was the wee hours of the morning and Corey hadn't even noticed.

Sleepy, he lay down and called it a night. For now sleep would be his only freedom. *Four more soul trains and a wake-up, I'm outta here!*

IN THE WORLD

Chapter 3

Corey was in his bedroom playing his Atari video game when his father yelled from the living room, "Corey! C'mere! Quick, hurry up!" Corey dropped his joystick and came running full speed through the two-bedroom apartment, toward the sound of his father's voice. At the entrance of the living room, he found his father, Mr. Dixon, a handsome brown-skinned man, seated on the edge of the couch, engrossed in the images that flashed across the screen of the big floor-model television. Going on in, Corey wondered what was so urgent to cause his father to yell like that.

"C'mere, Corey! Sit right here!" Mr. Dixon said, patting the plastic-covered love seat next to him. "Look, Corey! Look! Is this how you wanna be when you grow up? Huh?"

On the television, Corey saw two dirty black dope fiends with hands swollen the size of boxing gloves, shooting dope in an abandoned building, somewhere in Harlem. The program showing these junkies, *Like It Is*, was a weekly show hosted by pioneer black broadcaster Gil Noble. The show, known for addressing the problems facing the black community, was one of his father's favorites. And today it was examining the drug plague that was ravaging New York City.

"Is this how you wanna be when you grow up?" His father said as if he were pleading to his son.

"No, Daddy! No!"

Mr. Dixon stared at his son for a long moment, to see if his words and the grotesque scene being played out on TV were really affecting his son. They did, because from that day on Corey developed a phobia of needles. Whenever he went to a doctor for a routine checkup or flu shots, he had to be physically restrained. He became nauseous even at the scent of rubbing alcohol.

Corey sat down in a chair across from his dad, with a view of the TV.

"That's right! You better not ever let me hear about you foolin' wit no drugs. I'll break ya neck!" Mr. Dixon said seriously. "Using drugs is just like killing yaself, only slower. You'll die a thousand deaths. And before I see you do that, I'll kill you myself. Put you right outta ya misery. Drugs ain't never do nothing good for nobody. They just bring out the worst in people. Corey, the answer to your problems, to life's problems, can't be found in a bottle, bag, or vial. Because after the drugs wear off, ya problems will still be there. Getting high won't make them disappear. I don't need nothing to make me feel good. And neither do you." Mr. Dixon paused, then continued. "You know, the worst thing you could possibly do besides using drugs is sellin' drugs. Cuz then you just killing your own kind. God forbid, if you ever was strung out on drugs, I wouldn't want nobody sellin' drugs to you. So I damn sure don't want you sellin' no drugs to nobody else's kid."

Corey was all ears, looking back and forth from his father's face to the TV screen. Corey understood what his father meant. But what he didn't know was, his father had seen firsthand, in the late sixties and early seventies, the destruction of the black community. The death toll and carnage of young blacks lost to drugs. So many of his own family members and close friends had already succumbed to the temptation of drug use, addiction, or dealing. They fell into the trap of a fast-money lifestyle, which almost always led to prison or death. He'd seen drugs break up families, shatter dreams, and kill potential. He had successfully deterred all his children from drugs and the street life. Like every parent who wanted the best for their children, Mr. Dixon was no different. Since Corey was the last of his sons and the baby of the family, Mr. Dixon wanted to make sure Corey was on the right track. But he would soon find out that the tactics he'd used to keep his other children out of the streets wouldn't work on Corey.

* * *

In the midst of Corey's adolescence, this drug burst on the scene, more potent and addictive than any drug known before to man. When the crack cocaine epidemic hit New York City, in the summer of '85, New York became a city under siege. More affordable and a hundred times more habit-forming than regular powder cocaine, the rich man's high became a poor man's high. It became so widespread, so fast; crack's tentacles branched out from the inner cities to suburban America, touching people from all walks of life. The crack epidemic changed Corey's life and countless other black youths' lives forever.

* * *

The Dixon home was in Hillside Houses, a kinder, friendlier name for the projects. The reddish burgundy, four-story brick buildings stretched out over five city blocks. They were built going uphill, hence the name. Rectangular in shape, these housing projects were unlike the other circular death traps that dotted New York City's skyline. Although these projects were considerably smaller than the average New York City housing development, they were no less dangerous. Located uptown, in the northern part of the Bronx, each of their five streets led to one major thoroughfare, Boston Road. The Boston Road Crew became the moniker of all the local youths and drug dealers. Long before Corey's family ever moved to these projects, from the South Bronx, there was a Boston Road Crew known for producing a fair share of moneymakers, fighters, and even killers. The name and the legacy had been passed down from one generation to the next, from big brother to little brother, and sometimes from father to son.

Besides being an open-air drug market and hangout, Boston Road was lined; Hillside Houses residents didn't have to go far to shop. This area was self-sufficient. Unknowingly, the legal businesses fed the thriving drug trade, just by attracting new customers to their establishments daily.

The groups of black juveniles and young adults that congregated on Boston Road and the connecting side blocks—Wilson, Fish, Seymour, Fenton, and Corsa Avenues—appeared to be a wild and unruly gang. But upon closer inspection, they were something much more. They were a family, banded together to protect their hood from outsiders, to uphold their block's reputation and make some money.

A few feet away from the projects was an elementary school, P.S. 78, where all the project children attended. And where Corey and his friends frequently played anything from football to basketball, after school and in the summertime. This was their refuge. Today they were playing another popular ghetto game, called skelly. The game was played with a large square board usually marked on the ground with spray paint or chalk. Boxes marked on the board were numbered 1–13. The only other thing needed for each player was a top, which was filled with clay or wax to give it weight. To win, one needed good eye-hand coordination and a nice touch. On this humid summer day, Corey was getting the best of all his friends, Will, Lil Marco, Lord, and Swift.

"Killer!" Corey shouted as his top entered the center of the blacktop board. He cautiously lay on the hot ground, not caring if he messed up his white tank top, to get a better aim at Lil Marco's top.

Squinting his eye, he looked through a hole made by touching the tip of his index finger to the top of his thumb.

Then Corey violently launched his top and got the better of the collision, knocking Lil Marco's top out the box and off the board.

Corey grinned and shot back. "Boy, if I tell ya, I gotta kill ya." Then he lined up Will's top and fired, knocking it out of the box too. Systematically, he went backward on the numbered board, knocking all his friends' tops out of the box. He was well on his way to winning the game—and then came trouble.

The neighborhood bully, Omar Patterson, aka O, was riding past the schoolyard when he came upon Corey and his friends. Short, husky, and dark-skinned, O was a troublemaker who stayed in the street and was always in the middle of something. Corey was just coming off the steps; he decided to try him.

"Oh, shit!" Lil Marco cursed under his breath as he watched O ride his chrome BMX dirt bike down a short flight of steps that led to the schoolyard.

At first Corey didn't take notice; he was too busy concentrating on the game. Then O did a wheelie across the board. "Yo, whut da fuck you doin'?" Corey asked as O narrowly missed running over him. "Can't you see we playin' here?"

"Man, fuck dat game!" O replied. "I do whut da fuck I wanna do. Who gon' stop me? Y'all know what time it iz!"

Vexed, Corey got up from his squatting position. He knew O was directing this challenge to him. He knew O's style. If you showed him any sign of weakness, he'd be on you like stink on shit. And if that happened, Corey could kiss the rest of his summer good-bye, because O would run him in the house every day from now on. He had to make a stand, it was either fight or take flight. Corey didn't want no trouble, but he damn sure wasn't gonna run from it either.

Seeing that a fight was about to jump off, the other skelly players stepped back a few feet to give O and Corey room to do their thing. At one time or another they had all had verbal or physical confrontations with O, so they kept silent to see how Corey would handle himself.

"Ain't da one! I ain't scared ya ass," Corey exploded, putting up a brave front. Some people automatically assumed that just because Corey was quiet, he was soft.

"Let's get busy," O said confidently as he got off his bike and leaned it up against the wall. Calling Corey's bluff, O was prepared to do whatever. He placed his dark blue Yankees hat on his handlebars and tucked in his gold rope chain, preparing to fight. Tall and skinny, Corey was built the exact opposite of O. The fight looked like a physical mismatch, even before the first punch was thrown. But O had the advantage of being the more experienced fighter of the two; he'd been in countless scraps. The battle scars on his face were evidence. Butterflies in the pit of Corey's stomach were working overtime. This always happened to him before he fought; he was scared. But fear was natural and motivated him to fight harder. A thin line separates the hero from the coward.

"Nigga, let's stop singin' and start swingin'," O stated as he walked up on Corey. "Now we gonna see if ya heart iz as big as ya mouth, pussy."

"Bring it! I got ya pussy, nigga! Ain't nuttin' between us but the air," Corey told him.

"Ooohhh! He poppin' crazy shit. I know you ain't goin' fa dat!" Lord said, instigating. Lord liked nothing more than to instigate a fight. He didn't care whom it was between, as long as it wasn't him.

Amongst the scattered tops, the two combatants stood in the middle of the board. Holding his hands high, as he'd been taught, Corey protected his chin. O countered with a low crouching style of his own. Moving aggressively toward O, Corey was determined to take the fight to him even though he was outweighed by fifty plus pounds. He wanted to see what O had. He couldn't possibly be hitting harder than Corey's older brothers. They had done a good job of toughening him up, preparing him for days like this, by play-fighting with him.

Corey threw a weak left jab, followed by a wild right hand, both of which missed badly. O avoided them easily, finishing with a smile as he did.

"Datz da best you can do?" O teased. "If it iz, you in trouble." O's swagger was unmatched. He talked a good game, but if you listened to him talking trash, you were already defeated. It seemed as if he'd been holding his own since he came out of his mother's womb. With no father or brothers to run to, just a little sister, he learned to fight the hard way, by fighting older dudes. So now fighting was fun to him, especially when he fought someone his own age.

"I got something fa ya ass," Corey countered, infuriated by the smart remark. He began throwing a flurry of punches, till he tired himself out. Seeing this, O went on the attack. He threw a fake punch, and then bum-rushed Corey. Picking him up to his chest level, O body-slammed him down hard on his back, on the blacktop. Toying with him, O let Corey get up without striking him.

The fall hurt like hell, but Corey refused to let O see him in pain. "Why you gotta wrestle for?" Corey growled. "Whut, can't you beat me with your hands?"

"Nigga, ain't no rules in fighting!" O replied sharply. "I'll bite ya ass if I got to."

That's right! Point well taken, go all out too. Corey thought to himself. This was a classic matchup, one that pitted a boxer, Corey, against a street fighter/wrestler, O. Whoever could impose his will on the other would win the fight.

After getting up off the ground, Corey was determined to fight smarter and be less careless with his punches. Flicking out his jab, he began to use his huge reach advantage to keep O at bay. The whole time he kept his right hand cocked, ready to drop a big punch the first chance he got.

Using a crouching style, O bobbed and weaved, trying to avoid Corey's long jab. Then he made a mistake, coming up out of his stance too soon. Corey capitalized on this, tagging him in his eye. Then, using a trick of his own, Corey faked a kick, which O reacted to by dropping his guard. In an attempt to block it, he left himself wide open. Taking advantage, Corey caught him with a hard overhand right, splitting O's lip, filling his mouth with blood.

Now it was Corey's turn to talk shit. "Yeah, nigger, whut's up now?" he said confidently. "You can't fuck with me!"

"You got dat! Dat's a good one!" O admitted as he spat out some blood. It was his turn to feel a little pain and embarrassment. O couldn't believe that he'd fallen for an old trick like that.

For close to an hour, in the hot summer's heat, they went at it. Neither boy gained a clear-cut advantage. At times it was hard to tell who was winning and who was losing. The tide turned continually. They fought hard; reputations were at stake. O was expected to win, while Corey was determined not to lose. This was Corey's trial by fire, his rite of passage onto the block, his defining moment.

Each blow Corey connected with or was hit with, his inner circle of friends, Will, Lil Marco, and Swift, silently cheered or winced. Except for Lord, they were all pulling for him. Lord openly rooted for O. "Yeah, O, dat's right, get 'im!" Lord yelled every time it appeared that O had the advantage.

Lord and Corey had never gotten along from day one. They spoke to each other, but nothing more. Their personalities clashed. Lord was loud and obnoxious, Corey was low-key. But even Corey was surprised that Lord was so out with his attitude toward him. They hadn't even bumped heads lately. Lord perceived O as having more style and more going for him. Corey took Lord's cheerleading as a sign of disrespect. He made a mental note to check Lord later. He vowed to himself to get him later.

The guys fought until they were both dead tired; neither would give in. Physically and emotionally drained, they moved slowly almost by sheer willpower. They both ended up on the ground, each clamping the other tightly in a headlock. Corey couldn't do nothing with O, and vice versa.

Having seen enough, Will signaled Swift, and together they pulled them apart. With someone else stopping the fight, they both saved face. "Aiight, dat's enuff!" Will said. "It's over!" Exhausted, neither of them objected.

"Hope you don't think it's over between you and me, cuz it ain't!" O declared as he got on his bike and rode away.

"Whatever!" Corey shouted back. He was hyped up. "Come back, we can finish dis shit now!"

O ignored him and continued to ride away. Corey's friends surrounded him, giving him congrats, pounds and pats on the back.

"Yeah, boy, you got busy!" Lil Marco exclaimed, proud of his homie.

"Yo, Core caught dat nigger lovely wit a stupid fake," Swift admiringly added as he reenacted it.

"Word!" Lord chimed in, trying to act as if he were on Corey's side all along.

Corey glared at Lord; he couldn't believe his audacity. "Yo, get da fuck outta my face, you punk muthafucka!" he angrily stated as their faces came within inches of each other. "Yo, don't say nuttin' ta me no more. I don't fuck wit you like dat. I heard you jumpin' all on O's dick."

"Yo, I wuz jus' . . . ," Lord weakly replied.

"You wuz jus' what? Whut, nigger?" Corey demanded. Everyone else just got quiet. "You played yaself. Step da fuck off for you catch a beat-down!"

Lord was speechless. There was nothing he could say in defense of himself. He stood there looking stupid. No one dared come to his aid. He was dead wrong. He scanned the eyes of each person in the schoolyard. Their faces and eyes registered the same thing. *Leave!* they all seemed to say in unison. Lord was merely tolerated by them, while Corey was genuinely liked.

"It's like dat?" a dejected Lord asked, seeking a reprieve.

"Yeah, it's like dat!" Lil Marco stated, speaking for everybody, officially kicking Lord out of the crew. Stomping off, an irate Lord swore he would get even with them all, someday.

Chapter 4

The sunrays streamed through the wide-open window, through the sheer white curtains, settling on Corey's face. As hard as he tried to ignore it, he couldn't. The heat beat on his face like a drum, till he finally awoke. Though the sun hadn't reached its peak yet, it was getting too hot to sleep. Opening his eyes, he simultaneously winced from the sharp pain exploding in the back of his head. This was the morning after the fight and he was still feeling the effects. Reaching a hand to the back of his head, he felt for a knot, which he was sure had formed overnight. One touch confirmed what he already knew.

Slowly, he rose and sat on the edge of his bed, meditating, trying to gather his bearings. Corey put his face in the palms of his hands. He prayed the mild headache wouldn't turn into a migraine. He may have won the battle yesterday, but this morning his body was losing the war. Getting himself together, he headed straight for the bathroom. Once there, he opened up the mirrored medicine cabinet. His eyes scoured each shelf till he found what he was looking for, Extra Strength Tylenol. Taking two capsules, he washed them down with a handful of cold water.

While he waited for the Tylenol to take effect, Corey attended to his hygiene, washing his face and brushing his teeth. After that, he strolled around the house, wearing nothing but a pair of white Fruit Of The Loom briefs. Weekdays during summer vacation were always like this; while his parents were at work, he had the run of the house. Both his parents worked long hours in an effort to make ends meet. Mr. Dixon was a former auto mechanic who had just recently been hired as a city bus driver, after years of waiting. His mother, a former homemaker, now worked in an old folks' home, as a nurse's aide. They typically worked six days a week, while Corey did whatever he wanted to do. For eight hours a day, he raised himself.

The pain in his head subsided and he realized that he was hungry. He searched the refrigerator for a quick snack. He bypassed last night's leftovers and anything else that he had to reheat or cook. He decided to eat some Cap'n Crunch cereal, which he poured into a big cake bowl, drowned it with milk, and began to munch out on. Slurping and smacking, he enjoyed every mouthful. The miniature cuckoo clock mounted on the wall read ten o'clock. *Damn, it's early. I bet ain't nobody outside yet,* Corey thought to himself. He got up to look out of his bedroom window. Other than the kitchen, Corey's room was the only one that faced the street. There wasn't a soul in sight on the block except for some maintenance men, going from building to building making repairs.

After giving up all hope of seeing anybody, Corey caught sight of Will. He moved quickly, darting in and out of the street and between parked cars. *What's he doing?* Corey wondered. He watched Will with great interest, trying to figure out what the hell was going on. It didn't take long to find out. A few moments later, Diesel, one of the older drug dealers from the block, appeared, followed closely by a scrawny white boy with dirty-blond hair, wearing a pair of tight, faded blue jeans and a dingy white T-shirt. They both entered the same building where Will had gone. Shortly afterward, the white boy reemerged by himself, flagged down a ride, and drove off. Then Diesel exited the building, alone, and headed back around the corner to the avenue. Next, Will slid out of the building and took a seat on the stoop. "*Ooot, ooohhh! Ooot, ooohhh!*" Corey hollered loudly, using the official block call. "Ay, yo!"

Echoing off the building, the noise traveled way down the street to Will, and as soon as he heard it, he knew who it was. Nobody hollered quite like Corey. Getting off the stoop, he walked into the middle of the street; waving his hand in a circular motion, he beckoned for Corey to come outside.

Acknowledging him, Corey flashed a two-fingered peace sign. Since he was already up and had nothing better to do, he figured he'd go chill with Will on the block. Quickly Corey got dressed, putting on a brightly colored Hawaiian shorts set, with his white fisherman hat, with a pair of white-shell-top Adidas. Grabbing his keys, he was out the door.

* * *

Inside the project building lobby, Corey and Will exchanged pounds and greetings.

"Yo, whut up?" Corey cheerfully said. "Whut you doin' outside dis early? Ain't ya ass suppose ta be in summer school?"

Will smirked. "Man, fuck summer school! I'm tryin' ta get paid."

Get paid? Corey pondered. *Get paid how? Doing what?* He hadn't the slightest idea what Will was talking about. Corey was green, green as grass in the summertime, he had no street smarts. Compared to Will, Corey lived a more sheltered, family-oriented lifestyle.

"Yo, I'm out here holdin' Diesel's work," Will said.

"Work?" Corey asked, confused.

Will looked at his friend and shook his head. He couldn't believe how someone so book smart could lack so much street knowledge. "Drugz!" he snapped. "*Work* iz just a slang word we use fa drugz on da block. Yo, dat means I'm holding Diesel's drugz. Now, did I make myself clear? Or do I have ta spell it out? God damn, Core! You gotta start hangin' on the block more often, so you'll know what time it iz. You be playin' too much ball and watching TV twenty-four/seven. Word!"

"Nigger, you buggin'! I know whut time it iz," Corey fired back, trying to convince his friend that he was down.

"Stop frontin'!" Will joked. "Ya momz and popz got ya ass in check."

"Yeah, right!" Corey managed to say. "If you say so."

Will laughed out loud at a stone-faced Corey. Then Will changed the subject. "Yo, come wit me up ta da roof for a second. I wanna show you something."

Corey's mood shifted from frustration to curiosity. He hightailed it up the steps behind Will. They both reached the rooftop in record time, a little winded, though.

Once on the roof, Will pulled out a black zippered pouch. He opened and tilted it slightly, shaking out a few of its contents into his cupped hand. Corey huddled close to him to get a better look. From where he stood, the stuff almost looked like candy.

He picked up one of the pretty colored vials for further inspection. Corey's eyes focused on two unevenly shaped, white, rockish-looking objects. "Yo, whut'z dis?"

Will paused for a minute. "Dat'z dat new shit! Dis whut e'rybody's sellin' or smokin', crack!"

Corey had only seen drugs on the news, after a major drug bust. He knew about cocaine and weed, but not crack. "Crack? Whut da fuck iz dis?"

"Yo, it ain't nuttin' but regular powder coke, cooked up with baking soda to make it hard. So they can smoke it. Jus' fa holdin' dis gee pack, Diesel gives me one hundred dollars a day. Plus free food. A hundred dollars fa doin' nuttin', it'z easy money."

The wheels in Corey's mind began to turn, as if he were struck with a bright idea. His eyed sparkled with interest. The significance of the moment was not lost on him. A hundred dollars a day was a lot to some grown men, let alone a thirteen-year-old kid from the projects. Corey wasn't spoiled, but he didn't have everything that he wanted. He had everything he needed, but now that was taken for granted. Corey was probably one of the most fortunate kids in the projects. He was being raised by both of his parents and, being the baby in the family, reaped material benefits that his older siblings had never had. Living in a two-parent household, Corey had more parental guidance and financial security than any of his friends. He didn't have to do illegal activities to get the bare necessities in life. Yet he yearned to do what his friends did, run the streets. Corey was intrigued and asked for more information about Will's job. He was enthused by the thought of making some fast money.

"Damn, nigger, you act like you wanna get down or something," Will said. "Corey, you know ya popz will whip dat ass."

"How he gone know?" Corey pointed out. "My momz and popz work all day, e'vryday. Besides dat, fa a hundred dollars I'll take a ass whipping."

Will doubled over in laughter as he pictured Mr. Dixon whipping Corey's ass, right there on the block. Will knew that there was a good chance of that happening because Mr. Dixon was an old-school, big mean-looking father, no-nonsense type of guy.

"Slow ya roll. Play at ya own risk. Jus' chill wit me fa da day and peep how shit goes. And later, if ya still interested, I'll hook it up wit Diesel."

"Bet!" Corey exclaimed.

For the next few hours, Will popped in and out of the building on Diesel's command. All morning long and early into the late afternoon, they moved endless gee packs to a string of customers.

* * *

Corey observed every move that they made from the staircase window. And just as his friend had told him earlier, it appeared to be easy money. Will actually did nothing but hold drugs and money. He didn't make a sale, he didn't rush customers. Occasionally, he ducked a passing police cruiser. To Corey it seemed as if Diesel were taking all the risks and Will were reaping all the rewards. But in all actuality, it was the other way around—as with the rest of the older drug dealers on the block. Diesel had recently begun to aggressively recruit neighborhood youths for the drug game. They were expendable fall guys and flunkies, earning sneaker money while the dealers kept the real money for themselves. At this time not even the police were aware of the heavy juvenile involvement in the drug game. As the day wound down, Will and Corey sat safely inside the building staircase, eating shrimp fried rice and egg rolls from the Chinese take-out restaurant around the corner.

"See how sweet this iz?" Will bragged with a mouthful of food. "Money, I get paid e'ryday jus ta hold work, stay outta sight, and eat Chinese food. And dat's definitely better than going to summer school, summer camp, or goin' down South."

Busy eating, Corey merely nodded his head in agreement. He'd already made up his mind, that he wanted to be a part of the game.

"Oh, yeah, I almost forgot ta tell you," Will remembered. "We gotta basketball game today in da park."

"Against who?"

"Last night afta you went in, I ran into dose up-da-hill ass niggers at da pizza shop," Will explained. "And they wuz poppin' crazy shit, like they could beat any five I get. So I set up a game, jus' ta shut dese niggers up. It's Corsa Avenue versus Fish Avenue, up da hill vs. down da hill. You know e'rybody, whut?"

Pausing for a moment to think, Corey weighed his options. If the game was as big as Will said it would be, then everyone, including O, would surely be there. And he would definitely have to fight him again. This time in front of everybody, including O's friends too. And if he got the best of O, chances were he might get jumped. But as long as Will, Lil Marco, and Swift were there, he wasn't really worried about that. There was no doubt in his mind that they'd help. *Fuck it!* he thought to himself. If he had to rumble O again, so be it. He wasn't about to let O stop him from going where he wanted to go. "Yeah, I'm playin'!" Corey assured Will.

Will cracked a smile. "Fa a minute there, I thought you wuz gonna fess, I thought you wuz gonna say no."

"Ya thought wrong!" Corey sharply retorted.

"Oh, yeah, check dis out," Will whispered. "Ya man Lord iz gonna be playin' too."

"Wit who? If he on our team, I ain't playin'. I don't like dat two-face nigger!"

"Calm down," Will said. "He's runnin' wit them."

"Good. I really don't wanna be round 'im, afta da shit he did yesterday."

"Word. He did play his self. I couldn't believe dat shit. But he's two-faced like dat. When he found out dat I wuz runnin' wit Diesel, he started playin' me crazy close."

"Dat'z how he is," Corey agreed. "He's a wannabe."

Sensing it was about quitting time, Will looked out the staircase window, sticking his head between the bent iron safety bars for Diesel. From this view he could see the block bustling with people, returning home from work via the bus or subway. Soon he spotted Diesel alone bending the corner, coming directly toward the building.

"Ay, yo!" he yelled loudly. "Come down and open up da fuckin' door."

Will turned to Corey and said, "C'mon, I'll hook it up now."

Leaving the empty soda bottles and Styrofoam food containers on the steps, they went downstairs. Reaching the lobby, they could see a huge, blurry black form through the frosted Plexiglas window in the wooden door. Turning the doorknob, Will let Diesel in. Corey took a seat on the steps, silently observing.

In walked Diesel with his menacing presence: big barrel chest, long, thick arms, and close-cropped hair filled with grease and waves. He towered over them.

"Yo, lemme get dat work," Diesel ordered. "Shop closed! I'm out. Shift jus' changed and all those supercops getting ready ta hit da block. Murry, Wong, and all da rest of dem faggot muthafuckas." As Diesel spoke, his eyes cut over at Corey as if he just now noticed him. "Yo, who dis?"

"Oh, dat'z my man from down da block, Corey," Will said, cosigning for his friend.

Diesel stared intensely at Corey. His face looked familiar to Diesel, but he couldn't place it. "Ay, yo, shorty, where I know you from?"

"I live on dis block," Corey answered. "But you probably thinking about my big brother. They say we look alike."

"Yeah!" Diesel wagged his big black finger. "Chris! Dat'z ya brother. I knew I knew you from somewhere. Word ta mother, you look jus' like him. Yo, iz he still in the army?"

Corey's oldest brother, Chris, was somewhat of a legend in the neighborhood, well-respected for his fight skills. In his teenage years he was somewhat of a thug, captivated by the street life. But he was smart enough to heed his father's warnings and get his act together. Smart enough to know there was no future in the streets. So immediately after graduating from high school, he enlisted in the army. Chris was one of the lucky few who dabbled in the game and walked away seemingly unscathed.

For five long years he was gone, and during that time Corey's other brother, Courtney, followed in his older brother's footsteps and joined the service too. Corey was left to fend for himself. He felt somewhat abandoned by their back-to-back departures. Truth be told, had Chris been around, Corey would never even have entertained the thought of getting into the drug game for two reasons: One, Corey loved and looked up to his big brother too much to ever let him down. Two, Diesel respected Chris too much to ever involve his little brother in the drug game. But time and distance tend to make people forgetful and disrespectful, giving them the courage to do the things they wouldn't normally do.

"Yeah, he still in da army. He be home fa Thanksgivin' or Christmas, on his thirty-day leave."

"Yo, tell 'im I said whut'z up, next time you talk ta him," Diesel said sincerely. He turned his attention back to Will.

"Huh!" Will said as he shoved a big bankroll into Diesel's hand.

Diesel flipped through it, taking a mental tally of the cash. Things seemed to be in order, so he peeled off Will's pay and handed it to him. And since he didn't want Corey to feel left out, he gave him a twenty-dollar bill on general principle.

"Yo, Diesel, check dis out," Will began. "My man tryin' ta work. Let 'im take my spot sometime. I already showed 'im whut he gotta do. He knows whut time it iz."

Aside from being a juvenile, Will was one of Diesel's most valuable workers. By living on one of the most drug-infested blocks in the area, Will became a valuable asset. He routinely stored large sums of money and drugs in his house, unbeknownst to his elderly grandparents. And the location of his building was perfect, giving Diesel quick access to his packages of drugs and guns. He had Diesel's trust. So, whenever Will told him to put somebody down, Diesel did.

"Aiight!" Diesel agreed as he stuffed the money into his pockets. "See ya tamorrow mornin' same time." He turned to leave the building, then suddenly spun back around. "Ay, yo, Will, go put da resta dat work up now! Before ya ass do anything. Next thing ya know, ya dumb ass will forget. Then ya get knocked on a humble. You'll be callin' me collect from Spafford, cryin'."

Doing what he was told, Will and Corey walked across the street to Corey's building. He didn't want to go inside his apartment, for fear that his mother might keep him in or have him run an errand. Will opened up his mailbox and locked the drugs inside. He knew they would be safe.

That done, they headed for the park. On the way there, Corey was overcome by a funny feeling he just couldn't shake, like something was about to happen.

Chapter 5

Centered in the middle of the projects was the park, a typical ghetto playground, equipped with a small wading pool, benches, swings, slides, monkey bars, and, of course, a basketball court. In the summertime when you couldn't find whomever it was you were looking for, chances were he was in the park. It was the place to be.

The place was packed and abuzz with excitement, from spectators and players alike. Everybody who was somebody in the projects was there. After spending most of the day cooped up in the house, trying to beat the heat, watching reruns on TV, people were glad to be outside catching a summer's breeze. Groups of fly girls and B-boys gathered in certain sections, while others lined the fence that separated the court from the playground, anxiously awaiting the game. Being that Corey and Will were the last two players to show up, all eyes were on them.

"Yo, it's crazy people out here!" Will said as they made their way through the crowd.

"Word!" Corey agreed. He made eye contact with Monique, far and away one of the finest and flyest young girls in the projects. She returned his gaze with an inviting look of her own. She and Corey were casual acquaintances, on hi-and-bye terms. They knew each other from school. But Corey secretly had a crush on her. With the park filled to capacity, the game took on a greater meaning, the stakes were raised. Bragging rights were on the line. Everyone playing in the game wanted to shine and show off in front of the girls.

"Y'all niggers ready or whut?" Will announced as he stripped down to his tank top. "Y'all already know the teams. Let'z get busy!"

"Shoot ta die!" someone suggested. "Make it, you take it."

Corey and his teammates, Lil Marco, Swift, Will, and another kid named Head, watched attentively player from the opposing team attempted to make a free throw, to determine which team would get the ball first.

"Our ball!" Will yelled after the shooter missed badly. "Da game goes ta thirty-two by twos. If da game get'z tied up at that point, then you gotta win by four. Respect all calls! And call out da score afta each basket made." He loudly announced the rules of the game up front so there wouldn't be any arguments or discrepancies at the end of the game.

There were no qualms from either side about the rules; they all were in agreement. The Corsa Avenue squad took off their shirts, bearing their still-developing upper bodies. Now it was official, shirts versus skins. The game started off slowly, with each team taking turns, missing shots. Then things began to pick up as they traded baskets. After they'd felt each other out, the game shifted to an up-tempo, open-court, run-and-gun hectic pace. The kind of game that kids in the hood loved to play. The emphasis here was on style, scoring points in dramatic fashion. Making an easy move look fancy and a difficult move look easy. These two teams were playing to the oohs and aahs of the crowd.

On his team, Corey was the man, scoring points in bunches, in every way imaginable. Single-handedly he kept his team in the game. On the other side, they played more team ball, spreading the wealth; everyone was involved. But Lord was heated because Corey was stealing the show. Thinking that he could shut him down, he and a teammate switched men. Now he was guarding Corey man-to-man, and Corey welcomed the challenge. Corey took the switch personally; he didn't even wanna be on the same court as Lord, now he was guarding him. He didn't just wanna play well against him; he wanted to embarrass him in front of everybody.

"Gimme da rock!" Corey pleaded to Lil Marco. Receiving the ball in the high post, he waved off a pick set by Head. He took two dribbles, then jab-stepped, creating enough room for him to release his picture-perfect jump shot. "Face!" he called out, as the ball swished through the net.

"Sixteen up!" a tall, rough-looking boy shouted. The

game was at the halfway point and already a sense of desperation seemed to be setting in. With the game tied, Corey grabbed a defensive rebound and bought the ball up the court himself. Though he was not officially the team's point guard, he handled that extremely well. Like most New York City kids, he made dribbling the ball an art form. Slowly he came toward Lord, bouncing the ball low between his legs, exaggerating his dribble, then in a blink of an eye, Corey raised up and flashed his trademark killer crossover dribble. He momentarily froze Lord as he swooped to the hoop for an easy basket. The crowd went wild. "Core-ree!" one girl sweetly screamed out. Jogging back up court, he glanced in the direction of the call. He caught Monique's eyes silently singing his praise. Corey was even more pumped now.

"Yeeahh! Dat'z right, he can't fuck wit you." Lil Marco cheered as he patted Corey on his behind. Corey received high fives from the rest of his team as he headed up court.

Undaunted, Lord got the ball on the next play and hit a long rainbow jumper. Right back at you, it seemed to say to Corey. The crowd responded wildly, further fanning the flames of animosity. This game was turning into a one-on-one battle. It seemed as if every time they alternated possessions, it resulted in a score. And with each score the screams got louder, more hysterical. This alone was enough to inspire the players to play that much harder, to be more aggressive. Tempers started to flare.

"My ball!" Corey said after being hacked by Lord.

"Ya ball?" Lord questioned, looking at him as if he were crazy.

"Yeah, my ball!" Corey insisted. "Yo, I'm telling you, don't foul me like dat no more."

"Whut?" Lord barked, trying to sound tough.

"You heard."

When Corey didn't score, Lord turned and laughed at Corey, taunting him as if he had cheated him out of something. This unsportsmanlike conduct further antagonized the situation. Corey wished he had beaten Lord up yesterday, as he'd started to. Now he knew what he was gonna do.

"Point!" An opposing player shouted out after his team scored.

Trying his hand, at some late-game heroics, Lil Marco put up a wild shot, then watched as it hit nothing but air, igniting a fast break, the other way.

"Yo!" Lord hollered with his hand held high as he raced up the court. Unable to make a play on the ball, Corey watched as the outlet pass sailed safely over his head, into the outstretched hands of Lord.

With a chance to win the game, to be the man, Lord moved swiftly up the court. But out of the corner of his eye, he could see Corey gaining ground. This was what he wanted, this would make the victory that much sweeter. Not only would he score the game-winning points, but he'd do it on Corey. Lord leaped off his left foot, gliding toward the basket. At the same time, Corey jumped, hell-bent on stopping him.

Like two runaway trains on the same track, they met in midair and collided violently. Faking like he was going for the ball, Corey clotheslined Lord, dragging him out of the air, kamikaze-style, sending Lord free-falling hard to the blacktop, on his back. “Blat!” went Lord’s shirtless upper body as it slapped against the ground. He never got the shot off; the ball bounced harmlessly out of bounds. The crowd looked on shocked, unsure of what they were seeing.

“Now, whut, big mouth?” Corey snarled as Lord lay crumpled on the ground. Corey got up, stood over him, and began to taunt him. His voice was alive with hate. He was letting it be known that he’d meant to do that.

“Damn!” an opposing player barked. “Dat’z fucked up. You ain’t hav’ta foul ’im like dat.”

“Yeah, dat’z fucked up!” someone else added as he ran up court to aid his fallen teammate. “Y’all Fish Ave. niggers always gotta put shit in da game. Specially when y’all see y’all about ta lose.”

“Whut? Fuck you!” Will said, coming to Corey’s defense. “Y’all don’t want no beef wit us.”

Already salty because they were denied an opportunity to win the game, the opposing team became enraged by Corey’s blatant disrespect of Lord. By this time, more and more of their homies had gathered to watch the game, now outnumbering the Fish Ave. team. Under normal conditions they wouldn’t dare go up against them, but when chumps gang up in packs, they tend to gain courage. Suddenly they began hopping the fences, surrounding Corey and Will. Quickly

Lil Marco, Swift, and Head ran up court, pushing their way through the crowd.

"Get da fuck away from my man!" Lil Marco cursed. "Y'all ain't doin' nuttin' ta him."

"Y'all a lil deep now, all of a sudden y'all think y'all tough?" Swift shouted.

Seemingly from out of nowhere, O rode up on his bike, followed by a few older drug dealers from the block. Having spotted the large crowd from the street, they'd decided to come into the park and investigate.

"Whut da fuck y'all Corsa Ave. niggers think y'all doin'? I know y'all ain't tryin' ta roll on 'em?" O strongly implied as he threw down his bike. Walking up to some of the main perpetrators, he gave them an icy stare. With O and his goons on the scene, they suddenly punked out.

"I'm sayin', O . . . ," one kid tried to explain, copping a plea. "Dat nigger Corey started it. We wuz all ballin', then he—"

"I ain't tryin' ta hear dat shit!" O snapped, quickly cutting him off. "I don't care who started it. I'ma finish it. He wit me. So whoever got beef wit him, got beef with me too!" Lifting up his oversize T-shirt, O exposed a black, snub-nosed .38 tucked in his waistband. He made sure everyone saw that he was strapped. "Now, if y'all don't want no trouble, I suggest y'all break out before I start bustin'! Leave in peace or leave in pieces. However y'all wanna do it."

Unable to press the issue, the whole Corsa Ave. entourage began to disperse, retreating to their own part of the project. This wasn't the first time they were at each other's throat over some nonsense. But as usual, they got the short end of the stick. Even though they lived in the same projects, things got geographical at times.

Having recuperated from his fall, Lord got up and walked off with them. Even though he was from Fish Ave., he no longer wished to be associated with them. In essence, he was banished from his own block, by his boys he grew up with. As he walked away, he shot a long, dirty look at Corey. One that let him know it wasn't over between them. This was a lifetime beef.

Before anyone else could get next to Corey, O threw his arm around him and walked away a few paces. "Now da beef iz squashed between us. Fa now on we roll together," O said. "Man, I hope there ain't no hard feelings between us. I had ta try you, ta see where you wuz at. Even though you live on da block, I had ta see if you could represent it." After overcoming the initial shock of O coming to his rescue, Corey felt good. He was down. He had respect on the block. Over the last few days, he'd earned some serious stripes.

Corey coolly replied, "Cool. We both did whut we had ta do. One a dose things." Having declared a truce, Corey and O embraced, that was that. And this was the start of a true friendship. Seeing that nothing more was gonna happen, everyone began exiting the park. Corey, O, Will, Lil Marco, Swift, and Head, all strolled off together. Passing a group of remaining girls that included Monique, they heard one girl say, "Damn, Corey, I didn't know you had that many friends."

He grinned and thought to himself, *I didn't know I had this many either.* Now the whole block had his back.

Summer hadn't even hit full swing yet, and already Corey had been involved in more than his fair share of drama. This was just the tip of the iceberg.

Chapter 6

Corey was more of an observer than a participant in his first summer in the crack game. Familiarizing himself with the cops, customers, and slang, he cleverly mingled amongst the dealers and fiends on the block, while holding packages on his person. He was just one of the numerous kids who were out on the block day and night. With no summer youth jobs or camps to attend, this was their summer vacation. They wanted to be in the middle of the action and excitement. Nothing excited Corey more than being on the block. Even if Corey wasn't dealing drugs, he'd probably be out there anyway, just hanging out—but maybe not as much. The difference now was, he was getting paid to be on the block—like most of his friends, also involved in the drug trade. By working for Diesel, he was slowly becoming his property. When Diesel was putting money in someone's pocket, he thought he owned him. He thought that gave him the right to talk to him any way he wanted to as well. One late evening, while Will and Corey were attempting to sneak off the block to head for a block party, trying to avoid Diesel, they ran right into him. As they turned the corner, he stood right there. He had unsuccessfully looked for them all day and he was furious.

"Ay, yo, Will, where da fuck you been all fuckin' day?" Diesel roared, directing all his rage at him. Will was more critical to his drug-dealing operations than Corey. "All fuckin' day I been holdin' dis fuckin' pack on me. Will, I'm tellin' you, if I get fuckin' knocked, I'ma murder you!"

Even though Diesel wasn't talking to him, Corey was still very much intimidated by his tone of voice and body language. An overgrown bully, Diesel frightened some grown men. Just by the sound of his voice, people knew he meant business. Suddenly Corey began to wonder just what he'd gotten himself into.

"Yo, Diesel, you buggin'! 'Member, I told you yesterday dat I had to go somewhere wit my family?" Will said, reciting a lie. "Dat'z where I wuz all day."

"You always gotta excuse fa somethin'. But you sure iz real fresh ta be runnin' an errand. Let me find out that you lyin' and you gonna catch a beat-down fa fuckin' up my paper. Got mad work sittin' in ya cribs dat I can't even get to."

"Yo, I told you I wuz goin'," Will insisted. "Ain't my fault if you don't remember. You coulda got dat work late night if you really wanted it. I had ta go out to see my family. It was my grandmomz anniversary. Whut, I'm supposed to tell my grandparents no? I ain't goin'! Damn, you act like a nigga don't gotta life outside da block. I know I told you yesterday,

I wuz gonna be ghost, fa da whole day. But you neva listen. Then you wonder why shit getz fucked up. . . ."

The lie Will told sounded so convincing, it was beginning to make sense to Diesel. There was some truth to it. Diesel ran his drug ring with an iron fist; he wanted all his workers to be at his beck and call twenty-four hours a day. Diesel began to have second thoughts about screaming on him the way he had. Still, he had to play his role and let Will know who was boss. "I don't know who da fuck you think you talking to," Diesel snapped. "But ya betta watch ya fuckin' mouth. I'ma let ya lil ass slide dis time, but don't let it happen again. Don't let ya mouth write a check ya ass ain't cash . . . bitch ass nigga."

Will was relieved he'd got over on him. To him, Diesel was a pushover.

"Yo, whut'z up with you?" Diesel asked, glancing over at Corey. "I know you're workin', right?"

Corey knew from the bass in his voice, Diesel wasn't asking him, he was telling him. Passing on the offer wasn't an option Corey wanted to exercise. He didn't wanna run the risk of getting smacked. He didn't know what Diesel was liable to do. "Yeah, I'm workin'," Corey reluctantly said.

"Here!" Diesel said as he pulled a black pouch filled with crack out of his groin and shoved it in Corey's hands. "C'mon!" he ordered.

Marching around the corner, Corey gazed over at Will and shrugged his shoulders, giving him a so-much-for-that look as he walked away. His only consolation was, at least he would be getting paid tonight. Will winked at Corey and headed for the block party, as he'd planned.

* * *

Early Friday evening, the sun was setting, leaving faint streaks of red in the sky. The neon and fluorescent store signs were ablaze on the avenue, illuminating the city sidewalks. Blinking signs attracted the eye to pizza places, liquor stores, and bodegas. In the midst of it all was the open-air drug market, attracting customers like moths to city lights.

"Yo, Corey, c'mere!" Diesel summoned. His voice was so pleasant, alarms went off in Corey's head. Diesel was acting out of character.

Weaving his way through a crowd of people, Corey followed Diesel around a corner. Corey caught up and Diesel wrapped his huge arms around him. "Listen." He pointed. "See dat car right there? Da black Jetta?" Corey had noticed it circling the block, as if the driver were looking for someone in particular. "Dat'z one of my best customers. Her name is Kelly. Her people got paper. She lookin' fa me, but I don't feel like fuckin' wit her tanite." Feeling uneasy, Corey felt his heart begin to beat a little faster; he didn't like the direction that the conversation was going. "Yo, take a few of dem things and see whut she wants. Matter fact, tella you got my thing," Diesel said smoothly in a con man's voice, making the task seem simple.

Corey wasn't going for it though. Serving customers was uncharted waters for him—a big step that he didn't want to take. He couldn't afford to be seen selling drugs. If word got back to his parents, they'd kill him. He hadn't been in the game a hot month yet and already he was being told to do something serious.

"D-D-D-Diesel," he stuttered. "I neva served nobody before."

In a flash Diesel's whole demeanor changed. "Muthafucka, you do whut da fuck I say! And hurry up, before I slap ya fuckin' head off. And you won't get paid!"

Corey felt stupid, humiliated for having been screamed at in public. Now he thought everyone was looking at him. In truth, only a few people were on the block, most of whom paid Diesel no mind. Everyone knew that he was loud. To save himself any further grief or bodily harm, Corey decided to do what he was told. Plus, he wanted to get paid. Paid for missing out on all the fun at the block party. Corey walked over to a dark spot and removed the pouch he had stuffed down his groin. Dumping out a handful of crack, he bent down and stashed the pouch inside a parked car's bumper. He went to the corner to flag down the Jetta while Diesel faded into the shadows to watch the transaction from a safe distance.

"Kelly!" Corey yelled, frantically waving his hand at the passing car.

Suddenly, the brake lights came on. She came to a stop, then reversed, pulling up alongside him. Rolling down the passenger window, she asked, "Who you?"

For a minute Corey was speechless. He was stunned by the beauty of this young lady. *Was she was on drugs?* he wondered with surprise. Her light brown skin glowed, her cornrows were thick and nicely done, and her pearl-white teeth were perfect. "I'm Cee," he told her, not wanting to reveal his real name. "Diesel's man."

"Well, where he at?" she inquired impatiently. "I been drivin' around lookin' fa him, he suppose ta meet me."

"He had to go do something real quick. He ain't out here. He's takin' care of some bizness. I got his thing, though. Whut you want?"

She opened the car door. "Hurry up, get in!"

Corey quickly climbed into her car and they drove away. The interior of the car was alive with a strong pine aroma, from the half dozen pine-tree air fresheners dangling from the rearview mirror. Wanting to get out of the hot spot, Kelly drove across Boston Road, away from the projects, toward the private house side. As they rode, she cut her eye over at her baby-faced passenger. *Damn, they got babies out here selling drugs now. What is this world coming to?* she thought to herself.

She double-parked in the middle of the next block and killed the lights. "Lemme see whatcha workin' wit." The whole time she was scheming on how she could use his inexperience against him; how she could beat him out of some get-high.

Corey began to fidget in his seat, constantly checking the side mirror for any signs of the police. Her request caught him off guard. "Huh?" he replied.

"Yo, you gonna lemme see ya product, or whut?"

"Yeah, it's flavor," Corey said.

"Dat'z whut they all say. I wanna see for myself. Boy, how old iz you anyway?"

"Ole enuff!" Corey snapped. "Stop rappin', cop and bop."

"Old enuff ta do whut?" she sarcastically asked. "You can't pee straight."

"Whatever. Listen, I ain't tryin' to hear all dat. Let's do whut we came to do, so save it."

"Nigga, pleaze! You ain't had pussy since pussy had you. Now, answer my question. How old iz you?"

Corey stared at Kelly defiantly, then said, "You askin' too many questions, homegirl. Whut you, five-0 or somethin'?" His age was always a sensitive subject for Corey, because he always wanted to be older than he really was. He couldn't wait for his facial hair to start growing so he could look a little older. Childhood was too restrictive for him; he was in a rush to be an adult.

Kelly had a good sense of humor, and she laughed off his reference about her being a cop.

Corey relaxed a little. "Here!" he said, placing all the vials of crack in her hand as he continued to stay on the lookout. "Hurry up too, I ain't got all day."

She couldn't believe her luck. He was really green. This was gonna be like taking candy away from a baby. Examining the merchandise, Kelly fingered through the vials, looking for the fattest and most packed ones. Fantasizing about freebasing, she pictured her lips wrapped around the stem of a glass crack pipe. Ever since that fateful day her girlfriend convinced her to take that first hit, she'd never stopped chasing that exclusive high. Unbeknownst to Kelly, she'd never achieve that euphoric feeling ever again. Without Corey even noticing, a switch was made. Having copped crack from Diesel earlier that day, she'd saved some empty vials for the sole purpose of beating someone. Being that the vials were the same color, Corey was none the wiser. Dropping a few of his real vials in her lap, she slipped them in her pocket and replaced them with some vials of fake crack, made of Ivory soap. Kelly had carefully carved the soap to look like crack rocks.

"Pay you tomorrow, I promise!"

"I can't do that," Corey informed her. "No credit! Straight paper!"

"C'mon, pleeaazzze!" she whined like a baby, while she clutched the fake product in her closed fist. "Diesel, I'm one of his best customers."

"I ain't Diesel. It'z cash and carry wit me."

"Pleaazze! I'll do you a favor if you look out fa me." She began to have second thoughts about sexually propositioning someone so young. "Ummm, faget it, I'll get it from Diesel later."

"Yo, lemme get dat work, since you ain't buyin' nuttin'," Corey coldly stated.

"Oh, it'z like dat?" she complained. "Wait till I tell Diesel how you tried to dis me. He gonna scream on you, watch!"

"Listen, homegirl, I ain't got time fa ya bullshit. Now gimme my shit! Tell 'im whut ya want, he ain't my popz."

"Little boy, Cee, or whutever ya fuckin' name iz, wit ya smart-ass mouth." She fidgeted in her seat as if she had to pee or something. "Nigga, you betta respect ya elders." After handing over the product, she reached over and pulled the latch on the passenger door, helping him out.

Corey got out of the car and slammed the door in her face.

"Fuck you, bitch!" he hollered as he walked away. "You fuckin' beggar! Come back when you get a nickel over lunch money."

Kelly flipped him the finger and pulled off, tires screeching. She had the last laugh anyway. She'd burned him out of some crack.

When Corey got back to the block, he told Diesel what had happened, sparing no details.

"Yo, you mean ta tell me dat you sat there all dat time and dat bitch ain't spend no fuckin' money?" he asked. "I knew she wanted some fuckin' credit. Dat'z why I didn't serve her. I'ma have ta put her in check, she gettin' carried away wit dis credit shit. I'm surprised she didn't ask ta suck ya dick."

"Huh?" Corey replied.

"If you say 'huh', you heard. Yeah, dat triflin' ho suck a mean dick. When she gives head, she gives good head! Nobody does it like her. She'll have a nigga strung out givin' up all hiz product. Word! She should getta trophy fa dat shit. Anyway, fuck her. Always remember, bizness before pleasure. Get ya money first, then have ya fun. Otherwise you hustlin' ass backwards."

Corey was intrigued by the thought of having such a pretty girl like her perform oral sex on him. Something about her appealed to him, even though she had that nasty attitude.

"Look, fa future reference, so you'll know, if a customer ain't buyin' nuttin' or ain't sellin' you somethin', make 'em step off. Cuz if ya listen to them crackhead muthafuckas long enuff, they'll talk ya outta somethin', or into somethin'," Diesel advised. "Now go grab da stash and put dat work back. Then go post up in da Chinese restaurant. As I need it, I'll come get it."

The rest of the night moved along smoothly. Diesel sold his drugs and Corey got paid.

Chapter 7

An unmarked police car came to a screeching halt on the corner, catching Corey and company by surprise. Two white, stocky plainclothes officers sprang out of the vehicle and boxed them in, strategically positioning themselves just in case anybody got a bright idea about running.

"Everybody up against the wall!" the fat white cop commanded. "Move it."

Assuming the position was nothing new for these street-corner pharmacists or any inhabitant of high-crime and drug-infested areas. At any time people could be harassed, subject to frisks, searches, whether they were breaking the law or not. Many times they were just guilty of living in the neighborhood.

Corey's heart pounded steadily against his chest. He was dirty; he had a pack of crack hidden on his person. He wasn't alone; so did Swift. He had a mouthful of crack vials stashed beneath his tongue. If worse came to worst, he'd swallow them. But only as a last resort. Corey's group and a few other drug dealers were lined up spread-eagle against the wall. This was routine. If they were clean, they had nothing to fear. If not, they would surely be arrested and charged.

"Yo, Officer, whut we do?" Will demanded to know. "Why y'all messin' wit us? Is it against the law to hang on ya own block?" When he was clean, he liked to play head games with the police. That way they wouldn't mess with him when he was dirty.

"Ya loitering!" one cop strongly replied. It was the best excuse he could come up with. "And that's against the law, smart-ass."

"Loiterin'?" Swift repeated, amazed. "We live on dis block, so how am I loiterin'?"

Neither cop bothered to respond. They just went about their business as if they didn't hear him. One cop began to search the detainees, while the other stood watch, like a prison guard. Roughly, he kicked apart their feet, making them all spread their legs as far as they could without falling. They didn't take too kindly to being questioned about what they perceived as their duty. Going down the line, each person was thoroughly frisked, turning up a variety of things in the young men's possession.

"Whose pager is this?" the fat cop asked Will, waving a black pager in his face.

"My momz'," Will said, lying. "She let me use it so she can contact me when she needs me."

"Oh, yeah?" the fat cop exclaimed. "Well, tell ya mother business is bad today. I'm confiscating the pager. Tell her to come to the precinct if she wants it back." He placed it in his pocket.

Will didn't say a word, he just sighed. He knew these types of things came with the territory. Another smart remark from him might lead to a beating and his arrest on trumped-up charges.

"Where you get all this money from?" one cop questioned someone else, leafing through a wad of cash. "My popz gave it ta me ta pay da phone bill. I'm on my way to the check-cashing place right now, Officer."

"Yeah, right. That must be one helluva phone bill. There's at least eight hundred dollars here. Where'd youz call? Africa?" The cop laughed at his own joke. "You know what? I don't believe you. How come you ain't got a phone bill on you?" He paused. "Tell you what, tell ya dad ta come down to the precinct and pick up this money. And don't forget ta tell him ta bring the phone bill or some paycheck stubs—if he got any."

Everybody knew what that meant; the cops were keeping the money. It would never make it to the precinct. No drug dealer in his right mind would go down there to claim it. This was a shakedown. The cops knew these kids wouldn't or couldn't complain formally about stolen drug money. It was the drug dealers' word against theirs. One by one, after each person was searched and questioned, he was free to go. But instead they chose to stand across the street and watch the harassment of their friends to make sure the police didn't plant anything on someone and to see how the drama unfolded. Going down the line, the police repeated their searches till Corey was the last person remaining on the wall. By this time, a small group of innocent bystanders had gathered on the scene. Running both his hands all over Corey's body, the cop vigorously patted him down. Playing a hunch, he grabbed a handful of Corey's testicles. Jackpot, he found something. "Turn round!" the fat cop ordered as he violently whirled Corey around. Not waiting, the cop stuck his hand down the front of Corey's pants to retrieve the hidden contraband. "What's this?" the fat cop said, pulling out a big black pouch from Corey's crotch. Even before he opened it, he knew what it was. One look inside confirmed that. "Bingo, got one! I knew somebody had something. Everyone wanna play Mr. Innocent."

Corey's worst fear was confirmed, he was busted. "Turn round," the fat cop barked as he prepared to arrest him. "Place ya hands behind ya back."

As the metal bracelets were forcibly slapped on his wrists, Corey thought his heart would explode. He was in trouble, big trouble. After being placed in the unmarked patrol car, Corey caught the sorrowful glances of his friends. As bad as they wanted to help him, there was nothing they could do. He was on his own. Ducking down in the backseat, Corey gave them one last look of frustration. Corey was just another bust. Just another black face. Just some paperwork and overtime.

"You guys must think y'all are invisible or something. Standing on the same damn corner every day," the fat cop said. "It don't take a rocket scientist to figure out what's goin' on."

The other cop added, "We could go on vacation for about a month, come back, and y'all would still be right where we left ya. I'm willin' ta bet my last dollar on that. Guarantee it!"

Corey stayed silent. He didn't care what they thought or

had to say. In his world the police were the enemy, the streets taught him that. He knew better than to engage in a conversation with them. Besides, he was more worried about what his father would do to him.

Instead of going directly to the precinct, the cops cruised the neighborhood, circling the block several times, showing off their prisoner. This was a warning to all the other drug dealers on the block: *This could be you.* As they entered the next block, a crowd had gathered in the middle of the street. They formed a circle around a little black girl, who lay motionless on the ground, apparently the victim of a hit-and-run. Adhering to their call of duty, the cops quickly responded. They both exited the car, leaving Corey alone. This was the chance he had been waiting for. Immediately he went into action. Double-jointed, Corey maneuvered the cuffs down near his ankles, then stepped through them, bringing them in front of his body. Cautiously he looked around to make sure the coast was clear. Then he climbed over the front seat and bolted out the driver's door. In the midst of all the commotion the cops never saw him fleeing through the projects. Corey ran like the wind, propelled by his fear. Knowing the projects like the back of his hand, he fled to a nearby crack house.

Bang! Bang! Bang! Corey beat on the door like a madman. "Smokey, open up!"

Inside the apartment, the occupants came to a sudden standstill. At first they thought the hard pounding on the door was the police, and that this was a raid. Till they heard a childish voice pleading for admittance.

"Who?" Smokey growled. Somebody was messing up his

business. He had just finished cooking up a couple of ounces of crack and was now about to smoke some. He was the neighborhood crack cooker, working daily for all the local drug dealers to feed his own crack habit.

"Me!" came the reply. Corey knew Smokey from the block, copping crack.

"Me who?" Smokey demanded, as he approached the door. Tall and husky, he was unlike your average crackhead. He kept his weight on despite smoking a lot. Smokey was as black as charcoal briquettes. His eyes stayed bloodshot from the many sleepless days and nights he spent getting high. All he did was smoke crack, everybody called him Smokey.

"Corey!" Corey shouted, while impatiently waiting for the door to open.

"Shop closed!" Smokey said firmly as he eyed Corey through the peephole. "Come back later. I'm busy right now."

"Yo, Smokey!" a voice called from the kitchen. "Let 'im in."

Complying with the order, Smokey began to unlock a series of dead bolts, latches, and locks that ran down his door, finally letting Corey in.

"Five-O . . . knocked me . . . I jumped out da car!" Corey blurted out as he tried to explain himself to Smokey and catch his breath.

"Ay, Corey, c'mere!" a familiar-sounding voice yelled from the kitchen. Following the sound of the voice, Corey was happy as hell to see O's face.

"Yo, whut da fuck happened ta you? Whut'z up wit da handcuffs?" O asked.

"Yo, five-O blitzed the corner inna unmarked car." Corey recounted the whole story.

O listened intently to the events that had led to Corey's arrest, but his mind was more focused on getting his friend out of the handcuffs. "Smokey," O called. "Listen, go to da hardware store and getta small hacksaw." Going into his pocket, O pulled out a twenty-dollar bill and handed it to him.

"You gon' bless me when I get back, right?" Smokey asked sheepishly.

"Stop fuckin' fiendin' all da time!" O snapped. "I got you. Now get da fuck outta here. Go!"

Smokey went on his mission to get the necessary tool to free Corey. He didn't care how O talked to him just as long as he kept feeding him crack.

As soon as Smokey left, Corey and O were able to speak freely. "Yo, you'z lucky!" O said. "But you know five-0 iz gonna be lookin' fa you like crazy. Especially on dis shift. You gonna have ta take a serious chill pill."

"Yeah, I know," Corey admitted. "But right now, I'm dyin' ta get outta these tight-ass cuffs."

"Yo, who knocked you? Wuzn't none of the regulars, right?"

"Nah! It wuzn't nobody I knew. It was two new jacks, O'Brien and Long."

"Neva hearda 'em," O declared. "So you might be cool. You know we all look alike to them. But whatcha really gotta worry bout iz ya momz and popz finding out. You know how fast news travelz in the projects."

"Word! You right. But I can't do nuttin' 'bout dat. If my people say somethin' ta me 'bout it, all I'ma do iz lie. Say it wuzn't me. Dat'z 'bout all I can do."

"Right! Right! Dat'z ya best bet. Deny e'rythin' ta da end. Or put da blame on somebody else. Dat'z whut I always do if I were in ya shoes. Fuck it! It'z betta than admittin' ta it. At least dat'z whut I'd do if I were in ya shoes."

As the conversation went on and on, they discussed various ways of getting out of this predicament. Before they knew it, Smokey was coming through the door, seemingly empty-handed.

"Where da fuck iz da hacksaw?" O roared.

Smokey smiled, revealing rows of yellow teeth, and then from underneath his dirty black sweatshirt, he produced a brand-new hacksaw. "I got it!" Like a true crackhead, he'd stolen the tool and pocketed the money.

Laying the hacksaw on the small dinette table, Smokey stepped back and waited like an obedient dog for his reward. "Now bless me one time," he said, rubbing his hands together. "I'm tryin', tryin' ta beam up ta da *Enterprise.* See Captain Kirk and 'em."

The kitchen table was cluttered with drug paraphernalia—a triple-beam scale, empty crack vials, and a pack of single-edge razor blades—plus two ounces of crack, sitting directly in front of O. He grabbed one ounce and chipped off a sizable chunk, placing it in Smokey's filthy hand. His eyes widened with anticipation. He cradled it as if it were a baby, not wanting to drop a precious crumb.

"Now, whatcha gimme fa dis?" Smokey asked, pulling out the twenty-dollar bill O had given him earlier.

"Smokey, you outta fuckin' order!" O complained, breaking him off another nice-size chunk. "Here! You greedy bastard. One day you gon' fuck 'round and bust ya heart."

As Smokey scurried out of the kitchen to smoke his crack, he said, "Underneath da sink there are a chisel and a hammer. In case you need it."

"Why you ain't been tell us dat before?" O replied as he retrieved the tools. Quickly sizing up the situation, he told Corey, "Get on da floor and spread ya hands as far as possible." Corey lay on the floor, spread his wrists, and watched while O carefully pounded at the small chain links. After a couple of powerful strokes, the chain gave away.

"Now fa da hard part," O announced.

Corey exclaimed, "You tellin' me?"

Reexamining the handcuffs for the thinnest part, the weakest point to attack, O went back to work. The vigorous sawing back and forth created friction, heating up the metal cuffs.

"Ouch!" Corey cried as the cuffs began to tighten around his wrists, threatening to cut off his circulation.

"My fault! I know it hurtz, but hold on. I'm almost done."

Lowering his head, Corey gritted his teeth and bore the pain till the job was done. Together they pried the handcuff off. Repeating the process, they freed Corey's other hand. Rubbing his wrists, he grimaced from the pain.

"Now you gotta wait till da shift changes before you leave," O advised. "There's probably an APB out on you. I'ma send Smokey ta da block ta get you a change of clothes. You might get bum-rushed wit dat on."

"Huh!" Corey acknowledged him. "Whut da fuck we gon' do up here in da meantime?"

"We gonna bag dis shit up. You know how ta bag up?"

"Nope!"

"Well, you about ta learn." Step by step he began breaking down the game to Corey. He explained how to properly use the scale and the common misuses. All the tricks of the trade were laid out so Corey could avoid getting beat. It was one big show-and-tell. Though they were the same age, O was a seasoned veteran of the drug game. He had gotten involved out of necessity at a young age. Now he was selling for himself, while his peers were satisfied with working for older drug dealers. His heart and ambition set him apart from all the other kids his age; he was always willing to go all out on his own. And he always thought big.

"Yo, lemme ask you somethin'?" O said. "How long you plan on workin' fa Diesel?"

"I don't know. Neva thought about it."

"Well, it'z time you did. Diesel da type a nigger dat'll keep you under his wing faever. I'm tellin' you now, you gotta stop fuckin' wit him. You'll neva get paid—unless you like chump change. Fuck whut ya heard, e'rybody tryin' ta get paid and have they own work and workers. Dat'z e'ry nigger on da block dream, ta have his own crew of lil niggerz workin' fa 'im. To move up from flippin' bottles, ta ounces, to a key . . ."

For hours they rapped, with O dominating the conversation, giving Corey a deeper understanding of the game.

"Fuck Diesel. He be jerkin' niggerz. When I use ta work for 'im, I use ta rob him blind. Tappin' da work and stashin' money. Here's whut ya need ta do. Start savin' up somethin'. And here's whut I'll do. When you get a couple hundred, I'll put you down wit me. We'll be partners. You know two headz iz betta than one . . ."

Chapter 8

Same shit, different summer. Corey was up to his old tricks. The game was coming at him fast and furious. After successfully laying low, then managing to break away from Diesel, he took O's advice and they pooled their money and became partners. Almost a year later, now they were officially a team, two hungry renegades, chasing sales and running customers on the late night.

"How many you want?" Corey asked Smokey. Possessing a have-drugs-will-travel attitude, Corey went anywhere and everywhere to make a sale. At this moment he was inside Smokey's apartment.

"Three," Smokey said as he watched Corey like a hawk. "Dis still da same stuff I cooked up fa y'all, right?"

"Yeah!" Corey said, shaking out a couple of vials for Smokey to choose from.

Smokey began to salivate at the mere sight of all the crack vials. His lust for the drug began to temporarily cloud his rational thoughts. Here he was with no money and a strong urge to get high. He was praying that Corey would look out and give him something on credit.

"Yo, man," Smokey began. "Lemme hold somethin' till Friday. My check'll be here then. I'm good for it. You can even hold my ID."

"Yo, don't fuckin' tell me you called me way da fuck up here and ain't got no money?"

"I'm sayin', man, look out fa me. I looked out fa you befo. 'Member, I ran you dat big five-hundred-dollar sale, dat dude bought ya whole pack, and you didn't even give me no P.C." Smokey was trying to jog Corey's memory, recounting some of the favors he had performed for Corey in the past. "Man, I always take care of you. You can't do me dis favor? Huh?"

But his pleas fell on deaf ears. Corey wasn't trying to hear it. He refused to give Smokey credit for fear that he would put him on the fuck-you payment plan. Corey would have to track him down to get paid. "I ain't got it like dat!" Corey snapped.

Angered, Smokey suddenly snatched the package of drugs out of Corey's hand.

"Whut da . . ." Corey's voice rose. Instinctively he rushed him. But he was no match for a grown man. Especially a drug-crazed crackhead like Smokey. He manhandled him, flinging Corey around like a rag doll.

"I'm tired of beggin' ya ass. I tried ta be nice and come ta you like a man," Smokey stated, making up an excuse for doing what he was about to do. "Now I'm takin' all dis shit."

After getting up off the floor, Corey charged him again. "Betta gimme back my shit!"

"Go 'head, I'm tellin' you," Smokey warned as he tossed Corey to the floor again. "Fo I hurt you."

"Yo, gimme my shit! You ain't got nuttin' comin'!"

"Nigger, you owe me! As many times as I done shit fa you and you never gave me shit? Dis mine."

"You crackhead muthafucka! You think you just gon' take my shit like dat? Nigger, you must be crazy. I'ma make you kill me up in here."

Corey was out of his mind, but he meant every word he said. Like a hurricane, he came at Smokey again, swinging his fists wildly. But the punches that landed had little or no effect. Smokey still managed to fend Corey off and clutch the package at the same time. To let him know he meant business, Smokey cocked back and unleashed a powerful blow. The force behind the punch dropped Corey, sending him flying into the kitchen.

Dazed, Corey sat up on the floor and tried to shake it off. He couldn't believe that Smokey had actually hit him like that.

"Go 'head," Smokey advised him. "Don't make me hurt you over dis lil bit a shit."

Regaining his sense, Corey suddenly realized where he was. He quickly scrambled to his feet and flung open the utensil drawer. Reaching inside, he grabbed the biggest butcher knife he could find.

Simultaneously, Smokey made a break for his bedroom, with Corey in hot pursuit. He narrowly missed stabbing him in the back. Making it to his bedroom just in time, Smokey slammed the door in Corey's face.

"Open da fuckin' door, you fuckin' sucka!" Corey demanded as he pounded and kicked on the door.

Inside the bedroom, Smokey had already begun to barricade himself in. Using a heavy oak dresser and his queen-size bed, he blocked the door. Settling in, he prepared to smoke Corey's crack and wait him out. Meanwhile, Corey was taking out his anger and frustration on Smokey's apartment, leaving the place in shambles. The he went to find O, to tell him what had happened.

"Smokey did whut?" O asked in disbelief after being roused from a weed-induced sleep.

"Da nigger Smokey iz fiendin'. He snatched my whole pack!" Corey explained. "He wuz mad cuz I wouldn't give 'im no credit. I tried ta fight 'im, but da nigger was too big fa me. He kept slammin' me." Corey recalled the incident, and O listened, his anger slowly rising.

"I don't believe dat nigger," O snapped. "We gon' get 'im though. We gon' get 'im."

One thing about O, if he was your friend, he had your back no matter what. You could be dead wrong, and he would still be there to support you. He'd help a friend in need even if it killed him. "Yo, just chill up here till it getz dark. Tanite we'll take care of Smokey. By then he'll be fresh out of crack and fiendin' fa more," O said.

Later that night, dressed in black hoodies, O and Corey went on a mission, staking out Smokey's apartment from the roof of a building directly across from his. Inside the candlelit apartment, they could see someone resembling him, moving about. Corey was armed with a baseball bat; O had an old .22 long, which resembled a .38. They patiently waited for Smokey to emerge from his crack den. They knew sooner or later he would.

Finally after about an hour, Smokey left his hideout in search of some more crack. Either his stupidity or his unquenchable appetite had placed him in immediate danger. From the rooftops they trailed him, watching Smokey go from crack house to crack house. Then as soon as he made the mistake of going to a more secluded building, O and Corey came off the roof to hide behind some parked cars, waiting to ambush him. After coming up empty-handed on his quest for crack, Smokey exited another building. They crept up on him and jumped him. Corey hit him in the knee, chopping him down, to keep him from running. Once on the ground, Corey had him right where he wanted him. Corey beat Smokey unmercifully. "*Aaahhh!*" Smokey screamed as he rolled on the ground in pain.

"Whut comes around goes around, Smokey!" O said between laughs.

Wielding the bat like a maniac, Corey went crazy. Pounding Smokey's body to a bloody pulp. The sickening sound of breaking bones could be heard as the bat broke through Smokey's weak defense.

"*Aaahhh!* You got it!" Smokey yelled at the top of his lungs, trying to draw attention to the attack while he received a taste of street justice.

"Shut da fuck up!" O commanded, whipping out his gun. "Shut up fa I bust ya ass."

Loud whimpers escaped from Smokey's lips. He cried crocodile tears as Corey continued to work him over. "Aiight! Chill dat'z enuff!" O said, bringing the onslaught to an end, stopping Corey before he caught a body.

As they left the scene of the crime, Corey stepped over Smokey and gave him a swift kick in the nuts for good measure. "Dat'z fa punchin' me in the face, you fuckin' crackhead!"

Smokey moaned, almost passing out from the excruciating pain exploding in his stomach. To add insult to injury, O stood over him and fired a slug into the fallen figure, hitting Smokey in the right buttock.

* * *

Back at O's house, in the comfort of his room, he and Corey celebrated their beat-down of Smokey. "Yo, you heard da way dat nigger wuz screamin'?" O giggled. "All da bitch came out of him."

Corey confessed, "Man, I wuz tryin' ta kill dat nigger fa strong-armin' me like dat. Do you think he'll tell?"

"Tell?" O confidently replied. "Then where he gon' live? He ain't stupid. . . . Oh, dis ain't da first time he caughta bad one. He been shot and stabbed crazy times. Smokey must think he got nine lives da way he keeps beatin' people outta drugz."

"Fuck 'im!" Corey added, trying to convince O he didn't care. "He got whut his hand called for. Brought dat on his self."

Putting a blunt in his mouth, O struck a match, sparking it up. Inhaling and exhaling, he created thick clouds of smoke. After taking a few more puffs, he passed the blunt to Corey.

Corey hesitated before taking it. His mind flashed back to

something his father had told him years ago: One thing leads to another.

"Ay, yo, you sure ya momz ain't gonna say nuttin' about dis?" he asked, stalling. Looking for a reason not to take a toke.

"I got dis!" O assured him. "I run things here. Jus hit da shit, you wastin' some good smoke."

Caving in, Corey put the blunt between his lips and pulled. He pulled too hard and the smoke rushed to his lungs, choking him.

The weed had already begun to take effect on O; he fell back on his bed laughing hysterically. "Slow down," he chuckled. "Fa you kill yaself. Dat ain't no dirt weed, dat'z buddha!"

Corey coughed so hard, it sounded as if he were gagging. When he finally stopped, he took a few more pulls and passed the blunt back. The coughs had amplified his high. Now he was beginning to feel nice.

Taking a series of long drags, O suddenly shifted the mood. The weed took him from silly; it made him serious. It made him think. Think and talk crazy. "Yo, Corey," O whispered, squinting his eyes, protecting them from the smoke. "I die fa you."

The statement came from out of nowhere, catching Corey completely off guard. He was stunned.

"You my man," O continued. "Like da brother I neva had. I ain't gonna let nuttin' happen ta you, if I can help it. Know what I'm sayin'?"

"Word, I hear ya." Even though Corey was high as a kite, he could still relate.

"Anybody could kill fa anybody," O stated. "But only a few people will die fa you. Will you die fa me?"

Without hesitating Corey replied, "Withoutta doubt!" Their feelings were mutual. He knew O was willing to go all out for him, and that this wasn't just idle talk. O had mad love for Corey, and he couldn't help but reciprocate that love.

O smiled. "Dat'z whut da fuck I'm talking bout. All fa one and one fa all. We gon' do dis. Watch, we gon' get large. Yo, I swear ta God, if anything wuz ever ta happen ta you, God fabid, I'ma murder somethin'. I'ma putta nigger six feet deep. And if anything wuz ever ta happen ta me, God fabid, if a nigger ever ta body me, I want you to take 'im out. I don't want nobody walkin' dis earth dat murdered me."

"Word ta mother!" Corey swore. "I'll handle dat."

Chapter 9

It was another hot, scorching summer, both literally and figuratively. This afternoon there wasn't a soul in sight; the usual subjects had vacated the block. And for some reason, there was a heavy police presence, patrol cars circling left and right. This was just one of those days when the police decided just to shut things down. A show of force. On this day Corey found himself out on the block looking for customers. But by being the only drug dealer outside, he caught some curious stares from the cops. Quickly he nixed any idea he had of selling drugs. Only a fool would take a chance like that, on a day like this. So Corey made a detour into the corner store, which also served as a game room. He decided to kill some time doing one of his favorite things, playing video games.

"Hey, Ms. Torres. Lemme get four quarters," Corey said, slapping a dollar bill on the counter.

"Hi, Corey!" she excitedly replied in her thick Spanish accent. "How you been? Haven't seen you lately. Hope ya not out here getting in trouble." Ms. Torres was like a foster mother of the block. She'd had her store in the neighborhood for so long, she'd known all the bad guys when they were good little boys. Everybody loved and respected her.

"I ain't doin nuttin'," Corey assured her, then collected his quarters. With his coins in hand, Corey headed toward the back of the store.

"Keep ya eye out fa me, please, Corey. Don't let anybody steal nuttin'," she yelled out, then turned her attention back to the soap operas.

"Aiight!" he replied, walking down the narrow aisle, past the chip rack, the pastry display case, and the shelves filled with Goya products. Hidden way in the back were the video games.

Placing all his quarters in the Ms. Pac-Man game, he watched it register four credits. *Damn!* Corey suddenly cursed when he noticed that someone had taken down his high score. *Who the fuck is Mo?* he wondered. Now he was determined to put up a new high score. Hitting the one-player button, Corey watched and listened as the sound effects blared and the screen came to life. When the game started, he used his special pattern to gobble up everything on the board. Clearing board after board, he earned free men. Time flew by; Corey became completely engrossed in the game. He never noticed when another player walked up on him, until he caught a hand, out of the corner of his eye, placing a quarter upon the video game, signaling next.

"Oh, you tryin' ta get my high?" a soft feminine voice said.

Glancing over in that direction, he noticed that it

was Monique. "So you Mo, huh?" he asked, continuing to play.

"Yeah, dat be me!" she said confidently. "I'm da best Ms. Pac-Man player 'round here!"

"Oh, yeah? Let'z see about dat." Quickly Corey ended his game, killing off all his remaining men. "Now let'z play head-up, ta see who'z really da best," Corey challenged her.

"Bet."

Surrendering the joystick to her, Corey stepped aside to watch Monique play. Effortlessly she cleared board after board, accumulating lots of points. It seemed that the more difficult the game became, the better she got. A good thirty minutes passed before she made a careless mistake that cost her to lose her turn. Then Corey grabbed the game's controls and went to work, smoothly maneuvering his man. As he played, he talked to the game to hype himself up. He surpassed her score. Back and forth they went as the game turned into a hard-fought battle. When Corey's hand began to cramp, he decided he'd played long enough. This game could go on forever, they both were that good. So he purposely attempted a risky move and it backfired, costing him the game.

"Yeah!" Monique happily exclaimed. "I won! I told you, you wuzn't betta than me."

"I let you win," Corey countered. "I didn't have ta make dat move."

"Yeah right!" Monique said, her hands on her hips. "Whateva you say! You jus' a sore loser."

Watching Monique go through the motions, rubbing it

in, Corey couldn't help but smile. She still looked fine with her baby hair done and the rest pulled back in a ponytail. She wore a pair of sandals. "Yo, you hungry?" he suddenly asked, not knowing where the words came from. "Cuz if you iz, we can go ta da pizza shop. Everything on me."

Monique shot him a funny look as if she were gonna turn him down and tell him off. "C'mon, loser, I wanna slice and a soda," she said sarcastically, marching toward the front of the store.

Leaving the candy store, they made their way to the pizza shop. After paying for their order, Corey escorted Monique back to her building, at her request. Once inside, they sat on the steps eating and talking. "Corey, I usta think you wuz so conceited."

"Me? Conceited? Only girls and pretty boyz act conceited. And I ain't either."

"You don't think you pretty or cute?"

"Babies are pretty. Monkeys are cute. And men are handsome."

Monique rolled her eyes. "Well, excuze me! . . . But like I said, boyz do get conceited. Cuz da only time you ever said hi ta me wuz when I said hi ta you first."

By deliberately ignoring her, Corey had gotten her attention. "I thought you wuz stuck-up," he revealed. "E'rybody be jockin' you e'ryday. Didn't think you even noticed me."

"Boy, you somethin' else," she said, sucking her teeth. "How could I not notice you? You wuz in all my fuckin' classes."

"But I wuzn't all up in ya face!" Corey shot back.

"Whateva!" she sighed. "So, whut, you don't like me?"

Like you? Corey thought to himself. *Girl, I had a crush on you since day one. If only you knew.* "Whut'z dere not ta like about you?"

"Oh!" she said with confidence. "I thought so. . . . You know whut, outta all these boyz 'round here, I ain't neva heard nuttin' 'bout you havin' a girlfriend. But you probably sneaky though, jus' like da rest a dem. I wonder . . . I wonder, who ya girl?"

"Ain't got one!"

"Yeah, I know. I already did my homework on you. Jus' wanted ta see if you wuz gonna lie on ya dick. Corey . . . you wanna be my boyfriend?"

"Huh?" Corey couldn't believe his ears. "Was that a question?"

"You heard me! Now do you or don't you?"

"Stop playin'!" he joked.

"Do it look like I'm playin'?" She was not smiling.

Corey quickly responded, "Yeah."

"Good!" she exclaimed. "Fa now on, we boyfriend and girlfriend. So don't let me catch none of dose nasty slutz up in ya face. Okay? Because I'm real jealous. So don't have me out here fightin' over you. Oh, yeah, one more thang, if I catch you cheatin', it'z over."

From that day on, they were a couple, spending as much time together as possible. When Corey wasn't with her, he was with O, running the streets, selling crack. Somehow he managed to divide his time equally, keeping both parties happy.

* * *

Weaving his way through the project's maze that summer, Corey ran into Kelly again.

"Yo, you gon' gimme dat or whut?" Kelly hissed.

So much had changed in her life since they'd last met a year before. Her crack habit hadn't robbed her of her good looks, but it had taken everything else. Her car and her dignity. Her family had disowned her. She was living in the streets, in different crack houses, selling her body to keep a roof over her head and to support her drug habit.

"Why you doin' this shit?" Corey asked. "Yo, you look too good ta be smokin' da pipe."

"Muthafucka," she snapped. "If I wanna lecture I'd go ta church, or rehab. Nigger, I'm tryin' ta get high. So iz you gonna gimme somethin' ta smoke or whut? I ain't got time fa no fuckin' lectures, especially from no drug dealer."

She was on it hard, Corey thought. "If I do dis fa you, whut you gonna do fa me?"

"Whut you want? I ain't got jack shit."

"How you gon' get somethin' fa nuttin'? You gotta gimme somethin'?" he asked, hoping she'd catch the hint.

Picking right up on it, she replied, "Whut you want? Some head? Dat'z da only thang I can give you. I'm on da rag."

"Aiight!"

"Where we gon' go?"

"Da roof!"

On the way up to the roof, they negotiated a price to be

paid in crack for her services. She wanted three vials of crack for a blow job; he thought the job was only worth one. They settled on two.

It was pitch-black on the roof, yet they managed to navigate their way to a secluded corner where it would be much harder for someone to stumble across them. God knows who walked these roofs so late at night. Laying her jacket down across the gravel, Kelly got on her knees and prepared to go to work. "Don't cum in my mouth," she warned him.

"Aiight, man!" Corey assured her as he whipped out his thing.

Grabbing his manhood, she guided it into her warm mouth. Feverishly she sucked, licked, and slurped, figuring the faster she got him to cum, the faster she could go about her business, smoking crack.

Corey was really into it, she was everything that Diesel said she was. He grabbed her head and rocked back and forth against her steady rhythm. At any moment he was gonna cum. As her head moved faster and faster, it happened. He exploded like a volcano, gagging her, filling her mouth with cum.

"Stupid muthafucka!" she barked after spitting out the cum. "I told you not ta cum in my mouth. Dat shit taste nasty. Dat'z gonna cost you two more."

Laughing, Corey put his slimy penis away. "I gave you whut I had. I ain't got no more."

"You betta go get two more!" she suggested strongly. "Uh-uh, I don't play dat shit. You gon' gimme two more! Shoot, you ain't gonna jus' do me like dat."

"Aiight, c'mon." Having quickly weighed his options in his head, Corey had decided against beating her. He knew how fast a female crackhead would cry rape to get even. So to avoid that, together they walked the rooftops to his building to get some more crack.

This would turn out to be a major mistake. By showing a drug addict where he lived, Corey was asking for trouble. Because just as with feeding a stray cat, she'd be back.

Chapter **10**

Corey's involvement in the drug game deepened, to the point where his grades began to slip and his behavior started to change. He lost his motivation to excel in school. Nothing excited him now more than the street life. He couldn't see himself undergoing the metamorphosis, but his parents did. His mother was the first to notice he was staying out. She heard the whispers and rumors about her son's alleged drug involvement. To keep the peace in her household, she never voiced her concerns to her husband. But every chance she got, Mrs. Dixon confronted her son.

"Corey! Corey! Get ya lazy ass up!" his mother shouted, yanking the sheet off his body. "Didn't I tell you last nite ta dump the trash in the incinerator?"

Peeking out of one eye, Corey desperately tried to focus on her face. But his vision was blurry. All he could see was a feminine outline dressed in hospital whites, standing over him.

"You hear me, boy. Get up. I don't know what the devil

has gotten into you lately. I gotta tell you three or four times ta do somethin'. And all ya father gotta tell you is once and you jump. You gon' start givin' me the same respect you give him. Boy, you so mannish, mannish till you stink."

Now he was awake. His mother had successfully ruined his sleep, screaming at the top of her lungs. She preached and scolded him at the same time, giving Corey a good old-fashioned tongue-lashing.

"Boy, all you wanna do is eat, sleep, and run the streets. You in the street so much, I think you gotta magnet in ya ass, pullin' you outside." She took a quick inventory of his bedroom. "And whose bike is that?"

"My friend's," Corey mumbled as he continued to lie in the bed, testing his mother's patience.

"Ya friend's? Everything is always your friend's. What I tell you 'bout bringin' stuff in this house that me or your father didn't buy, huh? Get that piece of junk outta my house! And don't bring it back. I don't care if the president gives you somethin', don't bring it in here. . . . Ya friend's this and ya friend's that. If ya friend jumps off the roof, you gon' do it too? Boy, you don't know what a friend is. Ya friend ain't ya friend."

As it stood now, Corey couldn't bring home anything he bought with his drug money. He had to stash all his valuables, dividing them amongst his girlfriend, Monique, and O. He'd purchased some gold jewelry—a four-finger ring and a big fat rope chain with a Mercedes-Benz medallion. His new clothes—Air Jordans, leather jackets, etc.—were at O's house until he could work them into his wardrobe.

"Don't just sit there looking stupid. Get up and get ready for summer school. Boy, sometimes you make me so sick. I dunno how the hell you go from the honor roll to barely passing. You sho is tryin' ya best ta get left back. At the rate you going, you gonna drop out. And if you do, pack ya bags. Cuz you getting the hell outta here. You ain't gonna be lyin' around here not workin' or goin' to school . . . Here!"

Taking a few dollars out of her pocketbook, she handed it over to her son. Reluctantly Corey accepted the money, even though he didn't need it. He felt guilty taking her hard-earned money. His partnership with O had become quite lucrative. But had he refused his mother's pocket money, it would only have aroused her suspicions even more.

"Straighten up this room. And get ridda that damn bike," she fussed as she left his room and exited the apartment.

"Yeah! Yeah! Yeah!" Corey said, mocking her, after he heard the door close. Then he got up and began to get himself together.

No more than twenty minutes had passed when the intercom went off. *Buzzz! Buzzz!*

Corey prayed that this wasn't his mother doubling back to check on him. He was in no mood for any more of her nonsense.

"Who!" he shouted into the intercom.

"Me. Kelly" came a muffled reply.

No, this bitch didn't, Corey mused to himself. She was way out of line for dropping by his house like this. He had specifically told her to forget where he lived.

Sticking his head out of the bedroom window, he yelled

down, "Ay, yo, whut da fuck iz you doin', comin' ta my crib like dis?"

"I gotta talk ta you," she shouted back, making it seem important.

"Fuck you want?" he questioned harshly.

"Can I come up and talk ta you?" she begged. "I don't wanna yell it out."

Against his better judgment, he buzzed her into the building. When she reached his third-floor apartment, Corey was already waiting for her in the stairwell.

"Kelly, whut da fuck iz on ya mind? Didn't I tell you not ta ever come here lookin' fa me? Bitch, you know whut my momz would say if she caught you ringin' my bell?" He cursed, calling her every name in the book.

"Damn!" she exclaimed. "I'm sorry. But you ain't gotta be talkin' ta me like dat. I didn't know it was like dat. I got some business fa you. I got dis white boy parked outside, he tryin' ta spend like three hundred wit you."

"Bitch, dis ain't no fuckin' crack house!" Corey exploded. "Don't be bringin' no fuckin' customers here. He could be da po-lease."

"Damn, my fault. I was jus' tryin' ta look out fa ya. Next time I'ma take him somewhere else."

"It betta not be a next time here. Where iz dis muthafucka parked?" He went to the staircase window.

Kelly had made up the whole story. She didn't have any customer waiting to cop from Corey. Whenever her craving for crack demanded it, she would make up anything to get you to put drugs in her hand.

Scanning the street with Corey, she said, "Oh, he musta pulled off. You know how paranoid dem white boyz get about bein' in da projects. . . . I'm sayin', Corey, maybe you and me can still do a lil somethin'. Like last time."

Enticed by her beauty, Corey began to think with his little head instead of his big head. The mere thought of the sexual act previously performed on him made his nature rise. He was horny. He hadn't had sex in a week or so. His girlfriend, Monique, wasn't putting out like that. "I'm sayin'," he warned, "make dis ya last time comin' here. I'm tellin' you if it happens again, you gonna have problems. Now, c'mon!"

Quickly he escorted her through his apartment, to his bedroom, to take care of business. As soon as she was done giving him oral sex, Corey quickly got rid of her. And again he warned her not to come back.

* * *

A couple of days later, as Corey headed home after calling it a night on the block, he saw his father walking briskly in his direction. The closer his father got, the clearer the bewildered look on his face became. Something was wrong because his father never came looking for him. If there was a problem, he'd simply wait till Corey came home.

"Daddy," Corey called out.

In his trancelike state, his father hadn't even noticed his son, even though they were on the same block.

"Oh, there you are!" Mr. Dixon said, relieved. "I was just gettin' ready ta go 'round the corner lookin' fa you."

"Fa whut?" Corey questioned as they began to walk home together.

Wide-eyed, Mr. Dixon announced, "The police came by the house lookin' fa you. They said that you sold some man some bad crack. And that he's in the hospital in critical condition. They said if he dies, you could get twenty-five to life. Corey, I know you ain't out there foolin' wit no drugs . . . is you?"

Corey's heart skipped a beat; he swallowed hard. This couldn't be real, he thought. But he wasn't sure if he was actually responsible or not. What day was his father talking about? Corey sold plenty of crack to a lot of people. He didn't know. Deep in his heart, Corey knew that someone had dropped a dime on him. Someone had to have, he reasoned. Because unlike everybody else on the block, he didn't have a nickname or an alias. He went by his real name. So it would be easy for anyone to implicate him.

Earlier that day, in a major drug sweep on the block, dozens of fiends and drug dealers had been arrested. But Corey had avoided this by being at the right place at the right time. Corey and O had been in Harlem re-upping.

"I don't know whut they talkin' 'bout," Corey lied, trying to play innocent. "It wuzn't me. I don't sell drugz."

"I hope for both of our sakes you tellin' me the truth," his father confessed. "Ya mother's upstairs all upset and cryin'. And you know how she gets. . . . The police told me to bring you down to the precinct for questioning or they gonna pick you up off the street themselves. I'd rather bring you down there than have them embarrass you like that. Now I'm gonna ask you one more time, is you sellin' drugs? Did you sell that man that stuff?"

"No," Corey snapped.

* * *

At the precinct, Corey was escorted, without his parents, to be questioned.

"Who do you work for?" one cop asked.

"Nobody! I don't sell drugs. And I don't know nobody who do," Corey insisted.

The cop grew visibly pissed. He wasn't one for smart-assed kids mouthing off. He went into his bad-cop role. "Look, son, don't play fuckin' stupid wit me. I've been workin' these streets too fuckin' long, longer than you been alive. And liars like you come a dime a dozen. So save the bullshit for your parents. I know your lyin', it's written all over ya face. Now I'm asking you again, who do you work for?"

With a nasty attitude, Corey shot back, "Fa da last time, I'm tellin' you I don't sell drugz!"

"Look at me!" the cop demanded. "Who do you think you're foolin'? You lil snot-nose bastard, I got informants that say you sell crack. And that they also say it was you who sold the bad batch of crack to that man."

The cop began applying more pressure, trying to get Corey to spill his guts and say something incriminating, something that could be used against him in a court of law. Corey refused to break, though. He was content playing around with the cop. He sat there cool as a fan, grimacing.

The cop continued, "You can make it easy on yaself now, if

you come clean and confess. I can talk to some people, maybe get them to cut you a break. Probation. A little slap on the wrist . . . Corey, we don't want you. We want the big man. The scumbag who's got all the little kids on the corner pushin' his drugs. Don't take the weight for the big man. He wouldn't do it for you. Why, he don't give a flyin' fuck about you."

Corey didn't buy into this speech for one second. No matter how much the cop tried to dress it up, he knew the cop wanted him to snitch. And he wanted no part of that. Like any streetwise kid, he'd rather die than tell.

Death before dishonor. In the hood there was nothing worse in the world than being labeled a snitch. There was a saying on the street: "Snitches get stitches, put in body bags and found in ditches." Besides, who was he gonna tell on? Himself? O?

"Your poor mother is downstairs cryin' her eyes out. And your dad is worried sick. So don't make this situation any harder than it has to be. Tell me what I need to know and then you can go home. Now, son, tell me, who do you work for?" the cop pleaded.

Slowly Corey responded, "I D-O-N'T S-E-L-L D-R-U-G-S."

"So you wanna play hardball, huh? You think you tough? Well, let's see how tough you are when ya candy ass gets twenty-five to life. When they send ya young ass way upstate to Sing Sing or Attica, and some big muscle-bound fag makes you his girl."

Corey had heard it all before, the scared-straight, booty-bandit, bread-and-water jail stories. And he wasn't the least bit scared. He already knew the real deal from the older cats on the block, who had already been up north, in the Bronx House, and on Rikers Island. In his young mind, he thought he knew how to do time.

The cop had no choice but to let him go, they didn't have any evidence to arrest him, yet; only hearsay.

"Go 'head, get ya smart ass outta here!" the cop yelled. "This ain't the last time you'll be seein' me. I promise."

Strolling out of the room with an arrogant grin on his face, Corey slammed the door behind him. He knew he'd beaten the system, at least for now. Outside the precinct and closer to home, things reached a boiling point between Corey and his father.

Mr. Dixon pulled off the street and parked. He said, "Don't hand me shit. You think you're so slick. I know you're lying and the cops know it too. You might not have done this, but you doing somethin'. The police ain't come by our house for nothing.'

"I ain't doin' nuttin'," Corey said, straight-faced.

"Corey, you must really think I'm stupid, huh?" You don't think I ever was a kid? You think you the only one that ever lied to his father? When I was young, I lied to my father too. What I tell you about lying? You only lie to people you scared of."

Wearing a defiant look on his face, Corey just stared at his father from the backseat of the car. And being that Mr. Dixon was from the old school, he took his son's facial expression as disrespectful. A direct challenge to his authority.

He reached over the seat to Corey with the intent of knocking some sense into him. He stopped himself, got out of the car, and opened Corey's door. Mrs. Dixon got out too. She stepped between her husband and son. "Let go a me, Janice," Mr. Dixon angrily said to her through clenched teeth. "He thinks he's a man, I'ma beat 'im like one."

"No, John, please!" Mrs. Dixon cried. "Don't do this, please."

Standing his ground, Corey continued to look at his father as if he were crazy.

"What, you think you a man now, nigger?" his father yelled heatedly, trying to wriggle away from his wife's grip. "You think you grown now? Then leave, nigger! Go on, leave!"

This was the way out Corey had been looking for, his excuse to leave home. A free ghetto pass to run the streets and sell drugs, all day and every day. Just like some of his fatherless friends did. Taking one more rebellious glance at his father, he turned and began to walk away. He had no idea where he was going; all he knew was, he was going.

"No, Corey! No, baby! Please don't go!" his mother pleaded.

In the Dixon household, Mr. Dixon was a dictator. Whatever he said went. He was hard but fair. But Corey was becoming disenchanted with the spell his father had cast over the rest of the family. He knew his father didn't know it all. Corey wanted to be his own man and make his own decisions. So walking away from his father wouldn't be a problem. But his mother's cries froze him in his tracks. Only his mother's love brought him back, back to reality.

"Baby, don't go." She embraced him. "C'mon, y'all, let's cut this foolishness out. C'mon, let's all get in the car and go home. Everything is gonna be alright."

Back at the house, after Mr. Dixon had calmed down, he sat Corey down again. "Listen, Corey, next summer you'll be sixteen, and from then on you'll be considered an adult in the eyes of the law. So everything you do from then on goes on your record. And your record is like your skin, you gotta wear it for life. Your record will dictate what kinda job you can get, how you'll live, and your future. Son, don't trade tomorrow for today. Don't mortgage your whole future over some nonsense now. It ain't worth it. There's only two things ready for you now: jail and the graveyard. Which one is it gonna be? If you keep doin' whatcha doin', you're going to end up in one of them."

His father's last statement hung in the air like a dark cloud. Corey had never contemplated his own mortality. Like so many youths, he was reckless with his life and liberty. He never thought either could be taken from him at any moment. And even with his recent run-in with the law, he still couldn't envision himself being locked down. He couldn't see three or four years down the road. He saw summer to summer. With no plans for the future, Corey was just out there, lost in the sauce. The adage held true here; youth is truly wasted on the young.

"Lemme tell you this story," Mr. Dixon continued. "I once had this friend named Melvin. Me and him was real tight. Man, we did everything together. His wife hung with my wife, and his kids played with mine. Then Melvin started sellin' drugs. Heroin was the thing back then. I didn't wanna sell drugs, and I didn't want that stuff around my family. So me and Melvin went our separate ways. But I still would see him from time to time. Man, he had everything, fancy clothes, expensive cars, and beautiful women. Yeah, Melvin was sittin' on top of the world. At least he thought he was. Eventually, Melvin started usin' the same drugs he was sellin'. He became his own best customer, a junkie. Everything he gained illegally, he lost. The same people he thought were his friends when he was on top turned their backs on him. Now I said that to say this: I ain't got much, but I'm working hard and saving up to get us outta these projects. I ain't gotta look over my shoulder for nothing. The cops ain't looking for me and nobody's after me. I ain't got much, but I'll tell you what I do got. I got a beautiful family and a peace of mind. And you can't put a price tag on those two things. So what you need to do is, stop tryin' ta be like ya friends. Stop tryin' ta be like those that appear ta be better off than others, and start lookin' at those worse off than you. You'll appreciate what you got even more. All those guys on the corner, they might have the latest clothes, jewelry, the newest cars, but let me tell you somethin', all of that is nothing. Not in the big scheme of things. Taste in cars, clothes, and jewelry change almost from year ta year. Those guys are gonna have to keep dealin' drugs to maintain that lifestyle. In the world nobody wants to settle for second best. Everybody wants to be 'the man.' To have the best of the best. But, Corey, there's more to life than material possessions. Those guys are in love with that stuff. In love with things not capable of loving them back. Things that may one day cost them their lives, because somebody wants what they got."

* * *

Nothing ever came of the alleged bad-crack case. The police never contacted the Dixons again. This should have been a wake-up call for Corey.

He did slow down somewhat. He stopped running the streets so much. He mainly hung around the house or at his girlfriend's. Understanding what Corey was going through, O continued to make money for them both, allowing Corey to appear as if he'd learned his lesson.

But the goody-goody lifestyle was boring him to death. He needed some excitement. Corey was soon back at it again, knee-deep in the game.

Chapter 11

O lured a crackhead to the roof of a building under the pretense of buying a bulletproof vest from him.

"Betta stay still," O said with a nine-millimeter gun aimed at the guy's head. "I'm telling you fa da last time, don't move."

"C'mon, man. Don't do this! Please, don't do it."

Corey stood to the side, watching the scene play out.

" 'Member dat VCR you sold me last week?" O asked as he squinted his eyes. "It didn't work. You beat me. You lied to me then. How I know you ain't lyin' to me now?"

"I'm sorry!" the man said, copping a plea. "I ain't know da VCR ain't work. I was sellin' it fa somebody else. They was lookin' out fa me. You know I always bring you good stuff. Dis da first time anythin' like dis eva happened—"

"Whut you so worried 'bout?" O stated, cutting him off. "You da one said da vest could stop forty-fives, nines, and some more shit. If it's all dat whut ya say it iz, you cool. But if it ain't . . ."

"Shorty, don't do dis," the crackhead pleaded. "Suppose you miss?"

"Yo, I heard nuff of dis shit!" O snapped. "Now hold ya arms out and stick out ya chest. I'ma 'bout ta bust off."

Reluctantly, the man did as he was told. Leaning against the wall of the next building, he closed his eyes and said a quick prayer. Praying to God almightily that O was a good shot. Or he was a dead man.

Continuing to line up the gun's sight, O zeroed in on his intended target, the man's chest. Then without warning, he squeezed off one shot from his semiautomatic. Resisting the urge to fire more rounds, knowing that one gunshot would only make people wonder—*Was that a gunshot?*—but two or three shots might bring the police. The slug found its intended target, slamming into the man's solar plexus. But most of the bullet's force was absorbed by the vest's shock plate. Still, there was more than enough power to knock the wind out of the man. Racing over to him, Corey and O didn't know if he was hit or not. They weren't too concerned about that either. They were more worried about the vest itself. Had it withstood the bullet? Could they depend on it during a shoot-out?

"Yo, you aiight?" Corey inquired as the man doubled over in pain. "You ain't hit, iz you?"

Gasping for air, the man was unable to talk. So he shook his head no.

"Aw, nigger, stand up!" O barked. "You aiight. Muthafucka, you'll live. Take my vest off now!"

"Boy, you crazy!" the crackhead whispered. "I ain't fuckin' wit you no more."

"Good!" O replied. "You betta come up outta dat vest fa I shoot ta kill, dis time."

Obeying the order, the man slipped out of the bulletproof vest and handed it over. O paid him in crack and he left.

Lately, O had begun stockpiling guns and ammunition. He bought almost every weapon that he came across, accumulating a small arsenal. Acquiring the bulletproof vest was like icing on the cake. Just having it in his possession made him feel invincible.

After securing the vest, Corey turned to O and said, "Damn, you sure iz buyin' up a lotta gunz and shit. Don't you think we got enuff?"

"We can neva have enuff gunz!" O shot back. "Dat'z like sayin' we got enuff money. Whut'z enuff? I'm tryin' ta get rich! Whut'z the point of gettin' in da game if you ain't? So how many gunz iz too many? Gunz iz protection. Gunz iz money. Gunz iz power."

This all-out fuck-the-world attitude was rubbing off on Corey. He followed O's lead, jumping back into the game headfirst.

* * *

Later that evening, when Corey came home to eat, he was greeted at the door by his mother. She was furious.

"Some lady came here lookin' fa you a while ago," she angrily stated. "I seen her before. And she's up to no good. She be out there in them streets at all hours of the day and night, foolin' wit them drugs. . . . I wanna know, what the hell she want wit you? Huh?"

Confused, he asked, "Who you talkin' 'bout? Whut'z her name?"

"Kelly!" his mother snapped. "I think that's what she says her name was. . . . Now, I wanna know, why she comin' to *my house* lookin' for *my teenage son?* Huh?"

Kelly? Corey thought to himself. *I'ma kill dat bitch! I told her not to come here no more. Now she did it.*

"Oh, Kelly is my friend's older sista," he quickly replied. "She probably came by here lookin' fa him, knowin' he be wit me."

"Don't hand me that mess!" his mother shouted. "You sellin' that stuff again. That's why she lookin' fa you, so she could buy some drugs. I ain't stupid. What ya father tell you about that? You ain't get enough of that, huh? You ain't gonna be happy till somethin' bad happens to you. Boy, you musta lost ya goddamn mind havin' some f-ing junkie come ta my house. Wait till ya father hears about this."

Enraged, Corey shot out of the apartment in search of Kelly. He was gonna beat her down. He'd told her several times not to come back to his house. But she hadn't listened. Her craving for crack got the best of her. Corey thought she had taken his warning as a joke. Since Kelly acted as if she hadn't heard him, she was about to feel his wrath.

"Corey, bring ya ass back up these stairs!" Mrs. Dixon hollered down the stairwell. "You hear me?"

Corey didn't listen, he kept on going. He wasn't gonna stop till he found Kelly. He was about to do something he'd live to regret.

Searching high and low, Corey checked all of Kelly's usual

hangouts—the block, the avenues, and various well-known crack houses. But he couldn't find her to save his life. By accident he came upon her in a building staircase.

Immediately, the nasty scowl that was pasted on Corey's face told Kelly she was in deep trouble. But be that as it may, she continued pulling on her glass crack pipe, with her eyes bulging out of her head.

"Bitch, didn't I tell you not to come to my house no more!" Corey hissed as he walked up to her. Then without warning, he suddenly launched a bloody assault on her, punching Kelly in the face, causing her to drop her crack-packed pipe.

"*Aaahhh!* Help! Police! Help!" she cried, creating a loud echo, while Corey continued.

"Whut, you thought I wuz playin' when I told you dat? Huh? Bitch, dis da last time you eva gonna dis me," Corey heatedly stated, landing blow after blow, savagely pounding on her, bloodying her face.

Had it not been for a nosy neighbor, Corey might have done some serious damage to Kelly. He was in a violent trance, completely disregarding that this was a woman, a black woman, that he was beating on.

"Hey, whut da hell's goin' on up there?" a man shouted, cautiously advancing up the steps. "Leave that lady alone. I'm callin' da po-lease."

The sound of the man's voice snapped Corey out of it. Before the Good Samaritan could reach the scene of the crime, Corey kicked open the door that led to the roof and fled, leaving behind a bloody mess. Afterward, Corey went straight to O's house, to tell him what he had done. And over forty ounces of beer and blunts, they laughed about the beating. Then later Corey went home.

And as soon as he crossed his apartment's threshold, his father pounced on him. "What the hell is on ya mind?" Mr. Dixon asked, pinning his son against the wall. "That lady came back by here again, all beat up. She said you did it. What you doin' puttin' ya hands on that woman like that? Nigger, you lucky she ain't call the cops on you." Held firmly against the wall, Corey couldn't move. He couldn't possibly explain to his father that Kelly had to be checked physically, because his father wasn't street. He didn't have that street mentality.

"Boy, I told you time and time again about ya nonsense. But you don't believe shit stinks," Mr. Dixon said. "This time you went too far. . . . You hardheaded! I tried to talk to you like a man, but you still won't listen. It's like I don't even know you no more. I don't know where you be or who you dealin' wit. All I know is this: you can't do it here no more. You endangering ya own life, as well as mine and ya mother's. You gotta go. Get ya things and leave."

The time had come as a parent to let go of his son's hand, to let him make his own mistakes. He had to let Corey face the dangers of the streets that he had so desperately tried to protect him from. As much as he didn't want to, he felt that he had to. Corey's behavior could no longer be tolerated. Corey had brought the street life to his door. What was next? He had to let go of his drowning son before he pulled the whole family under.

From her bedroom door, Mrs. Dixon watched, staying in her woman's place. As a mother and a wife, her heart was divided between letting her husband do what he felt had to be done and protecting her child. She knew her husband was right though, that something more had to be done.

Corey calmly walked to his room and began to pack. Quickly he gathered up as much of his stuff as he could carry.

Chapter 12

The frigid winter winds blew relentlessly; "the hawk" was out in full effect, making its presence known. Brutal weather conditions like these forced every sensible human being indoors, except drug addicts and drug dealers. Otherwise the block was like a ghost town. The few who did scurry about ran to and from the grocery story, pizza shop, and Chinese restaurant.

Corey raised his hand to his mouth to blow hot air on his frozen digits. Standing in front of the Chinese restaurant, he was armed only with a black, three-quarter, goose-down coat, a pair of tan North Lake boots, blue jeans, and thermals. But he might as well have been naked. Mother Nature cut through his weak defense as if it were nonexistent.

It's bleeding out here, he said to himself.

The rest of his friends and/or competition stood inside the restaurant nursing dollar soups, trying to warm up.

Out of the corner of his eye, he saw a customer quickly ride through the block. In a flash, he gave chase. The rest of the drug dealers followed suit, flying out of the restaurants, buildings, or wherever they were hiding. Corey was one of the first to reach the car.

"Danny! Danny!" they all seemed to shout in unison.

"I got dat fish scale!" someone yelled.

"My shit iz raw!" another hollered.

"How much you got? I'ma give you some play! These niggas got trash! Don't fuck wit them, you know me! My shit's official! Word!"

Huddling around the driver's-side window, they fiercely fought for position, just for the right to attempt to make this sell. Danny was a rich white boy, clean-cut corporate-America type, who spent nothing under a hundred dollars at a time. He was the type one could give credit. Danny was known as "good money" on the block. On a slow, cold night like tonight, drug dealers would literally fight—sometimes even kill—to make this kind of sale.

"Yo, get da fuck away from my custy!" a deep voice barked. "I'ma hurt one na y'all lil niggas. I'm tellin' you! Word ta mother! Y'all lil niggas betta stop bum-rushin' my people. Back da fuck up!" Diesel demanded.

He was the resident block bully, who threw his weight around every chance he got. Diesel used his imposing physical stature and loud mouth to intimidate the young and the weak. They heard him, but this crew was too hungry to heed his warnings. They didn't miss a beat.

"Oh, y'all lil niggas think I'm playin', huh?" Diesel furiously yelled, feeling totally disrespected.

Diesel was fresh out of a stint in jail. He had come home just in time to witness the changing of the guard on the block. The younger drug dealers, some of whom he had previously employed, now had their own product. This made Diesel have to sell his own drugs, hand to hand, to the junkies and fiends. While his peers in the drug game were either employing workers or had out-of-town drug gold mines, he was stuck on the block fighting young boys for sales. Mentally, it was killing him to be out here because, in his mind, he was larger than this. In his mind, he had made this block what it was. He had never imagined being disrespected by some young boys. Not now, not ever.

Diesel sprang into action. He began pulling the younger, smaller drug dealers away from the car. Like scrap pieces of paper he tossed one after another, until he had cleared the area, of all except one. Money Mike remained, almost oblivious to what was going on around him. He was determined to make this sale.

"Ay, yo, Mike! Nigga, didn't you fuckin' hear me? I'ma slap da shit outta you!" Diesel warned.

"Taste it, Danny!" Money Mike urged the customer. "My shit iz flavor! How many you want? I got it! Whatever? Lemme hop in." He was half inside the car window. Just in time, Money Mike looked up to see Diesel's huge hand coming down hard. The impact of the blow floored him. The sound of the smack was so loud it echoed off the project buildings.

"Get da fuck outta here! You bitch-ass nigga! I betta not see you out here no more tanite! Matterfact, no more! None of you lil niggas betta not make another fuckin' sale! Shop closed!"

Money Mike cowered meekly between the car and the cold concrete, as the ominous presence of Diesel towered over him. He feared that the vicious assault wasn't over. They were physically mismatched: Diesel was muscularly built and Money Mike was tall and lanky. Not until Diesel began to walk toward the other side of the car did Money Mike get up. He quickly got to his feet and staggered off. Loud laughs and snickers could be heard from the other drug dealers. It was safe to say that Money Mike's pride and manhood had taken a serious blow. The damage was done; to Mike, it could only be repaired by a bullet.

Outside the Chinese restaurant, a group of younger drug dealers reenacted the event.

"Yo, Diesel slapped da bullshit out of Money Mike! Like dis," one said, acting out both parts, exaggerating every action and reaction.

They exchanged versions of the story and shared a good laugh at Money Mike's expense—unaware of the repercussions the incident would have.

* * *

On the next block, a few hundred feet away, Diesel stood in front of the corner bodega, counting his loot from a previous drug sale and talking to himself:

"These lil niggas iz outta fuckin' order round here! They must don't know who da fuck I am! Muthafuckin' Diesel! Lil niggas betta recognize! Dis my block! I run dis shit."

He never looked up while counting his cash. He kept talking to himself, hyping himself up. So he never saw Money

Mike turn the corner, gun in hand. Everyone else did, though. All the talk stopped and eyes focused on them.

"Yo, Diesel?" Money Mike said weakly. Even armed with a .38 snub-nose, he was still afraid of Diesel. His hand trembled as he raised the gun, taking aim at his intended victim's head.

"Yo, why da fuck you slap me? I neva disrespected you, let alone put my hands on you. You smacked me like a bitch. I ain't no ho! Yo, you think I'm pussy? You think I'ma herb? Huh?" he continued.

With an evil grin pasted on his face, Diesel paused from counting his money. Normally, Mike wasn't a violent person. But these weren't normal circumstances; the streets were watching and waiting to see how he would react.

"You bitch-ass nigga!" Diesel hollered. "You pullin' a gun out on me? Huh? Nigga, you pussy! You ain't gonna use it. You ain't got da heart! I'ma bout ta take dat shit from you and bust you wit ya own gun, faggot!"

The blood inside Money Mike's veins boiled. Diesel had just added verbal insult to physical injury. Mike wished he could crawl under a rock and hide. He felt he had no choice but to do what he had to do.

Taking a step toward him, Diesel reached for the gun; at the same time, a round went off. In slow motion Diesel seemed to stumble back. Shock registered on his face as blood began to gush from a gaping hole in his forehead.

A feeling of power surged through Money Mike's entire body. He began squeezing off shot after shot into Diesel's head and chest. He watched as Diesel's lifeless body fell to the ground. Then he stood over the top of the body, pumping shot after shot into it, until the gun's chamber was empty.

"Who's da bitch-ass nigga now!" Money Mike screamed. "Who? You fuckin' sucka! Run ya mouf now! Nigga, ya dead! I did dat! Me! Money Mike."

A thinking person would have fled the scene now. But Mike stayed, as if he were daring the law to apprehend him.

"Yo, Mike! Take da gun and be out!" another person hollered. "He dead! It'z ova! Run!"

Their request fell on deaf ears; Mike continued screaming at the corpse. He seemed oblivious to their pleas and the sirens that rose in volume as they came closer. Seemingly out of nowhere, blue-and-white and unmarked police cars screeched to a halt surrounding Money Mike and Diesel's corpse.

Officers drew their weapons and ordered, "Freeze! Drop your weapon and place your hands where we can see them."

Money Mike complied and dropped his gun. In an instant the officers rushed him from every direction, taking him down to the ground and handcuffing him. A group of spectators had arrived just in time to witness the actual arrest.

Money Mike seemed to smirk as he was being placed in the squad car. He seemed proud of himself.

"Fuck dat nigga!" Mike screamed out. "I bodied 'im!"

The police officers shook their heads. This was yet another case for their record books. It was unbelievable how these black kids took each other's life without a second thought.

* * *

After the meat wagon was called in to haul off Diesel's body, Corey and the rest of the drug dealers on the block headed their separate ways. The weather was still cold, but the block was scorching hot. The police presence alone would scare off all potential customers for a good while. The block was now crawling with cops, and that meant no money for a day or two. In any direction one looked, a police car was coming or going.

"Yo, guess whut?" Corey said. "Da nigga Diesel just got bodied!"

"Word?" O said. "How? Who did it? Who kilt 'im?"

"Money Mike!" Corey blurted out. "Shot 'im da fuck up!"

"Get da fuck outta here! Nah, not Money Mike. Fa real? He ain't no killa!"

"Da nigga Diesel smacked da bullshit outta him in fronta everybody though," Corey said. "Dat musta set him off. Maybe that embarrassed him or sumthin'."

"Okay! Dat explains everything. Men don't smack otha men. If you smack anotha man, dat means you had da chance to punch him but you chose not to. You thought so little of that man, he was a bitch to you, he wasn't a threat, you smacked him. Good for Diesel! He got his. He got what was comin' ta him."

"But, O, da nigga dead, kid! His fuckin' brains and blood is all over the sidewalk. He dead! Ain't no comin' back from dat."

"Listen, don't feel sorry fa Diesel. He got whut he deserved. He wuz a big fuckin' bully. Da nigga violated da code of the streets. You live by the code; you die by the code. I ain't gonna shed a tear fa da nigga. Money Mike did da whole block a favor. Word!"

No matter whom it befell or where it befell, death always put Corey in a somber mood. O on the other hand had lived the street life long enough though that it was placing a callus around his heart, causing him to be indifferent to it. The somber mood soon wore off and Corey kept his business and his body moving.

He didn't know that he was wanted for a direct sale of a controlled dangerous substance. This was the first year of "the Narcotics Task," and drug dealers in New York City were in for a rude awakening.

* * *

Weeks after the murder, the block returned to normal. The police presence slowly dissipated, and crack cocaine regained its place as the hottest product in this open-air drug market. Everyone had seemingly forgotten about Diesel's death and Money Mike's imprisonment. These two sacrificial lambs were distant memories in everyone's mind. Once again Corey was back on his grind, selling drugs like he had a license.

A Hispanic man in an old, beat-up two-door Ford Pinto circled the block again. He appeared to be looking for no one in particular. To Corey, he had *customer* written all over him. He was money and Corey wasn't going to let it pass him by again. He was on a serious paper chase. All money was good money to him. It all spent the same, dirty or clean.

"Yo, papi! Papi!" he called out as the car came to a halt in front of him. "I got them jumbos! How many you want?"

Corey bent down to avoid detection of any passing police car. Nervously, he looked up and down the block for any signs of the cops. He wanted to get this drug transaction over as quickly as possible. His motto was cop and bop.

"Lemme see whatcha got. Is it any good?" the customer asked.

"My jumbos are official. Home-cooked! None a dat big yeasted-up shit dat other niggas out here got. Look."

Corey passed the Hispanic man a small, clear, red-topped crack vial. He closely scrutinized the substance for authenticity. Assured of that, he proceeded to deal.

"How much is this? A dime piece?"

"Ain't no fuckin' dimes out here. Dat's a twenty," Corey shot back.

The man's lack of knowledge should have been a warning sign, a red flag, for Corey. On the street any legit customer knew the price of the product.

"How much is it?" the man repeated, as if he hadn't heard him.

"Twenty dollars!" Corey barked. "Are you deaf or sumthin'?"

"Can I get three for fifty?" the man begged. "Gimme a deal and I'll be back. I'll only cop from you."

"C'mon, man! It's hot out here. Gimme da muthafuckin' paper."

In one smooth motion Corey brought his hands to his mouth and spit out two more vials of crack cocaine, coated with saliva. Corey wiped them off, best he could, on his pants leg. Then they exchanged drugs for currency.

"Yo, good lookin' out!" the man happily exclaimed. "When I come back, I'll deal only wit you."

Whatever! Corey thought to himself as he walked away inspecting the fifty-dollar bill. He had been fooled by fake money before, the corners of a big bill taped to a one-dollar bill. He heard that I'll-be-back shit before. From experience he knew that crackheads were some disloyal people. Whoever they thought would give them a deal or had the flavor that they savored—that's whom the crackheads bought their product from. Their loyalty was limited to their next hit.

Corey walked back toward the avenue and posted up on the corner to wait on his next sale.

Corey watched closely as two other crack dealers on the corner participated in a slap-boxing match. This was a ghetto form of bravado, to test one another, something that the youths did to prove their manhood.

"Oooooh, he caught you lovely, Todd," someone instigated. "I know you ain't gonna let dat slide."

"Dat's right, Shiz, knock dat nigga's block off, kid! Yeah!" another guy yelled.

Corey was so engrossed in the match that he wasn't paying attention to his surroundings. Otherwise, he would have seen three unmarked police cars descending upon the corner. They closed off every avenue of escape before he knew it.

"Nobody move!" one cop commanded as law enforcement officials closed in on the group of teens.

Corey thought to himself, *Whoever it is they're looking for must be in crazy trouble.*

Soon it was clear exactly whom they were searching for, as they stepped directly to Corey and began to choke him. The undercover agent to whom he had made the drug sale had told the backup police units that Corey kept vials of crack cocaine stashed in his mouth. In arresting him, they choked him to prevent him from swallowing the evidence.

"Wha', wha'?" Corey couldn't get the words out. He didn't want to breathe and accidentally swallow a crack vial down the wrong part of his throat.

"Shut up! Spit it out!"

After a brief struggle, Corey momentarily broke their grip and swallowed the remaining crack vials he held under his tongue. Since possession was nine-tenths of the law, Corey hoped by swallowing the crack he had rid himself of any potential problem.

In the back of a nondescript cargo van, Corey sat shackled with numerous other crack cocaine dealers, as the police replayed their sting operation on countless other drug blocks in the area, arresting many offenders. The sweep caught everyone by surprise.

* * *

At the police station, it was the beginning of a long day. Corey and the rest of the other drug defendants were formally charged with the sale of a controlled substance. They were allowed their one phone call, and then they were thrown into tiny holding cells while everyone's paperwork was completed. This was the worst part of being arrested and was known to criminals as bull-pen therapy. Many men have cracked while sleeping in tiny, cold, crowded cells, on hard wooden benches, where more often than not you had to fight just for breathing room.

Corey handled it like a champ. He was shuffled from one police precinct to another, then transported to the 161st courthouse, known as central booking. This was where a defendant was arraigned in front of a magistrate judge. This was the last stop for most. They were either remanded to jail for their criminal acts or they were set free, most times to commit the same crime again.

"The People of New York versus Corey Dixon," the court official said. Corey wondered how many times she'd had to say those same words. He was alone and felt, literally, against the world. He felt a tinge of fear in the pit of his stomach and didn't like the sound of what he was hearing.

After two days of sleeping in the bull pens, Corey now stood in front of the judge in roughed-up, wrinkled clothes, looking somewhat disoriented.

"How do you plead?" the court official asked.

"At this present time the defendant wishes to plead not guilty, Your Honor," his public defender said.

Corey stood stone-faced and silent before the judge as the district attorney solemnly read from the police report. Listening closely, Corey heard him stretch the truth and tell a few lies. He read Corey's whole criminal history, as if that sheet of paper accurately painted a picture of Corey the person. To hear him tell it, Corey was public enemy number one or a menace to society. After being subjected to this pack of lies, Corey had no choice but to take it personally. Evilly, he glared at the district attorney with hatred in his heart.

"Your Honor, my client is still in school," the public defender stated. "And I think you would be doing this young man a major injustice if you remanded him to Rikers Island."

The judged weighted the validity of each argument, then

remanded Corey in lieu of a five-hundred-dollar bail. Corey was devastated as the handcuffs were slapped back on his wrists, and he was led back to the bull pens by two court officers.

Almost immediately bond was posted for him. His good friend and crime partner O had posted bail.

Never in his life was Corey so happy to see his friend's face. They hugged and exchanged greetings.

"Yo, kid, I thought I was goin' ta da Island fa a minute there. I didn't see you out in da courtroom or nuttin'," Corey exclaimed.

"Man, just cuz you ain't see me, don't mean I ain't there. I had to talk to some bails bondsmen just in case. And good thing I did. Look how they played you? A fuckin' five-hundred-dollar bail! Dat's crazy!"

"Word up! Dat shit wuz foul!"

"Yo, let's go git sumthin' ta eat. I know you hungrier than a muthafucka. Fuck wit dem hard-ass cheese sandwiches."

"Definitely! I'm starvin'! Ready to munch out!" Corey exclaimed.

* * *

Corey had his day in court after his initial arrest on drug charges. Corey's case was waived from Bronx Criminal to the State Supreme Court.

The courtroom was damn near empty on that cold winter day. Only a few concerned family members and friends of other defendants were seated scattered about. O was amongst those who braved the elements to lend his friend some moral support. He was there to show that, yes, someone did love and care about this young black boy. O felt that this was the least he could do, since they had fallen on some hard times, taking loss after loss in the drug game. They had failed to stash enough money for an adequate lawyer for Corey's defense. They had committed a cardinal sin, known in the drug game as hustling backward.

O was not alone in showing support; he was just the only person Corey had asked to be there today. He didn't want his girlfriend there to make an emotional scene in the courtroom. That was the last thing he needed right now.

So he never told her exactly what day he was scheduled to appear in court. See, Corey knew what she didn't. He was going to jail. He had accepted that he was going to jail months ago. He had already plea-bargained and pled guilty to the drug charge; as a consequence the state dropped the assault case against him. It didn't matter how much his girlfriend prayed and tried to stay optimistic. The question now was, for how long would he be locked up?

Corey didn't tell his parents what was going to happen either. He didn't want them to know for various reasons. He feared his father might say, "I told you so," and that his mother would worry. She didn't deserve that from him. He had brought this on himself and he planned on dealing with it by himself. He wasn't about to drag anyone down with him.

The Honorable Judge Lawrence B. Brown III was presiding in his case. A murderous, chaotic scene had taken place in his courtroom months ago, so security was beefed up. Court officers were in full force. A repeat performance was out of the question.

The spectators watched as each prisoner, one by one, was led from the cold holding cells beneath the courthouse like a funeral procession. Soon it would be Corey's turn to learn his fate.

He felt as if he were watching each man in front of him being put to death and knew he was next.

Corey huddled on the cold wooden court bench in the corner with O and his public defender as he heard his court docket number called. They rose to take their places behind the defendant's table. Before doing so, he made eye contact with O and nodded his head, as if to say, 'I'm ready for whatever may happen.'

Corey's gesture was bold, but inside he was scared to death. Secretly O too was afraid for him.

The whole process seemed surreal. Before he knew it, he was standing before the judge, his mind a blur. All he would remember would be them saying, "The People of New York versus Corey Dixon. Docket number 38-5503." And once again that statement blew his mind.

This was a sentencing hearing for Corey so there was no need for the district attorney to assassinate Corey's character. Still, the public defender put up a feeble attempt to sway the judge's already formulated decision. What was about to happen was going to happen; no amount of words from either side would change that.

"Well, Your Honor, since the last time my client appeared, he's managed to keep his nose clean while out on bail. My client is young, seventeen years old, and he has made a few mistakes in his lifetime, but he stands before you a changed man," the public defender said weakly. "I feel it's in the best interest of the court to sentence this young man to probation verses little, if any, jail time."

Going through the formalities, the judge let the public defender speak his piece. Then it was Corey's turn to address the court.

The judge asked, "Do you have anything to say before the court passes sentence on you, young man?"

"Yes, Your Honor," Corey announced as he nervously shifted his body weight from one foot to another.

Not one word that was about to be uttered from Corey's mouth was planned or rehearsed. His speech came purely from the heart. He didn't like to speak publicly but he felt that no one would fight harder or speak better for his freedom than he would.

"I, I stand before you today for sentencing, not to deny my guilt or to proclaim my innocence." He continued, "But to ask that Your Honor have mercy on me in this matter. With that being said, I place myself at the mercy of the court."

"Are you finished, young man?" the judge interrupted; he clearly wasn't moved by Corey's makeshift speech.

The judge had heard this song before, from far more persuasive defendants; just like Corey, they were also guilty as sin. He didn't see an ounce of remorse in Corey. In his estimation the only the thing Corey was probably sorry for was getting caught. Judge Brown was quite sure Corey, had he not been arrested, would have kept on plaguing the community with his drug-dealing ways. He was a thorn in society's side that had to be properly dealt with.

Corey was caught off guard; he thought the judge would at least hear him out.

"Ummm, yeah! I mean yes, Your Honor," he stuttered. "I'm finished."

The judge looked down from his ivory white tower, called the bench, upon Corey with an expression of sheer disgust.

"If you are looking for mercy, Mr. Dixon, then, sir, you are surely in the wrong place," the judge spat. "I'm in the business off dispensing justice. Protecting society from scoundrels like you!"

At this point, Corey wished he could crawl under a rock and hide. Had he known how the judge would respond to his words, he would have remained silent. The volume and tone of voice the judge used caused him to cringe. Right then and there he knew it would get worse before it got better.

"And furthermore, I beg to differ with the positive picture that your Legal Aid lawyer has painted of you. Oh, you're no angel, young man. You're a bad kid whose only lament is getting caught. I've seen your kind before. You people start out with minor crimes, then before long you graduate to murder." The judge began to shuffle paperwork back and forth on his desk.

A nervous look appeared on Corey's public defender's face. He took the judge's action as a sign he had already made up his mind and was ready to move on to the next case.

Looking down upon Corey in pure disgust, the judge continued, "You're nothing more than a gun-toting crack dealer. A hazard to both yourself and society. By the way, young man, where are your parents? Your mother? Is she here in the courtroom with you today?"

"No, sir. She's not here with me today because I didn't tell her that I was being sentenced today. I have already caused her too much pain." Corey lied unconvincingly, "She's very sick. She has a bad heart."

The judge exploded, "And I suppose you don't know why? She's ashamed of you! That's the real reason. Your mother didn't accompany you today because she's ashamed of you! Her youngest son in the highest court of the land! I hereby sentence you to a minimum sentence of three years and a maximum sentence not to exceed six years. My only other wish would be that I could impose an even more severe punishment than that. But I am bound by the sentencing guidelines. Let me warn you, Mr. Dixon, if you should ever have the misfortune of setting one foot in my courtroom again, I'll do everything in my power to make sure you never see the light of day again! Bailiffs, remove this poor excuse of a human out of my sight! Next case!"

Corey thought, *This is what the color line, the racial divide, looks like. This is where it breaks down to the powerful versus the powerless, persecutor versus the persecuted, the oppressor versus the oppressed.*

Corey stood still, dumbfounded and unsure of what had just transpired. *Three to six years.* Those numbers kept racing through his mind, along with the resounding, chilling voice of the judge.

He was supposed to get "a slap on the wrist." At least that's how his public defender had put it. That's why he'd copped out to the crime in the first place. But what he hadn't realized was that his sentencing was solely up to the discretion of the judge and the prosecutor. His public defender had given him bad advice, had sold him out. Corey had just gotten railroaded. He was now state property.

Corey wasn't really sure how much time he was actually going to serve. All he knew was he had to serve a minimum of three years before he was even eligible for parole. All he knew was that he would no longer be called by name, only a number. All he knew was that he couldn't even see that far down the road. Never in his entire life had he fathomed the thought of where he would be in three years. Now he didn't have much choice. Either he put an *H* on his chest and handled the situation, or he could take the cowardly route and hang himself.

One thing was for certain: nothing in Corey's seventeen years of existence had prepared him for what would come next.

[illegible]
[illegible]
[illegible]
[illegible]
[illegible]
[illegible]
[illegible]
[illegible]
[illegible]
[illegible]

[illegible]
[illegible]

TIME

Chapter 13

Surrounded by water, a stone's throw away from La Guardia Airport in Queens, New York, Rikers Island penal compound is one of the largest in the world. Corey would temporarily be housed there while he awaited a transfer to a state facility. Rikers Island was as dangerous as any state prison in America. It was like a boot camp that would prepare Corey for his tour of duty in the state prison system. This was gladiator school.

"Don't serve time, let time serve you!" one sign read.

These signs were everywhere. Corey had seen this sign or heard the saying countless times. And he never really understood its true meaning.

The minute Corey set foot on Rikers Island he was on full alert. To be alert meant seeing trouble before it came your way. Being alert meant staying alive. He knew he had to watch his own back. He'd heard all the horror stories that drug dealers from his block had brought home with them. Only the strong survived here; the weak were robbed and/or punked. They were made to wash clothes and extorted for packages or commissary goods. He was determined to enter jail just as he'd come: unmarked and respected.

"Save all those mean looks fa population," an older inmate said to a group of "new jacks." He was mopping a long prison-corridor floor. He was tired of all those mean stares the new arriving inmates shot at him.

C-76 was the name of the housing unit to which sentenced inmates were sent. Corey was immediately placed in four upper, a "new jack" dorm for adolescents, because of his age. He was surrounded by kids from ages sixteen to twenty-one. They were from every part of the city imaginable. Every face Corey saw was unfamiliar to him, except for some kid he'd met after he'd gotten arrested. His name was Shawn. They had managed to get caught on the same day, in different sections of the Bronx, where they both were from. Then they crossed paths again at court and in the bull pens the day Corey was sentenced. Shawn was sentenced to one year. Besides being incarcerated drug dealers, the Bronx was their common bond. Rikers Island and New York City were extremely geographical and territorial. It was about where you were from, you had to run with someone on Rikers Island, whether a group or a gang—you could not make it alone. So Corey and Shawn had made a pact, to watch each other's back in the bull pen.

Corey walked into the new jack dorm with several other sentenced inmates, carrying his bedroll—a small green army cover, two dingy white sheets, a pillowcase—and a roll of toilet tissue. All eyes seemed on him.

"Yo, Shiz, whut'z up, baby boy?" Corey yelled to Shawn as he placed his things down on an empty bunk.

Shawn was doing some push-ups in the corner and had not seen Corey come in. "Oh, shit! What's up, kid?"

"Chillin'!" Corey replied. "Just came in."

"Yo, how you livin'? You aiight? Want some commissary or somethin'? You smoke?" Shawn asked, bombarding Corey with question after question.

"Nah, I don't smoke, kid! But I could use some deodorant and soap, baby oil, and some shower slippers."

"Kid, I got you! Don't worry 'bout it! And I got some eatz fa you too."

"Yo, I'm gonna give it back to you once we go to commissary. I got some paper in my account."

"Core, don't sweat dat! I'm aiight! I got a lil store. I be jugglin' cigarettes and food. Cigarettes on the juggle. No juggle, no struggle."

As they were talking, another inmate walked up on them and stood nearby. Corey assumed that Shawn knew the fellow and vice versa. They continued talking.

"Yo, why don't you let my man try on ya sneakerz?" the kid said. "Whut size iz those? Huh?"

With a nasty snarl pasted on his lips, Corey looked at the kid with an expression that said, "You must be kiddin'. Get da fuck outta my face!" But he never said a word aloud. After hearing that statement, Corey knew that someone had sent this kid at him. He also knew from the street that the smallest dudes tend to start the most trouble. Corey would wipe the floor with "Shorty" if the need be. It wouldn't even be a fight.

"They yo size!" Corey snapped. "Get da fuck away from me! Before I—"

"Oh, you a gangster huh? Yo, everybody, we got a gangster in da house! Nigga, you betta wrap up whut you don't want broke up."

Before the kid walked away, he shot Corey a cold stare that said, "This ain't over."

"Yo, be on point tanite. Nigga's gonna try you fa ya kickz!" Shawn advised him.

Since Corey had entered the jail, he'd seen many admiring stares for the sneakers he wore. Air Jordans were a hot commodity on Rikers Island, to say the least. Some inmates were even willing to kill for them. He knew he would have problems over them; it was just a matter of time. Whether it be physically or verbally, he would be confronted.

"Yo, I'm goin' out fa minez! Ain't nobody takin' nuttin' from me! I'll fight anybody in here, one-on-one. You just watch my back and make sure nobody else jumps in, nobody tries ta sneak me, Shawn."

Corey didn't care who you were, who your brother was, or what your reputation or name was in jail or on the street. If you wanted trouble, then you stepped to the right person. He could hold his own against anyone. His block had instilled that type of confidence in him.

"You got dat! I ain't gonna let nobody move on you . . . Just get bizzy! Put a nigga head out!" Shawn replied.

Soon it was bedtime, the lights in the dorm were dimmed. The lone light that remained on was in the bathroom. Though everyone was physically in bed, no one was asleep. The word had been spread that there was going to be a fight tonight. Everyone anxiously awaited the battle, as if it were their favorite television show. Arguments and fights were a strange form of entertainment for these adolescents.

In back of the dorm, Corey sat up in his bed, fully clothed with his sneakers tightly laced, as if he were choking his feet. *If they wanted these sneakers, they were definitely going to have to take them*, he thought to himself. He was ready for any and everything. He was tense, the way he always got before a fight, but in the dark no one could see it. He was afraid, but not of anybody in the dorm; they all bled just like him. Fear of another man was the most despicable form of cowardice. And he was no coward, not by a long shot.

Periodically, an inmate circled the dorm; each time he passed Corey's bunk, he stared in that direction. Corey thought, *This is it.* This was the guy he would have to tangle with. No words were yet exchanged though.

Because Corey was a new jack to jail, he didn't know that this guy passing back and forth in front of his cell was a trustee from another dorm, doing his job. He was doing suicide watch, watching over the dorm while the other inmates slept. It was routine, to make sure no inmate new to the prison system had extreme problems dealing with confinement. They didn't want him or any of the rest of them to hang themselves in the middle of the night.

Corey watched time and time again as the inmate circled the dorm. Unsure of what to say or do, he kept quiet. As the time dragged on, the dorm fell silent. Sleep had overtaken everyone—including Corey.

Corey awoke the next morning, surprised to be in the

same position he had been in that night, back against the wall with his feet and legs propped up on the bed. He thought he had won the fight without even throwing a blow.

With no physical confrontations that Corey could see, he let his guard down.

Corey lay on his bunk engrossed in reading a novel, *Black Girl Lost* by Donald Goines. It was one of a few books he'd ever read on his own, outside of the required reading at school. He had remembered seeing his older sisters reading this book when he was a child. Only the book cover was different. Now here he was in prison, captivated by the same book. The author was writing about poverty, hopelessness, and crime. Corey had seen more than his fair share of these ills. This was part of his reality.

He consumed pages of the book at a rate he had never done before with any other. The book excited his young mind. While reading, his mind was free, he was again on the streets, not in jail.

Between finishing a chapter and starting another, he happened to look up, only to see three inmates headed directly toward him. A quick glance around and it registered that he was the only person around; the rest of the inmates were in the dayroom watching a movie or at recreation.

As they rapidly approached him, Corey quickly spotted a towel wrapped around one of the kids' hand and lower arm to conceal something. That could only mean one thing in here: he was concealing a shank under the towel. Corey would bet his life on it.

Corey tossed the book aside and rose up off his bed. He prepared himself for combat.

"Whut you wanna do fa them sneakers?" one would-be robber said.

The other two just stood around with menacing looks on their faces. Corey ignored the comment. He focused on the guy with the shank. He didn't want to get stabbed up. Still, he held his ground.

As if he could sense something was wrong, Shawn suddenly appeared from the dayroom. He saw Corey was surrounded and came running to his aide.

Producing a single-edge razor from his mouth, he said, "Ain't nobody jumpin' my man! One-on-one!"

Now that the cavalry had arrived and the odds were evened, Corey stepped up to the plate.

"Now, whut'z up, tough guy? Whut you wanna do?" Corey barked. His associate's sudden appearance eased his fears of being jumped or shanked. He could now rest assured that that wouldn't happen.

Without warning, Corey suddenly punched the kid in his face. Then the fight was on. For ten to fifteen minutes, they tussled unnoticed by other inmates or correctional officers. Corey easily whipped on his lesser skilled, yet determined opponent.

"Aiight! Dat's enuff! Yo, you got dat!" the kid said, conceding victory to Corey.

"New, fuck dat! I'ma fuck you up some more. Just fa even thinkin' you could fuck wit me," Corey announced.

"Yo, chill, Core! It's over!" Shawn said as he came between them. "Yo, Preme, get ya man and bounce."

Corey was hyped up now, he wanted to fight some more. But wisely Shawn was there to settle him back down.

"Yo, kid, leave dat alone. You gonna look like a bully if you keep whippin' dat nigga azz. And nobody likes a bully. Word ta mutha! Da whole dorm might try ta bum-rush ya azz. You proved ya point. You not da one! But you can't keep fightin' someone who don't wanna fight no more. Dat'z dead!" Shawn told him.

"Yeah, you right!" Corey said apologetically.

Corey served the remainder of his time on Rikers Island in relative peace, aside from a few fights here and there. He managed to keep his sneakers. He fought all comers and earned respect amongst the prison population; the word was out that Corey could hold his own.

After spending a few months on Rikers Island, the day came for Corey to be transferred upstate to a state correctional facility to serve his time.

* * *

Armed correctional officers closely watched as dozens of slow-moving prisoners boarded a big blue prison bus, known as the blue bird. Inmates of all shapes and sizes were shackled together with heavy metal chains, leg-irons, and a device known as the black box, which, once a pair of handcuffed wrists were inside, made it almost impossible for even the craftiest convict to pick the handcuff lock.

Corey stumbled along struggling to keep in step. He would never get used to these restraining devices, but somehow he managed to keep pace with the other inmates and board the prison bus.

Prisoners from every borough of New York City were

present and accounted for. There were even a few from out of state. They were mostly blacks and Hispanics, but some Asians and Caucasians were among them too.

"Watch your step boarding the bus," one correctional officer warned.

After the last of the inmates had boarded, a correctional officer went down the aisle and conducted a brief head count. He wanted to make sure that every last one of his precious cargo was accounted for. If even one wasn't, there would be hell to pay by both the inmates and the guards. The guards would be mad because they would have to go through the formality of searching for the missing inmate, and the inmates for having to be locked down until he was found. And the inmates would be equally upset to have their daily routine disturbed.

Finally, the time had come to leave. Corey took a deep breath; he was more than a little nervous—he was afraid. Going upstate, to prison, was almost like being sentenced to death to some inmates. Corey had heard the horror stories, in jail and from returning convicts, on the streets. He'd heard about the robbing, extortion, cutting, stabbing, and even rape. That stuff happened on Rikers Island too, but it was just child's play compared to what went down in the state prison system. The way he heard it told, the state system was a whole different breed of animal.

In the wee hours of the morning, the Department of Corrections whisked a busload of inmates to the state diagnostics center in Elmira, New York, to be classified for various security levels and to be housed at various institutions accordingly. As the bus made its way onto the highway, some inmates got their last look at New York City. It seemed to look so inviting and peaceful at this time of the morning. But they all knew that those same streets would be alive with trouble in just a few hours. Any kind of trouble you could think of.

"Shorty, where you from?" the older man asked. "Whut'z ya name?"

"Corey! Da Bronx!" Corey quickly replied.

"Mine's Melquan, I'm from Brooklyn. Do or Die Bedstuy! I don't mean ta be all up in ya bizness, but whut'z ya charge? You a stickup kid?"

"Stickup kid?" Corey repeated, unbelieving. "Do I look like one?"

"Ummmm, yeah!" the man joked. "I'm just fuckin' wit you. Just kickin' da bo-bo."

The two shared a lighthearted laugh. After breaking the ice, the older convict began to school Corey.

"Listen, Shorty, on da real side. Dis probably ya first time up north, so listen good. Never ever tell your bizness to a nigga you don't know. Or even to a nigga you do know. Dudes go some big numbers up north, some of them are comin' home Neveruary first. They gotta asshole full of time. They just waitin' for a nigga to run his mouth and tell his bizness. Next thing you know, you're reindicted or indicted on some shit you thought you got away wit. Niggas will tell on Jesus to save they azz. It ain't called snitchin' no more. It's called cooperatin'. So be careful. Da less people dat know ya bizness da betta it is fa you."

The advice he just gave Corey was indispensable. He filed

that away in his memory banks; it would become one of the many dos and don'ts, rules of survival, he would have to listen to, to survive in this strange new world.

* * *

The trip upstate appeared longer than it really was. The mood was somber on the bus.

"I'll be glad when we get ta where we goin'," someone said. "I hate all dis travelin' and shit. They can take me straight to my jail, lemme do my time, and lemme come da fuck home."

"I heard dat," another prisoner added. "I feel da same way."

Corey listened to the other inmates as they loud-talked on the way upstate. Before long, he and Melquan began their own conversation.

"Have you ever been upstate before?" Corey suddenly asked the older prisoner. "I'm sayin', how iz it?"

"I been doin' bids since you wuz in diapers and wettin' da sheets. I'm not new ta dis, I'm true ta dis!"

"So how iz it up there? Iz it like I hear it iz? I mean, iz it really dat wild?"

"Shortly, don't listen ta those bitch-azz, scared niggas. They heart pump Kool-Aid! They afraid of their own shadow. They shouldna never been breakin' law in da first place. I'm sayin' it ain't really no worst than the Island; same rules apply. Mind ya business and keep ya mouth closed. You know see no evil, hear no evil, and speak no evil. Don't loan nobody nuttin' and don't borrow nuttin' from nobody. God bless da child dat's got his own. Somebody try you, set da fuck off on them! If you don't, then nigga's gonna think you pussy. And then whole jail will be tryin' you," Melquan said, pointing behind him. "And believe me, you don't want dat. You might can fight, but you can't beat da world."

Melquan shot Corey a stern look to further emphasize his point. The duo fell silent as the corrections bus roared up the highway. Corey looked out the window at the blurry cars and trees.

Melquan continued, "And another thing—they got faggots and booty bandits upstate." Corey sat back. "But don't worry about dat, men recognize men! Muthafucka's think 'cause they fuckin' a faggot dat they ain't gay. Yeah, right! In my book ya'll both faggots. Whether you are pitching or back-catching, y'all both in da game. Understand? A man don't come to jail and suddenly realize he's gay. He been gay all his life, a closet homosexual. Maybe he had six sisters and he was da seventh. Somebody in jail just spotted his female tendencies and brought him out the closet. Point-blank!"

After a brief pause, Melquan continued, "Anyway, Shorty, you scramble, right? I mean, you sold crack. I mean, dat wuz ya thing. Da way you got ya paper, right?"

"Yeah!" Corey agreed. "I did a lil sumthin' sumthin'."

"Okay. You probably worked fa a nigga, right? At some point and time, huh?"

Corey threw his head back wondering where Melquan was going with this, then shook his head in agreement. "Uh-huh!"

"Well, I hope when you come home off dis bid, you'll be much wiser. Just like any other legitimate business, the real money is in ownership. The boss gets the lion share and the worker gets the chump change. You'll neva get rich working for somebody else. Yo, I love ta see those young black kids in the NBA, NFL, or Major League Baseball crack da bank and get all those millions. If they, da owners, couldn't afford them then, believe they wouldn't pay them. Every owner dat got a team is a billionaire or damn near one. So whut'z a couple million inside a billion? Nuttin'! Dat's like spillin' a drop a water out of a bucket. Who gonna miss it? Understand!"

Hearing the wisdom in the man's words, Corey began to pay close attention.

"After dis, if you should choose to go dat route again and break da law, never work for a nigga. Work wit a nigga. Use him as a stepping-stone, a come-up. Always keep ya eye on the prize, on ya own shit! In time thingz change. Roles reverse. Da weak become strong. Good turns ta bad. Boyz become men. Da only constant in life iz change. You won't be da same lil kid dat you came to da joint as. You'll grow physically and mentally. Ya mind-set will change. And so forth and so on. So wit dat said, be a leader not a follower! If you gonna be an Indian, be a chief! Shorty, jail ain't nuttin' but school. So learn. It's the School of Hard Knocks. Outside of a college university, an institute of higher learning, dis is the second-highest institute of learning on the face of this earth. Believe that!"

Though he had heard the man clearly, Corey didn't believe his last statement about jail being the second-highest institute of learning on the face of this earth. *It couldn't be,* he mused to himself.

Melquan continued, "A man gets two educations, one he

is given and one dat he teaches himself. You ever heard dat sayin', Shorty? Huh? I can't think of who said it, but it's true. Oh, how true it iz. You about ta see some things dat'll leave you physically, mentally, and possibly emotionally scarred for life. So be strong, trooper. Whut don't kill you will only make you stronger."

"Yo, Mel can I ask you sumthin'?" Corey said.

"Whut'z on ya mind? Ga'head, shoot."

"Yo, while you wuz doin' ya bid, did ya girl stick by you?"

Melquan smiled. He knew exactly where Corey was coming from. At one point and time, he was Corey. He was in love and incarcerated, and Melquan knew that could be detrimental to one's state of mind, if it wasn't controlled. In his time he'd seen lesser men take their own life, by hanging themselves, all in the name of love. And he'd seen men who had been incarcerated for so long, they'd become romantically involved with homosexuals. Being incarcerated took mental fortitude that some men lacked. In his mind he knew this young prisoner seated next to him would do neither of the above. At least he hoped not.

Corey interrupted him, "Mel, you ain't answerin' my question. Did she do da bid wit you?"

Something about Corey's presence said he was built to last. Something about his body language announced he was a survivor. Something in his demeanor said he was going to be all right, that he was going to make it.

"Kid, listen," Melquan began. "You don't need to have ya mind focused on no girl. Females come and go. Ya young, ya doin' time. You don't need ta be stressed out by no chick. You need ta have ya mind focused on getting' up out da joint! Makin' parole and shit."

"I know, but the more I try not to think about her, da more I think about her," Corey honestly admitted. "Man, I got a lot invested in dat girl. I bought her crazy shit. Jewelry, coats, Gucci bags and shit."

"Well, Corey, if nobody ever told you, let me be da first: kid, you can't buy love," Melquan said bluntly. "Love is made of many things. And material items ain't one of them."

This statement immediately stopped Corey from bragging any further. He realized what Melquan was saying was real.

Skipping the subject, Melquan joked, "Yo, you buggin' out, Corey. Yo, I done did time all kinds of ways. I did a bid wit a girl, witout a girl, and thought I had a girl. Da only thing I can tell you iz that you neva know. Time is funny like dat. It can make or break a relationship. It all depends on the individuals involved. How tight wuz da relationship before the man got incarcerated. Was it true love or was it pure lust? If you was takin' good care of ya girl, spoilin' her wit fly shit or you wuz dickin' her down on the regular, well, she gonna miss dat. She just like any crackhead or dope fiend, she needs her fix. Whateva it may be. And just think—you created dat monster. Da game don't stop 'cause a player gets locked. She gonna have to support her habit. Dat's human nature! It iz whut it iz. Corey, accept da fact she gonna fuck. As long she don't mess wit none of ya boyz or no nigga you know, it's cool! Just ask yaself dis: Whut would you do if ya girl wuz on lockdown and you wuz out in da world? Would you be fuckin'? If you look at it like dat, you can't be mad. As long as she writes, sends you pictures, packages, and money orders, then you aiight!"

The truth Melquan had just given Corey was a bitter pill to swallow. He couldn't imagine his girl having sex with someone else. But the thought dominated his every waking moment. The more he tried not to think about it, the more he did think about it. To his credit, though, he hardly ever let his thoughts manifest themselves into words. He kept his fears to himself. No one else cared anyway.

For the rest of the ride Corey rode in silence, lost in his thoughts.

Corey had now entered society's cesspool, where losers in life and love, the misguided, the lost souls, outcasts, misfits, and rejects were tossed. These closed and cramped quarters bred misery and despair. In an environment like this, negativity thrived. Prison was a killing field, a danger zone. Corey had better watch his step, anything could happen at any time.

* * *

Elmira Correctional Facility looked like a medieval castle to Corey. The prison bus finally came to a halt in front of a towering, electronically controlled front gate. Corey was glad that they'd finally arrived. A bucket was lowered from a watchtower. The armed officers who had escorted the prisoners from Rikers Island had to place their firearms into the bucket. This done, the prison bus was allowed entrance.

Sluggishly, the prison bus moved forward inside the prison compound to the designated area. Two tall, Caucasian, sloppily built correctional officers stood at the reception area entrance, chewing and spitting out gobs of tobacco. Though Corey had never laid eyes on them a day in his life, they appeared racist. They looked just like the Southern racists Corey had seen on film beating civil rights activists back in the sixties. They served as a sort of welcoming committee, a prelude to what was to come.

With the delivery of the new shipment of prisoners, the machine known as the system was now fed.

* * *

The last remaining task for the correctional officers from Rikers Island was to unhandcuff and deshackle the prisoners. From this point, they were state property and would have to deal with these hillbilly correctional officers from upstate New York. Correctional officers who were closed-minded to the prisoners' way of life. For the inmates and guards alike it was a culture shock. The good old boys had their own ways of dealing with New York City minorities, who they deemed unruly.

"Good luck!" one correctional officer whispered to Corey. "Don't let these rednecks play you out of position. Hold ya tongue and ya head."

Corey was taken aback by that statement; he knew if a guard wished him luck, things had to be bad.

After gathering up their restraining devices, the correctional officers from the city made a quick exit.

"Listen up, boys," one upstate officer commanded. "Y'all line up single file right here. . . . Strip down, butt-ass naked.

I want y'all to spread ya cheeks. Bend over, cough, and squat. . . . Do I make myself clear . . ."

The correctional officer went down the line; one by one, the prisoners complied. Corey was no exception; he did as he was told. He couldn't help but feel totally violated, as if a piece of his dignity or manhood had been stripped away. This was the first step in the dehumanization.

The prisoners were strip-searched; every imaginable cavity of their bodies was searched for contraband. Their heads shaved close to their skull. Their pubic hairs were sprayed for lice. At the end of this gauntlet was their reward: new green prison underwear, T-shirts, pants, and shirt. Every piece of clothing had been branded with black ink, with their state identification number. Now the prisoners no longer possessed a first name. They were inmate last name and state identification number.

The medical department awaited the prisoners once that was done. They ran a battery of tests on them. They tested the prisoners for everything from HIV to tuberculosis. When that was done, the psychiatric department had its turn.

"You ever felt suicidal? Has anyone in your family ever committed suicide?" the psychiatrist solemnly repeated over and over.

Corey quickly grew sick of answering his stupid questions. *Do I ever feel suicidal?* he thought to himself. *Are you fucking crazy?* He would never hurt himself, not even if he were facing life in prison. He loved himself too much. Someone else would have to end his life, because Corey was too much of a coward to do it himself. He loved living too much.

The last step was to see a classification counselor, who would determine exactly where a prisoner would be shipped from here, if anywhere. This was done by the prisoner's prior record, type of crime—violent or nonviolent—and age. All these factors were added into an equation before a decision was made. Since Corey was still an adolescent, he would be housed at Elmira Correctional Facility to take advantage of its GED program. All decisions were final. No prisoner really had a say in the matter. The only way a prisoner could get around this was to state that he had an enemy at a specific prison and give up a name of someone he knew was housed at that jail. Then prison officials were forced to keep both individuals separated for the entirety of their imprisonment.

"In case of emergency or death, who would you like us to notify?" the counselor robotically asked Corey.

In Corey's mind, it was almost a given that he was going home after serving his time. That he would leave prison the same way he entered, in one piece. The possibility of getting murdered or dying in jail never crossed his mind. For him it was unheard of—anyone except old timers, lifers, and people sentenced to death—dying in jail. Later on he would learn that death was always a possibility, an ever-present threat that lay in wait for any prisoner, at any given time.

"My mother, Janice Dixon."

"What's her address and telephone number?"

"Thirty-four fifty-four Fish Avenue, Bronx, New York 10469. Her phone number is 718-555-8366."

Now Corey's diagnostic process was complete. He and the rest of the newly arriving prisoners were placed in quarantined cells. There they were to wait for an allotted time, to make sure they didn't have any infectious diseases that they could possibly transmit to the rest of the prison population.

* * *

The temperature in the prison was a sweltering ninety-five degrees, but with the high humidity, it felt even worse. New York State was currently experiencing the first heat wave of the summer. That meant one thing for prison officials: violence was about to erupt. The sudden rise in temperature made a bad situation worse for the inmates. Extreme conditions like these made living inside the prison unbearable. Most of the prisons were built decades ago; thus they were not equipped with modern comforts such as air conditioners. An old prison like this one literally turned into an oven in the summertime.

The cells were so hot that the walls would sweat. Plenty of nights, Corey couldn't remember when or how he fell asleep. Being sentenced to confinement this time of year definitely had to fall under the category of cruel and unusual punishment. Being hot, miserable, and locked up made a deadly combination for most inmates. To the prisoners, summer wasn't summer until someone got stabbed.

"Michael Jordan iz betta than Dominique Wilkins!" one prisoner insisted. "Look how many times he led da NBA in scoring. And every time da Chicago Bulls play da Atlanta Hawks, Mike puts it on 'Nique. He be dunkin' on da whole team. Speakin' of dat, MJ even beat him in da dunk contest."

"C'mon now! Everybody know 'Nique was robbed. They

held dat dunk contest in Chicago! They robbed my man! You know it and I know it!" the other prisoner shouted. "Da last person dat did some shit like dat wore a mask. You make it seem like Dominique a bum or sumthin'? Like he don't be doin' work ta da Chicago Bulls or sumthin'? They don't call him da human highlight fa nuttin'!"

"Dominique a loser! What has he ever won? Besides a meaningless game or two? He never hit a clutch to win a big game. My man Air Jordan on da other hand, he hit a clutch shot as a freshman to win a NCAA championship. He got his own pair of sneakers, Air Jordans. When it's all said and done, Michael Jordan gonna be da best dat ever did it. Dominique will be washed up inna few years! As soon as his knees give out. All he can do iz run, jump, and dunk. He don't really got no game."

Talk like this could lead to an argument. Corey was in the big yard doing pull-ups on the bars as two prisoners, at a nearby picnic table, heatedly disagreed. From their tone of voice, something crazy was about to happen any second now.

"Nigga, you must be fuckin' crazy!" the man quickly snapped. "You musta lost ya fuckin' mind! Get off Michael Jordan's dick! Let dat man's nuts hang. You fuckin' homo!"

"Homo? I got ya homo. Right here! You know more about him, his statistics, than you do your own case."

The most important rules in prison are unwritten. These are the ones most critical to a prisoner's survival. Prison has its own yardstick to measure a man, one that separates the men from the boys, punks, and homosexuals. A lot more is at stake than just doing time. Here reputations are perpetuated or built, respect is earned or lost. To call a man out his name, especially calling him gay when he wasn't, in prison, was a direct attack on his manhood. It had to be dealt with immediately, with the punishment severe, or there would be hell to pay later.

The comment caught everyone's attention. If they hadn't taken notice of these two before, they did now.

In a blink of an eye, the Hispanic prisoner spit out a single-blade razor he kept concealed in his mouth. Once his weapon was in hand, he began to slice the black prisoner's face. Blood began to pour from the man's freshly opened gashes. Savagely the Hispanic prisoner kept slicing away, as if he were playing a deadly version of tic-tac-toe.

"I ain't da one!" he yelled while continuing to cut his victim's face. "I ain't the herb you lookin' for! Don't you ever try disrespecting me like dat in ya life, nigga! You hear me? Huh?"

In self-defense the black prisoner tried to throw up his hands, to shield his face. That didn't stop his attacker; he sliced his arms and hands too. He was determined to make an example of him.

"Somebody get dis nigga! Stop 'im!" the black man screamed. Gone was the bravado he'd possessed just moments ago.

It didn't take long for the correctional officer in the watchtower that overlooked the prison recreational yard to alert the other correctional officers who patrolled the yard. They couldn't see the melee from ground level due to the hundreds of inmates in the prison yard.

Quickly, dozens of guards descended on the scene. The Hispanic man was tackled. The black prisoner was taken to the prison infirmary. His wounds were so severe that from there he was taken by ambulance to the local hospital's emergency room.

That was the first of several startling events Corey would witness his first summer imprisoned. Dealing with this kind of thing was nothing compared to the physical separation from his loved ones, especially his girlfriend. His mind would constantly drift to her. He wanted desperately to hear her voice, to call her on the telephone. But her telephone number had a block on it. It didn't accept collect phone calls. So for now he poured his heart out on paper. And counted the days till she wrote him back.

The sheer brutality and violence of prison was something he was adapting to every day. Corey quickly learned that when in Rome, do as the Romans do. He'd be damned if he would come to a gunfight armed with a knife. Every fight in prison, the combants played for keeps.

One thing about prison life that one could never predict was what the next day would bring. It was totally unpredictable.

Chapter 14

DATE: Till the end of time
TIME: 3:00 AM
MOOD: Blunted da fuck up!
FROM: Ya muthafuckin' man, pots and pans, Brotha from anotha mothar, "O"!

Whut'z up kid? Troop, Troop how are you? Me, I'm aiight! You know me, moving, grooving, and manipulating. Work ain't hard, but da boss iz a bitch. Got da kite you sent ta me da other day. Anyway, I hope you still maintaining. I know you ain't letting none of them crab niggas front on you. I'm buggin' out kid! I know you can hold ya own. You ain't no slouch wit ya hands. Nigga, just stay on point. Don't let none of those crabs chop you across da face wit a ox. . . . I don't think ya girl would want you wit a big scar on ya face. (Just kiddin' nigga!) Speakin' of her, I saw her in front of da school and some nigga (I don't know who he wuz. Think he from da South Bronx some fuckin' where?) wuz tryin' ta push up on her. (Now I ain't sayin' she was givin' homeboy any rap. So don't start buggin' out!) You know I ran up on em and snuffed him. I beat him down, he couldn't fuck wit me. Even though you ain't out here, I'm still representing you to the fullest. Ain't nobody gonna violate ya girl or ya family. Not while I'm around. Core, you my nigga! (I told you before, I'll kill or die fa you!) Nigga, ya beef iz mine!

Enuff said about dat, yo ain't shit happenin' out here! Da block still da same. Same shit different day. There was a crazy drought out here. It lasted fa about a month. Yo, shit was so bad we was out here beating up fiends. Word up! Nobody had nuttin'! Da block was dry! So when a custy (we didn't like) came by lookin' fa some crack we would just rush him for rec. Fuck it! Wasn't nuttin' else to do! But now shit iz back ta normal. So I'ma be hit you wit those crazy fat money orders like I usta. Matterfact, I put a two hundred dollar money order in here wit dis kite. I also sent ya dat package off the other day. I put all dat shit in there you asked for, da squid, tuna, Jack Mac, cookies, candy and shit!

Yo, Corey I'm out kid! I'm tired than a muthafucka! Dat buddah got me mad sleepy! Hold YA Head! You'll be home soon.

Love, Peace and Hair grease

O

P.S. I know ya right arm gettin' cock diesel, cuz you beatin' ya meat like a muthafucka! (Ha! Ha!) Laugh muthafucka I know you want to!

P.P.S. Yo, you gonna bug off dis one kid! Guess whut I heard da other day? Ya man, Lord iz sellin' drugs now. (Dat'z bugged right? Imagine dat? Dat bitch ass nigga got some work too. Heard he got some money from some car accident he was in as a baby! He up da hill on Corsa Ave. pumpin'. I'ma get dat nigga! Word ta mother! I'm stick him up fa all his work! Watch!)

* * *

It was roughly 5:30 a.m. Corey waited for his cell door to be opened, and the chow line to be moving. He reread the letter again and again, as if the words would change. Like any inmate, he loved receiving and reading mail from the outside world. He smiled to himself as he read; it was almost as if he could hear his friend's voice. He was glad to hear from him as always. Besides getting letters from his girlfriend, he loved nothing more than getting mail from Omar. His letters provided Corey with crucial information about the block that nobody else could give him. Though he was physically in prison, Corey's mind was on the street. He yearned to know the latest gossip and happenings back home. It seemed to keep him alive until he returned there.

The mechanical opening of the prison tier's cell doors caught Corey off guard. Quickly, he folded the letter back inside the envelope and tucked it back under his mattress. Exiting his cell, he wondered what was on the menu for breakfast. No matter what though, he was going to eat it. He was that hungry.

One of the last inmates to leave the tier, Corey was

amongst the last to leave the chow hall. He and a scattered few other inmates from his tier made their way back to their respective cells after the rest of the population. As Corey turned a corner, he seemed to be in a blind spot, with no correctional officer in sight. Suddenly a deep voice said, "Oh, you thought I wuz playin' wit you!"

Corey turned just in time to see a long, sharpened piece of steel, known as a shank, being repeatedly plunged into another inmate's back. Though badly hurt, the victim had the presence of mind to flee his attacker. But Corey, unfortunately, was in his path of escape. Blood splattered onto Corey's prison uniform. It would look as if Corey had stabbed the guy.

The keen eye of the regular housing-unit officer working the tier spotted the blood on Corey's uniform. Corrections officers could sometimes sense something was wrong or out of place, like a mother with her child, after spending months and sometimes years around an inmate. The officer immediately called his supervisor. Within minutes dozens of correctional officers arrived on the scene. They went straight to Corey's cell. He was ordered to step out of his cell and place his hands behind his back. They informed him he was being placed in administrative custody. He was handcuffed and escorted to a segregated section of the prison known as the lockup or the box. Corey was placed there while prison officials investigated the incident.

* * *

The days Corey served in the box were relatively quiet, except for the noise that the chow cart made as it delivered the prisoners' meals. For about an hour, all that could be heard was the rattling of large turnkeys and the open and closing of slots, cut into the prison cell doors.

At night it was a different story. The inmates yelled up and down the tier all night. They screamed out the latest gossip and rumors from the street. Some inmates just talked for the hell of it. They had nothing meaningful to say. Corey on the other hand decided to remain silent. He listened to their conversations, letting them entertain him.

"Yo, Money, whut'z ya name again? And where you say you from again?" a husky-voiced inmate asked.

"Nigga, my name is T-money! And I'm from Brownsville neva ran, neva will!" the man strongly stated.

"Who?" the inmate asked again, baiting him.

"T-money! From *Brownsville!* Neva ran, neva will!"

"Neva hearda ya!" the inmate snapped. "Whut Brownsville you from? Brownsville, Texas? 'Cauze it sure ain't Brooklyn, you country muthafucka! Stop claimin' otha people'z neighborhood fa you catch a bad one, you lame!"

The entire tier broke out in laughter. They knew the man was perpetrating a fraud. He was really from a quiet town in upstate New York called Poughkeepsie. But he was ashamed to admit it. Prisoners from New York City outnumbered those from upstate in this jail. In a desperate attempt to fit in, he had lied about where he was from.

"Whut school you went to, huh? Tell me dat?" the inmate asked again.

"Ummmm, ummmmm," he stuttered, "I can't remember."

"How da fuck you gonna fahget some shit like dat? Huh?

Dat's like fahgettin' how ta ride a bike! You soft as drugstore cotton. . . . You ain't even from Bensonhurst! Even them white boys will fuck ya azz up out there."

More laughter ripped through the tier. Corey chuckled hard too. *Boy, there sure iz some funny muthafuckas in jail*, he said to himself. Now the rest of the tier joined in to further insult the man.

Then suddenly they all heard the sound of fumbling turnkeys. Everyone fell silent. Something was going on around there and they all wanted to know. Faces one by one were pressed against the bars in an attempt to see what was happening. The sound of a few pairs of feet could be heard echoing off the tier. Two correctional officers began walking down the tier.

"Corey Dixon?" one asked and announced all at once as they stopped directly in front of Corey's cell.

Corey lay in nothing but his boxer underwear in a weak attempt to beat the heat. He was startled by their sudden appearance at his cell door. He stood up. He hadn't heard anything further about the so-called investigation since he was first thrown in the box.

"Yeah, dat's me. Whut'z up, Officer?" he asked. "Whut you want?"

"Put some clothes on, the shift commander wants to talk to you," the correctional officer commanded.

He stood firm with Corey defiantly looking at him.

"Dixon, did you hear me?" the correctional officer asked.

"I ain't goin' nowhere to talk ta nobody!" Corey said loudly for everyone to hear. "I didn't see nuttin'! How many timez I gotta tell y'all dat? Huh? I'm new ta dis jail. I don't know nobody and nobody knows me. Soon as y'all get some info from one of y'all jailhouse snitches, if I go wit y'all and y'all should so happen to find out who really did it, everybody gonna think I'm da snitch! And then I'm gonna have ta take protective custody for the rest of my bid. Nah, no thanks! You tell the shift commander he wanna see me, I'm right here! We can talk right here in front of everybody!"

Corey knew the bold stance he had just taken might very well get him badly beaten by these two correctional officers. But he felt he had no choice. It was either get beat up by them or get labeled a snitch and possibly get shanked by the assailant or one of his friends.

"Dixon, put ya damn clothes on now! That's a direct order!" the correctional officer commanded.

He was tempted to have Corey's cell door opened. Then, he and his coworker would go up in there and adjust the young man's smart mouth, just as they used to do in the old days. In the late fifties and sixties, black prisoners that correctional officers didn't like, those who were outspoken, defiant, and unbroken by the system, were badly beaten or sometimes killed. Their bodies would then be buried in makeshift graves on or near prison grounds. When their families would become suspicious and begin to inquire about their loved ones, prison officials would simply say the inmate was transferred to another correctional institution farther upstate. Or they would doctor up phony release papers that said the prisoner had been released. Only in rare instances were their tactics ever uncovered, when the grieving family got up enough money to get a lawyer. Then they had to physically produce the inmate in question. Then and only then, half the truth would be told, that the inmate was dead. These types of incidents were widespread, across the state and the nation. The good old boy system ran roughshod over the inmates.

Hearing the direct order, Corey still didn't move. He meant what he said, he wasn't "goin' nowhere." Defiantly he stood his ground, preparing himself to deal with consequences of his actions.

Something in the young man's eye the correctional officer hadn't seen in a long time. Something that told him not to act on his thought. Something that told him this young black man before him was no pushover. He knew Corey would fight him tooth and nail, to the death if need be. The correctional officer was no spring chicken. Taking this hothead on was not worth risking his health.

He paused to contemplate his next move. He walked back and forth a bit, then said, "Boy, you sure are lucky! You better thank your lucky stars we didn't meet at another time and place." He stepped back to the corridor. "I'll let the shift commander make the call on this one. . . . C'mon, Harry!"

Unbeknownst to Corey, the man who had actually done the stabbing was also housed on the same tier, due to lack of space elsewhere. As a consequence, he had heard everything too. Corey's response would gain him a lifetime ally and a friend forever. Because he had stood up to the corrections officers and didn't crack under the threat of physical harm, Corey had earned his stripes within the prison population.

The word quickly spread that Corey was no snitch. That Corey had a lot of heart. A lot of inmates were only tough when dealing with other inmates. But he was cut from a different cloth than the rest of these young boys.

* * *

Back in the prison population, Corey seemingly began to adjust to prison life. He enrolled in the GED program, and after a few short months he passed the GED test. He became a teacher's aide. Corey began to work out and read the Bible religiously. He devised a rigorous exercise regimen. In the mornings he would go to the yard and lift weights—bench-press, curls, and shoulder presses. Then at night he would do calisthenics—push-ups, dips, and sit-ups. And on the weekends he would run the yard. Working out and reading kept Corey busy and more importantly out of trouble. He figured if no one knew him, his likes or dislikes, then people wouldn't know how to come at him. They wouldn't know how to offend him.

Corey released all his pent-up frustration and stress. He began to read other books besides the Bible. For him, reading opened up doors previously closed to him. Reading expanded his vocabulary and knowledge. He started out reading urban literature: Donald Goines, Iceberg Slim, and Terry McMillan. Soon he advanced beyond reading stories he could relate to; he also enjoyed reading about things and people he was curious about.

He read biographies of civil rights leaders, including Martin Luther King, Jesse Jackson, the Reverend Al Sharpton, and Dick Gregory, and about the Black Panther Party. He learned about all the lives that were lost and the sacrifices that were made for his sake. He learned about black culture. The more he read, the more he seemed to hunger for more knowledge.

Hardcover books had intimidated him all his life. The books were too high in page count for his tastes. He preferred thin, softcover novels. But now since he had time on his hands, since he wasn't going anywhere anytime soon, he consumed the pages of these books like a good meal. They were his food for thought. He was taking in thoughts and opinions of some of the greatest leaders and thinkers of the twentieth century.

Corey went from reading black literature to reading about white America and the conspiracy theories. He read about J. Edgar Hoover and the FBI's abuse of power. How he used his position as head of the Federal Bureau of Investigation to discredit and/or assassinate prominent civil rights leaders.

Corey read how Joe Kennedy made his fortune during the Prohibition Era, when selling alcohol was illegal. This man made riches untold, then took that money and invested it in Hollywood movie studios. He laundered his ill-gotten gains just as major drug dealers of today do. This same dirty money financed his two sons John F. Kennedy and Robert F. Kennedy when they ran for president. Corey thought the black man would never have the same kind of success doing anything illegal like that. The black man's American dream would have turned into a nightmare a long time ago, as his was doing now.

Through reading he discovered that some of the most successful people in the world, such as Donald Trump, never did well in school. But now his name was synonymous with money. Corey believed that Trump was a multimillionaire, but truly doubted that he was a billionaire. Corey figured that Trump's good name from making shrewd real estate deals, and his public persona, made the millionaire attractive to banks and other wealthy investors. Corey thought that Trump didn't really own all that high-priced realty in Manhattan. As far as Corey was concerned, Japanese businessmen owned the majority of those buildings.

He would rather believe that Trump had a long, long line of credit. Corey also learned that in the business world of America, it wasn't how much a person had in his bank account, but how good his credit was, that mattered. Some of the richest people in the world, such as athletes and entertainers, couldn't purchase a house unless they bought it outright with cash because their credit scores were that poor.

Reading made Corey feel that he was accomplishing something. He was seeing a task from start to finish and that gave him joy. He took many trips a week to the prison library.

Chapter 15

"Yo, Mo, you still goin' ta Skate Key tanite?" her girlfriend Denice asked.

"I don't know if I'm goin' or not yet. I'm waitin' on a call from Corey. I'm playin' my house close 'cause I don't want my momz to answer his collect call. You know how she be riffin' 'bout me keepin' in contact wit him. She thinks he's a jailbird and he's not neva gonna be nuttin'. But I don't care what she says, dat's my heart! My first luv!"

Monique was having a hard time adapting to life without Corey. Though she was trying to, the physical separation as well as the inconsistent communication was driving a wedge between them. On paper, her words never seemed to come out right. She visited him, loved seeing his face, but the short time they spent together was never enough. She ached with dread for the end. Then she had to go back home. She wondered if she'd ever touch him again. Corey was her bridge over troubled waters. He could comfort her and ease her fears like no other boyfriend she had ever had.

Though she had her physical freedom, she felt incarcerated too. She was doing Corey's time along with him.

Her girlfriend snapped, "Listen, Mo, I'm tireda hearin' 'bout Corey! Corey dis and Corey dat! I can't go here 'cause Corey said so. I can't go there 'cause niggas gonna try and talk ta me and Corey wouldn't like dat! You need to wake up and smell da fuckin' coffee. And get wit da program. Corey up north doin' a bid! A three-ta-fuckin'-six! He ain't comin' home no time soon. And who's ta say when he do get out he gonna still want you. Whose ta say he won't play you the fuck out! Just ask Tracey about dat shit."

Denice talked over Monique. "Her man came home from doin' eight months on da Island. He talked all dat lovey-dovey shit when his ass was in there. As long as her ass was bringin' him packages and sendin' him money orders and comin' up ta visit on da regular, everything was A-OK. He was talkin' dat tagether fa ever shit. It's all about them. You know no sooner than his ass hit da bricks, he flipped da script. He started fuckin' wit da next bitch. Monique, I'm tellin' you, don't get caught out there like dat! Don't be waitin' on no nigga ta come home from jail. They wouldn't wait fa you. You too young and pretty to be sittin' up in the house every fuckin' weekend. Live ya life."

Monique sat speechless, on the other end of the phone, as her friend had just given her the God's honest truth. Denice, she didn't hold anything back. Monique had never analyzed the situation like that. She was always in Corey's corner thinking about him. Now she had to ask herself, What about me? She had to live her life. Since Corey's arrest, her world had centered around him—doing for him and thinking about him. Without her other half, her life had become stagnant and stale. She had reached a point where she was tired of oppressing herself. Now she was going to start living again, hanging out with her girlfriends and going to parties.

"Yo, you right! I'm goin' out! Fuck dat shit! I'll be ready by nine thirty. Come in front my building in a cab and blow the horn," she announced.

"Bitch, you betta be ready too! Hope you ain't playin' no games. You know how slow ya ass iz! You be takin' all fuckin' day, tryin' ta look cute," Denice said.

What Monique didn't realize was that her friend, however good her intentions were, had succeeded in planting a seed of doubt about her relationship with Corey, which would eventually lead to the demise of their relationship.

* * *

" 'Bout time you came back, muthafucka!" Omar cursed to himself.

Looking down from the project rooftop, Omar gripped the .380 semiautomatic he had concealed in his hoodie's pouch pocket. He watched closely as Lord got out of a gypsy cab and entered his building. He had been waiting for months for this opportunity to present itself, to rob Lord. He knew Lord had just come back from a downtown re-up on cocaine. Last night Omar had got the word that Lord was out of product. Knowing every drug dealer needs product, in this case cocaine, to stay in business, O decided to get up early and wait for him to go re-up and return home.

Like most street-level drug dealers Lord kept cocaine and money stashed in his room in his mother's crib, as if he had a license to do so. This went against the hustler's credo "Never shit where you eat." Lord did this so often, packaging drugs in his mother's apartment, he never gave it a second thought.

Walking up the stairs, Lord searched his key ring for his apartment door key. He never heard the rooftop door open. Nor did he hear the soft sounds that O made as he took his position.

Lord reached his apartment door; quickly he undid both his locks. As he was about to enter his apartment, a hooded O appeared, gun in hand, pushing his way into the apartment.

The strong, stiff object pressed against his lower back immediately let Lord know what it was, a stickup. *Damn!* he exclaimed to himself.

"Aiight, nigga, you know what dis iz? Let's not turn it into a homicide," O announced. "Now give it up! Lemme get dat."

Instantly Lord recognized who it was. There was no mistaking it, this was O. And he had caught him dead to rights.

In a bold move, O removed his hoodie. He wanted Lord to know, if he didn't already, exactly who was robbing him. O feared no retaliation from Lord. He just knew that Lord was too afraid of him to do anything. But in the streets there is an old saying, "A scared person will kill you."

"Yo, whut da fuck you doin', O?" Lord asked. "Kid, I ain't neva done nuttin' ta you. So why you do dis?"

"Kill dat fuckin' noise! Give up da yayo, fa I put a hot one in you!"

By the tone of his voice, Lord knew O meant business. He didn't want to take a chance with his life and try O. To him, the amount of drugs he possessed wasn't worth dying for. So he decided to cut his losses and start over. He had money stashed away in his grandmother's house. He could get back on with that, Lord reasoned to himself. He took a deep sigh, glad that his mother wasn't home during all of this.

Lord reached in his groin area and removed a large plastic bag, filled with big chunks of a crystal-white substance, cocaine. He handed it over to O without even looking at his face.

"Nigga, if you wanna see me 'bout dis, you know where ta find me. I'll be right down the block on Fish Avenue. I ain't hard ta find!" O said in a sinister tone. "Remember, if you come lookin' fa me, you better be ready ta die. 'Cauze I'ma kill you!"

Threats of physical violence only work on people who believe that the would-be perpetrator will actually carry out the threats. Lord didn't believe Omar would act. Omar had ample opportunity to kill him now, with no witnesses around.

Omar gun-butted Lord in the back of his head, leaving him temporarily disoriented. Then Omar left the apartment, fleeing across the rooftop the way he had come.

* * *

"Ma'am, you have a collect call from Corey Dixon. Will you accept the charges?" the telephone operator stated.

"Yes," she said without hesitation.

"Hi, Ma!" Corey began. "You still comin' up dis weekend, right?"

"Yeah, boy, you know I am. Only thing keep me from comin' is God or bad weather."

"I been listening to da forecast on da radio. They say it suppose ta be nice dis weekend. I hope dat'z right. But you neva know fa sure."

"I know!" she agreed. "The weather upstate is always different from the city. It could be cold up there and nice down here."

Corey's mother had been there for him, every step of the way. Her actions now that he was in prision endeared her to him even more. Circumstances and absence made them grow closer. Corey's father, on the other hand, took more of a tough-love approach. Rarely did they talk. His father decided that he would not talk to Corey nor would he send him any money. He hoped that his son's incarceration would be his first and last. He prayed that his son would learn from his father's mistakes, as well as some of his own. Because he feared Corey might not live long enough, if he continued living the fast life, to make all the mistakes on his own. Corey figured his father was mad at him, so he in turn was mad at his father. Mrs. Dixon was awkwardly placed in the middle of a tug-of-war between her son and her husband, and it weighed heavily on her heart. Sometimes just to keep peace in the house, Mrs. Dixon wouldn't inform her husband of the illegal activities that had come to her attention about her son. Eventually when Mr. Dixon did find out, he would be irate. Corey became the main source of Mrs. Dixon and her husband's arguments. At times her husband didn't want to hear Corey's name mentioned in his presence.

"A, Ma, do me a favor. Call Monique for me on da three-way. I ain't heard nuttin' from her inna minute. She gotta block on her phone now. I gotta find out whut'z goin' on wit her."

While Corey waited, his mother clicked over to her other line and placed the call to her son's girlfriend's house.

"Boy, don't you go actin' all crazy on this phone," Mrs. Dixon warned. As soon as she made that comment, she knew that she had messed up.

"About whut, Ma? Why am I gonna act crazy on da phone? Fa whut reason? Huh?" Corey demanded. His instinct told him his mother was keeping something from him. He knew she couldn't hold water either, so he was going to pry the information out of her.

"I heard dat girl is pregnant!" she said.

The silence on the phone was eerie. Corey wasn't prepared for that information. Never in a million years did he ever think Monique would betray him in this fashion. He had the utmost confidence in her. This news was like a death in the family to Corey. How could he ever get back the time he'd invested in their relationship? How could he get back all the hopes and dreams he'd shared with her. This was more than just a blow to his ego; this was an internal wound to his heart. He had just lost the love of his young life.

"Whut? She's pregnant? By who?" he asked softly. "Why you didn't tell me before?"

"Boy, I didn't know for sure till I seen her last week at the supermarket. I didn't wanna worry you while you wuz away."

"But, Ma," he pleaded. "You suppose ta be on my side. I'm

ya son! Lemme know whut'z goin' on out there so I'm not in here lookin' like a fool. Thinkin' somethin' iz one way when it's anotha!"

"Hello?" Monique said, finally picking up the phone. "Who's dis?"

"It'z me, Corey! You know, ya supposed to be boyfriend."

From his nasty attitude, Monique could tell that something was definitely wrong with him.

"Corey, what's da matter wit you?"

"Bitch, don't play stupid wit me!" he exploded. "You know exactly whut da fuck's da matter wit me! You fuckin' pregnant."

Corey had taken a temporary leave of his senses talking like that, forgetting that his mother was still on the line with them. His heart was hurting.

"Corey, what da hell is wrong wit you, boy? Watch your mouth! I raised you better than dat," his mother interrupted.

He ignored her, choosing not even to address her. His mind was focused on Monique.

"Who told you I was pregnant?" she demanded.

"Don't worry 'bout dat!" he fired back. "Is it true? Huh?"

Though he knew the answer to that question already, he asked it anyway. As if his own mother had lied to him. He wanted to hear the answer from Monique's mouth. He desperately wanted for her to say it wasn't so. Unfortunately for Corey, these were words he would never hear.

"Yeah, I'm pregnant."

At that moment, Corey felt as though someone had

plunged a knife deep in his heart. He felt as if a piece of him had just passed away. For a few seconds he was speechless.

The blood in his veins boiled; suddenly he lashed out. "Bitch, I should kill ya muthafuckin' azz! Fa makin' me look stupid! I'ma get ya azz when I come home. Word!"

That was as much as he got to say before the line went dead. His mother wasn't able to tolerate any more cursing so she hung up, but she knew this was totally out of character for her son. Her heart went out to him. There was nothing she could do about his situation; he had to deal with it on his own.

Repeatedly, Corey attempted to redial his home number. But he received no response. There were more things he needed to say to Monique. He had more sorrow, anger, and pain to get off his chest. Today it was not to be.

Corey cried silently that night alone in his dark cell. He'd held his feelings in all during the day. Tears were a sign of weakness in jail. The wolves would smell blood and come try him.

He couldn't help but reflect on the good and bad times that they'd shared. Corey wished he could erase her from his memory bank. If he could turn back time, he would never even have messed with her in the first place. His regrets were many, and now he had to live with them. Corey resisted a strong urge to tear up every last photograph and letter she'd ever sent him. He decided to sleep on it. Maybe he would feel different in the morning.

The next morning Corey awoke to a tearstained pillow. He felt sort of relieved that he had got all of that crying out of his system. He felt a bit better, but for the next few days he still walked around in a daze. Nothing seemed to matter to him.

From that point on, Corey really began to focus on himself. He stopped letting anyone or anything dictate his happiness. He promised himself he wouldn't be happy because he had that car, chain, or girl. He decided to be happy just for the sake of being happy. Nothing material would sway this emotion one way or another.

* * *

Corey felt strange walking into the prison library; he hadn't been there in a while. Everything was still the same; the room was still cramped and smelled like an old house, due to the donation of old books, he supposed. The regulars still congregated there, the jailhouse lawyers, who worked on their criminal cases and other prisoners' cases for a small fee. A few homosexuals chose this place to rendezvous with their lovers. For Corey, it was a sanctuary away from the madness that went on in the prison yard and the housing units. Here he could get peace of mind.

"What's up, young buck? Ain't see you in a while. Where you been?" It was Tate, the inmate law librarian.

He was much like a law professor. He was not your typical convict. His thoughts ran deep. He could talk at length about anything from politics to religion. He stayed abreast of current events by reading papers and watching the news. There weren't many topics that he couldn't discuss. He knew a lot about New York State law. He could quote most laws word for word. The laws of human nature were what he studied more than anything, though; he studied the idiocies and tendencies of man.

He was a wise older prisoner who didn't say much to anybody. His demeanor told you he didn't take any nonsense from anyone. He was a well-seasoned veteran of countless prison tours. Unbeknownst to Corey, he had been watching him, his mannerisms, temperament, and what he read. Quietly he was impressed by all of the above. He thought Corey had a good head on his shoulders, so he extended an olive branch to him, in the form of conversation, to break the ice.

At first Corey didn't know whom the man was talking to, since they had never ever held a conversation. This guy was the silent type, not a man of many words. So it was a privilege to have him speak to him.

"Stressin'!" Corey admitted. "You know how dat go."

"Yeah, I know how that goes. Stress will make a young man old before his time. In the NA program, they have a sayin', 'Accept the things you cannot change. Change the things you can. And have the wisdom to know the difference.' . . . It goes something like that. I forget, but you get the picture."

"Ummmm, huh! I think I heard dat before. Listen, I need you to point me in the right direction. I want to appeal my case. I need to read some law books to see how that works."

Tate didn't know where Corey's sudden interest in law came from. But he liked to see younger inmates, in particular, take an interest in their own criminal cases. He always felt that no one will fight for your freedom harder than you will—not even high-priced lawyers and public defenders. Tate liked to see men take their destiny into their own hands. He had even seen a few prisoners find legal technicalities, loopholes in the law, use them to their benefit, and regain their freedom. He'd seen men exonerate themselves from life sentences. Tate was from the school of thought "Where there's a will, there's a way."

"First I need to know, did you go to trial or did you cop out?" Tate asked.

"I copped out!"

"Well, you don't have the right to appeal your case. You gave up that right when you plea-bargained."

Damn! Corey cursed himself. He now regretted taking the deal that the state prosecutor had offered. It looked appealing at the time, the plea bargain seemed to be in his best interest; now he saw that like most things in life, it was a trade-off, and it came with a price.

Going to trial with a criminal case was like playing a high-stakes game of poker, where the winner takes all. Most criminals were afraid to take this risk. They knew that the state had endless resources at its disposal, which it used to build its case against the defense. It was a known fact throughout the criminal realm that if one was found guilty at trial, then surely the judge would impose the maximum sentence. It was as if the state was laying a heavier penalty on the individual for exercising his constitutional rights.

Most criminals jumped at any plea-bargain offer, thinking they didn't stand a chance of winning a criminal trial. When faced with great amounts of time, even the most hard-core criminals turned to cowards.

Tate continued, "You only have one option left, it's call reconsideration. You can write a letter to the judge, listing the things you've accomplished since being incarcerated and how much of a changed man you've become. Basically, it's a bunch of bullshit. There are no guarantees. It's totally up to the judge, his own discretion, whether he'll take some time off your sentence or not. Your takin' a shot in the dark. Look at it this way, you got nuttin' ta lose and everything to gain. Ya freedom!"

Over the next few days, Corey and Tate put their heads together and drafted a letter, which was then sent to the judge. Corey anxiously waited. Within thirty days he received a response. His request was denied. Corey was crushed. He had to remember, as someone once told him, "What don't kill you will only make you stronger."

Through his trials and tribulations, Corey gained mental fortitude. Eventually, though, his heart began to harden. He started to feel like a product of his grim environment; he became criminal-minded, looking for ways to beat the system for robbing him of his youth.

Chapter 16

O was on his way home from a movie at Whitestone Theater, arriving on the block as the usual mix of drug dealers and crackheads milled around. This was a usual summer night in the projects. But he saw someone that he'd been missing.

"Stop the fuckin' car!" Omar barked at the cabdriver. "Lemme out right here!"

Omar couldn't believe whom he had just seen. Kelly. He'd been looking for her for some time now. She must have started getting high again. Word on the street was she had gone into rehab. She looked healthy. The rehab had put some much needed pounds back on her. She had regained her nice figure. But Omar wasn't interested in having sex with her. He had a score to settle. Kelly had told on his man Corey. He couldn't believe she was back out here as if nothing had happened. As if she wasn't guilty of violating one of the oldest rules of the game by snitching to the police.

Oblivious to what was about to take place, she stood carefree in front of a project building. With his head down, Omar quickly walked up on her before she could recognize him.

"Uh-huh! I got ya azz now, bitch!" Omar said as he snatched Kelly by her hair and dragged her into a building.

Everyone around her suddenly dispersed. They wanted no part of Omar or whatever she had done to him. No one lifted a finger to help her. They all turned a blind eye.

Dragging her by her cornrow extensions, Omar led her down to the basement.

"Oh, you like pressin' charges on my man, huh?" Omar yelled.

"They made me do dat. I wuzn't gonna go ta trial, if it went dat far," she cried.

"Yeah right, bitch! Who da fuck you think you talkin' to? You lyin' azz crackhead!" Omar cursed.

Suddenly, he began to viciously smack her in the face. Then his smacks turned into punches, as if he forgot she was a woman. He took her head and rammed it repeatedly into the wall, opening a nasty gash on her forehead. Drawing blood was not enough for Omar. He took things to another level. He pounded her head up against the wall one time too many. She soon lost consciousness. She would never regain it.

After he was done, Omar slipped out of the building, leaving her sprawled out on the floor.

* * *

DATE: Forever and a day
TIME: To get paid
MOOD: Zooted outta my mind!
FROM: Dat nigga you know and luv, O

Dear Core,

Whut'z up baby boy? Hope everything is aiight on ya end! Me, I'm chillin' like a villain. Yo, actually I been catchin' rec a last few weeks. I finally ran down on ya man, Lord. Yup, I robbed dat bitch-azz nigga. I ran up in his crib and got 'em. And I smacked him in the back of the head wit da joint, on GP. He mad pussy though, he didn't even try ta get back at me. I sec 'em sometimes and dat faggot just turns his head . . . Fuck 'em! I'm get him again! Dis time I wanna catch him fa ev'rything! So I gotta do it right! I stuck 'em fa 8oz's last time. I really wanted some paper too. And guess whut? I finally caught dat crack-head bitch, Kelly out there! I gave her da beat down of her life. I put dat bitch in da hospital. I did her dirty kid. Dat wuz fa you. Her tellin' azz got exactly whut she deserved. Snitches get stitches! Found in body bags and ditches.

Enough said about dat. I seen ya ex-wife Monique. She couldn't even look me in my face Core. I told her she crossed a good dude. Core I'm just waitin' on you ta give me da word and I'll stomp dat fuckin' baby outta her. But dat ain't gonna happen, you got alotta feelin' fa dat ho! If you should ever lose some luv let me know. And her azz iz mine. (I ain't never liked her anyway.) I let her live on ya strength. Word! I woulda be dissed her.

Yo, I put anotha money order inside dis envelope. You should be crazy straight by now too. You should have commissary stacked to the ceiling. I'm out Kid!

P.S.
If I should lead. . . . Follow me!
If I should hesitate. . . . Push me!!
If I should betray you. . . . Kill me!!!
Cauze I'ma super trooper!!!!!

Love, Peace and Hair grease
Omar aka O

* * *

Corey began to lift weights. It helped to relieve some stress and keep Monique off his mind. Months of lifting weights and eating three high-starched meals a day began to pay big dividends, turning Corey's body into a rock-hard physique. He was filling out fast. Other inmates began to notice too. His respect level went up another notch. Slowly, he was becoming a force to be reckoned with.

One day while working out on the dip bar, Corey was approached by a stranger.

"Yo, ya name Corey? Corey Dixon?" the man inquired. "You wuz in da box a few months ago?"

Corey recognized him. He was the shank-wielding assailant who'd stabbed the other inmate from Corey's tier. It had been about eighteen months since he'd last seen him. Corey wondered if he was just now getting out of the box.

"Why?"

"You, Corey right?" he asked again. "I wanna make sure I'm talkin' ta da right person."

"Yeah, dat'z me! Whut'z da problem?" he shot back.

Subtly Corey balled his fingers together forming a fist, preparing to defend himself, should that be needed. In prison anything could happen in a blink of an eye.

"Everything is cool! Ain't no beef or nuttin'. I was just comin' ta thank you fa bein' a real convict, not snitchin' on me a few months ago. I know you know whut I'm talkin' 'bout. Member when dat boy got shanked up and you went ta da box? Well, da wuz my work. I shanked him up. I ain't mean ta involve you in it, it just happened like dat. Wrong place, wrong time."

"You ain't ever gotta worry 'bout me tellin'. I ain't got out like dat. Dat ain't my MO! I ain't a squealer. Same way on da streetz, same way in jail. You know whut they say around here, snitches get stitches, found in body bags and ditches," Corey replied. "It'z a small thing. Shit happens. I wouldn't want nobody ta drop a dime on me. If I wuz you."

"Listen, if there's anything I can do fa you, let me know. I really appreciate you keepin' ya mouth shut. Most these niggas round here woulda been told! Corey, you true ta da game."

"Thanks. But I ain't do nuttin' dat I wouldn't want nobody ta do fa me. If the shoe were on da other foot."

"I hear you. Good lookin' out. Yo, by the way, my name Doc. You been gettin' busy wit them weights. I see you gettin' cock diesel around here. What you been eatin'? I need some of dat."

The comment brought a smile to Corey's face. He loved that other inmates were starting to recognize his hard work.

The man continued, "I need ta start workin' out again myself. Yo, you mind if I work out wit you? I need some motivation right now. You now how it iz when you startin' ta work out again. So whut you say, young buck? Can da old man hang or whut? I won't hold you back. I'll do whut I can do till I get back into da swing of thingz."

"Aiight, if you really serious! I'm not in competition wit nobody. We could work out tagether if you want. Meet me right here! I ain't gonna come lookin' fa you. I ain't got no problem wit dat. They just transferred my other workout partner anyway."

"Dat's a bet! I'll be out here tamorrow! Meet you right here."

* * *

Peace and quiet of sleep had taken over the prison. Corey lay curled up in a ball in his bed. He was dreaming that he was home. He began to awake. Keeping his eyes clamped tightly shut, he allowed his sense of hearing to dominate his common sense. Ever so gently he began to open his eyelids. That was when the reality of his situation hit him like a ton of bricks: he wasn't home at all. He had never felt so hurt in all his life. He yearned to be back on the block, back on the streets.

Unable to get back to sleep, he got up and began to write a letter to his father on a yellow, lined tablet.

Dear Dad,

I hope these lines find you and ma doing good. Me, I'm aiight! (Under the circumstances.) I know I haven't written you since I've been locked up. But I've been thinkin' bout you anyway. The reason I haven't written you is because, I remember something you always usta say, "When ya ass get locked up don't call me." I took ya words ta da heart and I didn't. Maybe that's a weak excuse to you, for not keeping in touch with my father. But right now it's the best one I got. After all I put myself here. I feel kinda guilty even writin' you let alone askin' you for somethin'. (Try and understand where I'm comin' from.)

Anyway, over the years I've been thinkin' bout you and me, us. I always wondered why you never told me certain things, about life. Now that I'm in prison, I'm discovering things through older inmates. I'm suppose to have learned these things from you, not them. And though I'm learning, picking up new things, it just ain't the same not comin' from you. I ain't layin' the blame on you though. I know I played a role in this, somewhere. I know we went through our trials and tribulations. But still and all, ya son needed to know certain things to make the transition from a boy to a man. (You understand me?) Anyway, hope you don't take this letter the wrong way. It was something I was just thinkin' about. There is no right or wrong answer, just ya explanation.

Well, I'm gone dad. Write back soon!

Love always,
Ya son
Corey

* * *

Four days later, Corey received a letter. When the correctional officer handed him an envelope addressed from his father, Corey was afraid to open it. He was just letting off some steam went he wrote that letter to his father. He had no idea that his father would actually reply. Corey's heart began to race. He tore the envelope open, hoping he hadn't offended his father.

He began to read the letter and everything and everybody around him faded away. His father's handwriting was barely legible, so he had to focus. It sort of looked like chicken scratch. Corey could heard his father's voice, echoing in his head as he read.

Dear Son,

How are you? Fine, I hope. Your mother and I are doing okay. (And so is the rest of the family.) Let me start off by saying, I'm surprised that you even wrote me. A few years have gone by without you and me communicating. Everything I know about you I hear from your mother. Do you know how that makes me feel? Like a step father. I know I said a few things out of anger. But I really didn't mean it. I love you, Corey you are my baby boy. Nothing in this world can take the place of you, in my heart. Do you know how hurt I be sometimes when you call home and ask to speak to your mother and never me? Not too good, I tell you. I know we didn't see eye to eye on a lot of things. Maybe you thought you knew it all. But at sixteen years old you didn't. All I was tryin' to do was, mold and shape you into a man. I had to make certain decisions for you till you were able to make good decisions on your own. I wanted the best for you. Can you blame me for that? Corey, I thought I'd have you a lot longer than I did, to help you become a man. But you started moving fast and hanging with the wrong crowd. And all the lectures I gave you, had no effect on you. Seemed like my words went in one ear and out the other. Putting you out the house was the hardest thing I ever had to do in my life. But it had to be done. Because you were out there involving yourself in something you ain't have no business being involved in, in the first place . . .

* * *

His father said more than a mouthful. Corey had never heard his father be so candid. He had never seen his father express his feelings like this and show his human side. His words chipped away at the stoic disciplinarian image that cloaked him. Corey came away with a newfound respect and understanding for his father. Corey wrote him again and his dad wrote back.

That one letter broke down the wall, allowing father and son to write each other often.

Chapter 17

Bap! Bap! Bap! came the knocks on the door.

Ms. Patterson looked out her peephole and saw the two white men; cops for sure. As she undid the locks, she wondered what her son had done now. She knew that this was the likely reason they were at her door. *But what can I do? Omar is too big and wild to control*, she rehearsed saying in her mind.

"Can I help you?" Ms. Patterson asked, giving attitude in her tone of speech and body language.

"Yes, ma'am. I'm Detective Peterson and this is Detective Riley, homicide division. We have a warrant for your son's arrest. We have reason to believe that he is the assailant responsible for the death of Kelly McDaniel."

Ms. Patterson threw her head back in shock. She had never expected anything like this. Her son was in serious trouble. Still she refused to disclose any information on his whereabouts. Though he was wrong by all accounts, Omar was her son. She just couldn't assist the police in apprehending him. She'd rot in jail herself first. She wasn't one of those righteous mothers who would turn their children over to the law the minute they broke the law. Admittedly, she knew, the crime her son was accused of was despicable. Still, as a parent, her job was to protect him at all costs.

Detective Peterson continued, "We also have a search warrant. Ma'am, could you step aside while we search the premises?"

The two detectives drew their guns and began a light search of the apartment. Their only concern was that Omar was hiding, armed, lying in wait. They weren't there to raid the house or search for anything else but him. As a matter of policy, if anything illegal, such as a gun or drugs, was in plain view, then one or all of the occupants would be arrested. They found nothing. They left Ms. Patterson their respective business cards.

The instant they were gone, Ms. Patterson paged her son on his beeper.

"Boy, I don't know whut da hell you done did, but da fuckin' police came up here lookin' fa ya ass. They wasn't just regular police either, they was detectives, from the homicide division."

The mere mention of the word *homicide* made O's heart beat a little faster.

"They came all up in the apartment with they guns out. Lookin' in every room, closet, and under the beds."

"Whut they want me for? Did they say?" he questioned her.

"Murder!" she shouted. "They said you killed somebody! Some lady named Kelly McDaniel."

Oh, shit! O thought to himself. *She died.*

"They have a warrant for your arrest. They want you to turn yourself in. They claim they just wanna question you. I don't believe them. Boy, don't even think about doing nothing stupid like that. I want you to go ta ya grandmother's house in Queens and stay there. Stay there till we can figure out what was really going on."

Omar hid out at his grandmother's house. He was officially on the run. But like most criminals, he was still in and out of his neighborhood. Returning to familiar surroundings was human nature. Besides that, he still had packages of drugs on the block. He had to check on his business.

* * *

The sun was ablaze, and the prison yard was sweltering with the high heat of summer. Most inmates didn't dare leave their tiers or cells. For security reasons, there were no trees in the prison yard, no shade, nowhere to hide from Mother Nature. This and the dead of winter was the kind of weather Corey loved to work out in. The springtime and fall, moderate temperatures, seemed to bring out all the wannabe and novice weight lifters and exercisers. Heat like this was a test. Most inmates don't like to work out in this type of heat. This allowed Corey the time and space that he needed to perform his exercises.

"C'mon, gimme two more!" Doc barked. "One! Two! Aiight, bring it home, I got it."

The muscles in Corey's chest bulged. His sweat-drenched white tank could barely contain him. He was so tight from doing repetitions on the bench press, he thought his skin would burst. Corey felt that if he had to fight at that moment, he wouldn't come out on the winning side.

"Now it's ya turn, Doc." Corey took his place behind the bench to spot him. "I'ma make you get every last rep by yaself too. Just like you did me."

"Oh, it's like dat, Corey?" Doc joked.

"Yeah, it'z like dat! Now let's stop rappin'. Ya stall tactics are incredible. Ready? One, two, three, dat's you, Doc!"

Carefully, Corey hovered over Doc, watching him and the weight bar. At the first sign of weakness he would assist him. Much to Corey's surprise, Doc turned out to be a worthy workout partner. Doc knew all the right buttons to push to get the most out of Corey.

When Corey thought he'd reached his peak, Doc would inspire him to go further.

"C'mon, old man," Corey commanded as he watched Doc suddenly begin to struggle. "Pusssshhhhhh! Dat's it! I got it!"

"Whewww!" Doc exhaled loudly. "I still got it! Corey, you see it! You can only hope ta look like dis when you get my age."

Corey just shook his head and smiled. But he had to admit Doc's body structure put a lot of younger inmates to shame. As they say in prison, Doc was "cut up like a bag of dope." Corey outweighed him by nearly sixty pounds. Doc had less body fat.

"Yeah, Doc, you got dat one off." Corey laughed. "I don't believe in role models. But you mine, old man, you minez."

"Dat's right, young buck! I can't think of a betta one ta have. Can you?"

"Na," Corey replied, stroking Doc's ego. "You da man!"

"Dat's right! Now repeat afta me. 'All we can't beat up—' "

"—'we gonna shoot up'!" Corey finished the well-rehearsed saying.

"Dat's right! You know how we do!" Doc said. "Let's take a few laps now. We done wit dis."

"Aiight, I'm comin', lemme grab my shirt."

After gathering up his items, Corey and Doc walked around the yard. This was something Corey didn't care to do too much of. Walking the yard made him feel like a dog circling inside its cage or owner's fence. True he was walking, but he wasn't going anywhere. But with Doc in tow, he knew the conversation would take his mind off what they were actually doing.

"Yo, Doc, why when a dude got an older state number than you, they think they betta than you. Why is dat?" Corey inquired. "Am I buggin' or whut? Do you see da same shit or whut?"

Doc replied, "I see it all da fuckin' time. Niggas iz brainwashed. It's all apart of bein' institutionalized. It's like a dude dat's done time before, he got a couple felonies on his record, and you ain't none, you're a new jack. He thinks he betta than you too. Just because he got a few bids unda his belt. Bust dis, when you really analyze the whole situation, all it really means iz dat he's worse at committing crime than you. Those type dudes kill me! They programmed. They inmates! We're prisoners! We being held against our will!"

"Word up! Yo, Doc, you so right. I hope I neva get like dat. I hope dis my first and last bid. They can have dis shit."

Changing the subject, Doc asked Corey, "Don't you go up for parole soon?"

"Yeah. Inna few weeks I see da board. I wonder whut them muthafuckas gonna do. You think they gonna cut me loose? I mean, I completed all the programs they asked me to do."

"Corey, ain't no tellin' wit them bastards. I see 'em cut loose muthafuckas they ain't have no business sending home. And give hitz to muthafuckas who deserved to make parole. Some strange things have happened up in dat room. So I can't call it. My advice ta you iz to prepare for da worst."

Corey heard Doc; at the same time he didn't. He wasn't trying to hear he wasn't going home. He believed wholeheartedly that he had done everything required to make parole. What more could they ask of him?

Doc continued, "I ain't tryin' ta bust ya bubble but, I just tellin' you how it is. You always here 'bout some bitch on the board whose kid wuz hooked on crack so they hard on drug dealers. Whateva ya crime iz, they come wit a story ta scare you wit. Dat be these hillbilly-ass COs spreadin' those rumors too. They think dat shit iz funny."

"Yeah, these crackers ain't right. They think a nigga's freedom iz one big joke." Corey expressed seriously, "My fuckin' life ain't no fuckin' joke. . . . Dat's whut really kills me 'bout dis place, a CO could come ta work wit a fucked-up attitude and fuck a nigga whole life up."

"Dat's true, but what can you do? Me, I just try ta stay outta their way. And hope they stay outta mine. They be power trippin'! They the same ones who got picked on, chased home, and beat up as kids. Now they got a lil taste of power. They become tyrants!" Doc explained. "You know whut they say though, if you don't like it here, you shoulda stayed ya ass home."

They were both breathing harder now. As they past the basketball court, Corey spotted a familiar face.

"Yo, Shawn! Shawn!" he yelled. "Whut up, kid?"

Shawn paused his game to look out and shouted back, "Yo, who dat?"

"Me, Corey! Ya man from central bookings and da Island."

Shawn had trouble recognizing Corey because he had gotten so big. He moved closer to get a good look.

"Oh, shit, kid! You done blew da fuck up! Whut you been eatin'?" Shawn marveled.

"Yo, money, you still playin' or whut?" an opposing player shouted. "You can talk to ya man later. We hoopin' right now!"

"Yo, when you got up here?" Corey asked.

"Yo, kid, I can't talk right now. We kick it later. Gotta get back to bustin' these niggas' ass. See you later."

"Aiight, Shiz, we kick it later. Lemme know if you need somethin'," Corey told him.

"I got you."

"Yo, Corey, who dat?" Doc asked once they'd moved forward a few more feet. "He from ya block? You know him from New York?"

"Dat's my man Shawn. I met him afta I got knocked by

TNT, in da bull pens. We been crazy cool ever since. We usta watch each other's back on da Island."

"If he cool wit you, then dat makes him cool wit me too," Doc said. " 'Cauze you my nigga! No question."

Corey and Doc continued to walk and hold a idle conversation. Suddenly, Corey spun around, thinking he heard somebody calling his name. But when he looked around, he didn't see anyone. He turned to continue walking.

"Yo, Corey! Corey!" a soft voice called again.

From a nearby picnic table, which doubled as a poker table, emerged a familiar face. Corey stared hard as the person came into view, as if he saw a ghost.

"Money?" he exclaimed softly. "Money Mike? Is dat you?"

"Yeah, it'z me kid! . . . Damn, Corey you got big. . . . How long you been down?"

"Close ta three years. I'm gettin' ready ta see the board soon. Yo, Mike, I ain't think we'd ever bump heads again. You know I wuz out there dat nite you bodied Diesel. Kid, you went all out. Word!"

Outwardly, Mike took the comment in stride. In prison, to be branded a killer was like sporting a badge of honor. Here, taking a person's life was what most inmates aspired to do. Mike would rather erase his memory of killing a man, but he couldn't. Sometimes he almost dreaded going to sleep. He saw Diesel's face every time he closed his eyes. If only people knew the consequences of committing murder, then they probably wouldn't do it. The law was one thing, your own conscience was another. Two lives were lost that day, Diesel's and his. He was the perpetrator and would never ever again be the same person that everyone knew.

Doc was studying Money Mike as they talked. He knew him from somewhere but he couldn't put his finger on it.

"Yo, c'mon, Corey, we gotta go!" Doc said forcefully, placing his arm around Corey's broad shoulders.

"Doc, whut'z up?" Corey asked, puzzled. "Can't you see I'm kickin' it wit my man?"

Doc reiterated, "Corey, c'mon! We gotta take care of somethin'! It's real important!"

"Whut? Beef?" Corey questioned.

"Just c'mon, man," Doc commanded.

"Yo, Mike, I'll talk to you later. Gotta see whut'z up wit dis . . ."

Doc remembered where he knew this guy from.

When they were safely out of earshot, Doc turned toward Corey and let him know what was going on.

"Yo, stay away from dat dude, he's bad news. I know dat's ya man from ya block and everythin', but he ain't right!"

"Whut da fuck dat suppose ta mean? Huh? Doc, I knew dis nigga all my life. Tell me sumthin'."

Doc fired back, "Yo, ya man got sugar in his tank."

"Gay?" Corey repeated out loud. "Mike's a faggot?"

How could his homie from his block go out like that? On the streets he'd never seen any signs of Money Mike liking men. On the contrary, he was Money Mike with lots of females, pretty ones at that. He wondered what the hell had gotten into him.

"If Mike ain't gay, then he definitely on his way," Doc said seriously. "I wouldn't put a bad bone on him like dat if it wasn't true. But you know how I know? We wuz up in Sing Sing together couple years ago. I seen 'im playin' them faggots real close up there. Every new homosexual dat they brought into the jail, ya man wuz on 'im."

"Word?" Corey was shocked. "He on it like dat?"

"Iz he?" Doc snapped. "Iz water wet? Iz a elephant heavy? Do a bear shit in da woods? Dat boy iz gay as da day iz long. But he probably don't believe it. He probably think just 'cause he fuckin' a faggot dat he ain't one. But you know whut they say, a pancake ain't done till you flip it! Betta believe it. Corey, just keep ya distance from him. Matter fact, cut him off. . . . Faget you ever known him, 'cauze association breeds similarity."

"Yo, I should go back over there and stomp dat bitch-ass nigga out! On GP, just fa disrespectin' our block like dat," Corey fumed.

"Na, don't even do no shit like dat! Why bust ya hand up on some chump? He might have dat shit anyway. Besides dat, you should never ever fight a faggot, because you have nothin' ta gain. If you win, you were supposed ta anyway. But if you lose, don't forget faggots are men too. . . . Da best thing fa you ta do iz, fly a kite back ta ya block. Tell all ya niggas whut da deal iz. . . . so if and when dat nigga do come home, all da broads in ya neighborhood know not ta fuck wit him. . . . 'Cauze he may fuck around and catch dat shit and bring back round da way."

The more Doc spoke, the more he made sense to Corey. From this point on, Money Mike was dead to him. He'd see him and wouldn't see him at the same time. If something were to happen to Money Mike tomorrow, he vowed to look the other way. Money Mike was on his own. Corey couldn't afford to tarnish his reputation by even talking to him. Corey knew that the silent treatment would kill him. In prison, it was rare that someone met a friend that he grew up with. Usually friends were forged over time, while in prison.

After getting over the initial shock of his former friend's sexual preference, Corey focused on his date with the parole board. His day was rapidly approaching.

Chapter 18

In broad daylight, Lord, surrounded by his team of drug-dealing thugs, brandished a small chrome .32 automatic. In the months since the robbery he had bounced back well. He had become a big man on the street. So, he figured the best defense was a good offense. He began to commit a string of senseless shootings. This was out of character for him but it was an effort to build a reputation for himself, as someone you didn't want to cross paths with.

"Where you want it? In ya hand or leg? Huh?" Lord asked. Talk ta me, nigga."

"Yo, Lord, I swear ta God. It wuzn't me who stole dat pack," the young man cried.

"I ain't tryin' a hear dat shit! If you didn't do it, why you disappear? Huh?" Lord shouted.

" 'Cauze I knew niggaz wuz gonna point da finger at me. I just got down wit y'all."

"No more rap!" Lord announced. "Step away from him, y'all. I'm about ta take dis nigga off dis earth."

Fearing that threat was real, the young man reluctantly stuck out his leg, far away from his body. Closing his eyes, he said a quick prayer. He hoped that the bullet didn't hit any major arteries, and that he wouldn't walk away from the incident with a severe limp. A light crackle of gunfire from the gun temporary interrupted his thoughts. Luckily for him, Lord's aim wasn't good, he merely grazed the thigh. The young man began to hop around, trying to shake off the effects of the shooting, as blood soaked his blue jeans.

After handing one of his workers the gun, Lord announced, "Somebody take dis bitch-ass nigga to da hospital. Get him up out of here before five-o come thru."

Lord wore a satisfied look on his face. He had just made an example out of the young man. And to top things off, he didn't leave the scene of the crime. An air of invincibility was surrounding him, he was starting to feel that he could take on anybody and come out the victor. He longed to avenge himself against O. It was only a matter of time before he retaliated against him. In his mind, O's day was coming, and a lot sooner than most people thought.

* * *

O was a fugtive, but it didn't stop him from showing up on the block. He was on the run from the law, but figured he had to do what he had to do—break the law—until captured. It wasn't as if the police were going to stop looking for him if he went legit.

For months he had moved around like a thief in the night, using darkness to shield himself from prying eyes. In a tinted-window hooptie, a black Honda Accord, the police couldn't tell who was inside his car. He never came around in the daytime.

With each passing day, O's appearances became more frequent. He truly believed that the police could never apprehend him in his own neighborhood, because he knew all the cuts and hide spots in the projects like the back of his hand. *I deserve ta go ta jail if they can catch me in my own neighborhood,* he often thought to himself. However, the main reason for showing his presence was a rash of losses in product and profit he was experiencing. His workers knew the type of legal problems he was facing, and some began to take advantage of it. This led to O making a surprise visit to one kid's home, smacking him up and threatening to kill him if O ever caught him on the block again. The kid took these words literally.

O took one more pull of the blunt and put it out in the ashtray. He then walked across the street to his mother's building, to make an unannounced visit.

"Lemme go upstairs and see Ma-dukes before I jet back ta Queens," he said to no one in particular.

Unbeknownst to him, sets of eyes watched him from an adjacent building's darkened hallway. Clothed in black army fatigue gear and black Timberland chukkas, the gunmen waited for just the right moment to strike.

The marijuana smoke O had previously inhaled must have dulled his senses, causing him to drop his guard. He never heard the other building door open and shut. While O fiddled with a ring of keys, the assailant quickly ran up on O, squeezing off two rounds in his head. Then he vanished into the night, avoiding identification.

With the sound of gunshots, lights soon began to flick on in the projects. Neighborhood busybodies appeared at their windows, just in time to see O's blood and brains lying on the sidewalk.

One of the neighbors knocked on Ms. Patterson's door to awaken her and tell her the news.

* * *

Corey was about to have his turn to dance with the devil—in other words, to go before the parole board. The thought of the parole board holding his fate in their hands rendered him unable to eat and left him feeling as if he were walking the plank.

"Hey, Dixon, you gotta drug charge, don't you?" the correctional officer asked as a few inmates waited on wooden benches in the hallway. "Well, it's not a good day ta be a crack dealer. One parole examiner's son killed himself smokin' dat stuff. She done gave out big hits to every drug dealer's parole case she's ever heard. Man, I sure wouldn't wanna be you."

That was the last thing Corey needed to hear. He stared blankly at the man and didn't allow his fear to register on his face. He thought to himself, *I already heard that lie before, buddy. Try to scare the next man.*

When Corey entered the parole hearing room, he was cautious not to bop or strut. He knew all eyes were on him, so he was careful not to display any of his street mannerisms. There was a time and a place for everything, and now was not the time or the place for that. He could be street in the yard or, better yet, on the street. From the onset he didn't like the looks of things. Three Caucasian hearing examiners sat in wait to pass judgment on him. Just as in the courthouse, he was not being judged by a jury of his peers. The parole board wasn't from his neighborhood or city. They didn't even understand his culture, so how could they possibly understand him and his reasons for committing crime?

After serving thirty long, hard months of a three-to-six-year prison term, he sat in a hard wooden chair with a perfect upright posture. A lone correctional officer was in the room for security reasons, just in case any inmate didn't agree with the decision that the board passed down and tried to get violent. His job was to protect the civilians against any potential threat.

Turning on the tape recorder, the lone female parole examiner began to speak. "The date is March fifteenth, 1992. We are about to begin the parole proceeding of inmate Corey Dixon, who is currently serving a three-to-six-year prison term for assault and a sale of a controlled substance, crack cocaine. How are you today, Mr. Dixon?"

"Fine, ma'am," Corey spoke.

That was the end of the pleasantries right there. The female hearing examiner proceeded to rip into Corey like a pit bull. She got straight to the point, pulling no punches.

"Being paroled is a privilege. Why do you think this hearing committee should grant you parole?" she grilled him, not giving him a chance to respond. "Besides those lousy pieces of paper in your base file called certificates, what have you done during your incarceration to merit your early release?"

Without giving it a second thought, Corey said, "I've

completed every program that the prison has prescribed that I take. I've been relatively free of trouble accept for one or two minor incidents."

The hearing officer erupted, "You call the stabbing of another inmate minor? It says here you were placed in solitary confinement for an extended period of time pending an institutional investigation."

"Yes, ma'am, but if you look in those very same base files, you will see I've been vindicated. The institutional investigation turned up no wrongdoing on my part. It was a case of mistaken identity, of me being at the wrong place at the wrong time."

"Oh, really, Mr. Dixon," she said sarcastically. "You got all the answers, huh? You're innocent I suppose. I bet you're doing time for someone else, right?"

"No, ma'am. That's not what I'm implying by any means. I'm merely stating the facts."

These were the last words Corey got to make to the parole board in his behalf. After that they each took turns cross-examining about every little sin he had ever committed in his life. They asked him cold, hard questions in hopes he would get caught in a lie. That way they would have probable cause to deny him parole and further degrade him. To them, the paper on the table, his rap sheet, told his whole life story. When in all actuality it was only partially true. There was no way in the world the paper could adequately describe his family life or his upbringing. His strong family values couldn't be described by mere words on paper, they had to be seen.

They excused Corey from the room while they rendered a parole decision. He was called back into the room in minutes. They had denied his parole.

* * *

A few days had passed and Corey was still reeling from the sting of not making parole. Corey opened a letter from his mother. He sat silently on his bunk, reading it.

Dear Son,

I haven't heard from you in a good while. (Not since you were told you were denied for parole.) Don't let those people worry you, take this set back as a sign from God. When he is ready for you to come home, no prison bars will be strong enough to keep you. Remember that. And stay strong Corey. It won't be long now. You'll be home sooner than you know it too.

Anyway, I have to tell you the real reason for writing this letter. A few days ago, they found your friend Omar, shot dead, in front of his building. The police don't know who did it or why. There are a whole lot of rumors running around, about who might have did it, but I'm not gonna speculate. Nobody knows for sure except God Almighty. They having a funeral Service Monday at McCall's. We contacted the jail to find out if you can go but they said no. It has to be immediate family, not friends. Corey I never been so glad in all my life to know that you were locked up during this time. Because you and that boy was real close. And yall probably would have been together that night. If you had been there that night, there might have been two dead people out there.

* * *

Corey's eyes filled up with tears. He couldn't bear the thought of never seeing his friend again, never laughing with him, never smiling at him. To him it was as if a piece of him had perished too.

His mind pondered who the culprit was. And each time he came to the same conclusion, Lord. He had the motives and resources to get it done. Corey's blood began to boil. He cursed the day that the bastard who killed his friend was born. There was no doubt in his mind that he would avenge Omar's death. *It was only right,* he mused. Corey had never forgotten the pact Omar and he had made. He vowed to uphold his end of the deal, whatever the cost.

Doc and Tate noticed the change in Corey ever since he gave them the news about the death of his friend. Doc gave him his space to grieve. Tate on the other hand took a different approach. He talked to Corey every chance he could get.

"Tate, whut really fucks me up about the whole situation iz, nobody iz doin' nuttin'. The kid who did it iz walkin' round like nuttin' happenin'. He a dead man walkin' fa real. When I get out, I'ma straighten it out."

Tate sat behind the desk in the prison library, rubbing his chin as Corey vented. He waited patiently till Corey was finished.

"First of all, I'm sorry to hear about ya homie gettin'

killed. But whatever happened, happened! Things happen for a reason. No one ever said we're suppose to know the reason why. You goin' home and shootin' or killin' somebody ain't gonna bring him back. You know, a wise man once said, 'He who plans revenge must dig two graves.' "

Corey listened to Tate, but his words had little effect on his mind-set. He knew he had made a mistake by mentioning his murderous intentions to his friend. Quietly he thought that old age was making Tate soft. Tate had somehow forgotten the code of the streets. Even the Bible preached vengeance, an eye for an eye. Tate's positive talk went in one ear and out the other. Corey was going to do what he had to do despite what anybody said.

It was clear from the beginning that Tate was dead set against revenge. He felt planning and plotting murder took up too much time and energy. He felt that going all out for revenge blinded a person to the reality of the situation. Certain sacrifices needed to be made; the avenger had to be ready to kill and die, if necessary.

Corey talked to Doc, who had a different idea on the subject of revenge. Doc lived and breathed the code of the street. He championed Corey's cause. He felt there was a time in everyone's life when one must make a stand and Corey's time had arrived. "You gotta stand for sumthin' or fall for anything," Doc often said.

"Doc, I'm tellin' you I know who did it, dat nigga Lord! I'll bet my fuckin' life on it!" an outraged Corey said.

Doc replied, "Ya probably right too. Ain't no secrets in da streetz, somebody knows sumthin', somebody saw sumthin'.

You just gotta apply pressure. Pressure busts pipes. One thing fa sure, drug dealers kill other drug dealers. Anyway, if that's how you feel in ya heart, then you know whut you gotta do. Somebody gotta die. Fuck dat leave-it-alone shit dat Tate iz talkin' about. I don't know whut he think this iz—a United Nations peace summit or sumthin'? Ain't no peace talks in da streetz. Whut he want, bygones ta be bygones? Well, it's too late fa dat. Blood's been spilt. I wouldn't tell you ta do nuttin' I wouldn't do. I'd rather live like a lion fa one day than ta live like a lamb fa a thousand."

Mentally, Corey digested Doc's words of street wisdom. Doc had told him exactly what he wanted to hear. He'd cosigned Corey's plans for street justice.

"Corey, before you go home and jump right into some beef, get you some paper first. You can't go ta war if you broke. You'll get slaughtered. All wars have to be financed. Go home and pretend you don't know nothin', then as soon as you get ya money right, make ya move. Make sure you do it right too. You don't want ta be peeking over ya shoulders. If you pull ya gun out, be ready ta use it. Be ready ta go all the way wit it," Doc advised.

Like a seasoned war general, Doc laid the foundation that would later become Corey's blueprint for attack. Over the next few months, Corey began to work out with a renewed purpose. This was basic training for him, preparing him for the drama that lay ahead on the street. With each repetition, each exercise he performed, he kept Doc's saying always echoing in his head: "All we can't beat up, we gone shoot up! Dead!"

Chapter 19

The annual summer-league basketball tournament was in full swing in the prison yard. Prisoners crowded around the basketball court, to see some of the best basketball players go at it. Many prisoners made bets on which team would win and by how many points. Packs of cigarettes took the place of real money as the currency being wagered.

Prison sports tended to bring out the worst in most inmates. Bragging rights were at high stake here. In competitive games like these, jailhouse legends were born. It seemed, though, that someone always found a way to take the fun out to the game. There was often a crooked referee, who purposely made bad calls in favor of one team. Sometimes it was the players themselves who, in the heat of the game, tended to foul too hard. The one rule to keep in mind when playing jailhouse basketball was, there were no rules; no blood, no foul. Intimidation was a key strategy. Two opposing players would jaw at each other on the way up court.

"Man, you couldn't guard me with a gun, yo. Y'all betta

put somebody else on me, 'cause I'm killin' ya man," a player boasted. "I'ma about ta do him dirty."

A player put up a wild shot and the rebound careened high off the rim. Shawn leaped high in the air, attempting to rebound. It appeared to be his for the taking. Then something bizarre happened. He lost consciousness. He hit the concrete court like a ton of bricks. Play stopped immediately as concerned prisoners rushed to his aid.

Late in reacting, Correctional Officer Miller made his way through the crowd, then ordered the inmates to back up. Radioing into the prison control center, he informed his superiors of the medical emergency. They, in turn, informed the infirmary.

Precious minutes passed as everyone waited for the slow-moving nurses to arrive. The prisoners began to grow rowdy as they watched the correctional officer do nothing.

"Help da damn man!" someone shouted. "Give him some CPR or sumthin', you fuckin' stupid cracker."

The officer felt uneasy. The inmates were pressuring. And though the inmate didn't appear to be breathing, there was no way in the world he was going to administer CPR to an inmate. He didn't know what kind of infectious diseases he might be carrying. He had a wife and kid to return home to after his shift. He couldn't possibly endanger their lives.

On the hot concrete, Shawn lay motionless; everyone who looked on knew he was doomed. Still they hoped their fallen comrade would make it. Prison was no place for a man to end his life.

With a wheelchair in tow, two overweight nurses huffed

and puffed their way over to the basketball court. They checked his vital signs, finding a weak pulse. Realizing this was a real emergency, they struggled to lift Shawn's limp, lifeless body into the wheelchair. As fast as they could, they made their way to the prison's infirmary. But it was too late; Shawn was DOA—dead on arrival.

* * *

"Yo, Corey! Corey!" another inmate shouted. "Yo, ya man just fell out in da yard."

"Whut? Who you talking 'bout—Doc?" Corey inquired eagerly.

"Nah, ya man Shawn!" the inmate replied quickly. "The nurses took him out in a wheelchair. He didn't look too good."

On this hot summer day, Corey was inside the prison library, searching for a good book to read. He needed a momentary escape from reality, considering all the drama he had been dealing with lately. Now he had more bad news.

"Word? Whut happened to him? How he fall? Somebody pushed him?"

"Nah, nobody ain't push him, he just went fa a rebound. He musta lost consciousness in the air. He just came down and hit his head hard. It didn't look like he was gonna make it either."

Corey only partially believed the inmate's story. What did he know? He wasn't no doctor or nuttin', Corey mused to himself. In his mind Shawn was still alive. He reasoned Shawn probably caught a seizure. He would be all right.

After a couple days in the prison infirmary, he'd be back in the prison population playing basketball again.

Game interrupted, the prisoners were sent back to their respective housing units. As Corey headed back to his tier, he saw an inmate trustee wheeling Shawn's personal possessions toward the prison control tower. Corey's stomach knotted. He realized that Shawn wouldn't be back. Shawn was just about to max out his prison sentence, next month. He was on his way home. He was so close and yet so far. Corey would never again in life feel the same way about the season again.

As word of Shawn's death spread around the prison, so did anger about what the prisoners deemed a senseless death. They were angry at the correctional officer on duty for not providing adequate medical attention, and they were angry at the slow-moving medical staff.

* * *

The following morning at breakfast a deadly silence permeated the prison mess hall. This was a show of solidarity for their fallen comrade. The tension was so thick inside the mess hall, you could cut it with a knife. Silence signaled death in prison, and that made correctional officers assigned to work the mess hall fear for their lives. They were trapped behind enemy lines, praying that a riot wouldn't erupt. Surely they were in grave danger.

But breakfast went on without incident and the prison administration breathed a collective sigh of relief. They thought they were out of the woods. But they were wrong.

* * *

Correctional Officer Miller used his vacation days to avoid coming to work for a while and because he liked to take extended vacations during the hunting season. But he returned a few weeks later to again patrol the prison yard. As Corey walked past him, Miller looked him over. As soon as the correctional officer turned his attention elsewhere, Corey punched him in the jaw, knocking him out cold. Then swarms of inmates followed suit, attacking correctional officers near them. The mayhem in the yard turned into a full-fledged riot, spreading throughout the jail. The riot squad was called in and shots were fired in an effort to regain order. Dozens of inmates and correctional officers suffered minor injuries.

The whole prison was on lockdown for months. The prison guards systematically began shaking down the cells, searching for contraband. Only those inmates who were trustees or worked in the kitchen were allowed out of the cells. And even they were assigned to make paper-bagged finger food for the prison population, breakfast, lunch, and dinner. The prisoner's didn't like being locked in, but they adapted. After a while they became used to it. They were suffering for a cause. The next generation of criminals would never have to deal with inadequate medical attention or medical negligence by prison officials, because they had demonstrated that they wouldn't take mistreatment.

Administrative investigations were conducted, and the instigators of the riot were found, charged, and transferred to different facilities. The prison was taken off lockdown and things went back to the way they were. Corey lucked out. He wasn't identified as one of the culprits.

* * *

As soon as Corey was permitted to, he returned to the library in search of more novels. During lockdown he nearly died of boredom. From now on he vowed to keep some reading material in the stash, just in case another riot ever happened.

"Whut'z up, Tate?" Corey greeted him.

"Well, well, if it isn't the big man on campus, Corey Dixon!" Tate sarcastically said.

"Tate, whut'z on ya mind, man? Talk ta me. I don't like da vibe I'm gettin' from you."

Tate carefully scanned the immediate area for anyone who might be within earshot before he spoke.

"Since you asked, I'll tell you what's on my mind. Corey, you musta lost ya goddamn mind. Pulling dat stunt you did in da yard. Nigga, you lucky one a these jailhouse snitches ain't turned you in. Betta thank ya lucky stars, boy. We all lucky ta still be alive. You know whut they coulda done ta us? You young niggas neva realize whut you do till the wheels are already in motion. Don't you know you can't beat the white man with physical force? They are the masters at dat shit. They are the most violent people on the face of this earth. They will squash you beneath their feet like a bug. And think nuttin' of it. They did it up in the Attica riots. The only way you can defeat them is with a pen. Haven't you heard the pen is mightier than the sword?" Tate spoke sternly, looking Corey directly in the eye as he did.

He continued, "Y'all did dat boy's memory a terrible dishonor. If you really wanna do something, do it legally! File a class-action suit against the jail. If you want, I'll show you how."

Tate hoped that Corey would take him up on his offer. He had grown so found of the young man, he wanted to help him help himself. He wanted to teach Corey how to use his brain instead of his brawn.

"I'm wit it," Corey replied. "Let's do dis."

Taking Tate's advice, Corey poured over the law books, looking for grounds for his suit. When he found them, together he and Tate drafted the class-action suit themselves. They filed in the federal court system. Now it was a waiting game; they waited for the courts to hear the case.

* * *

Corey knew something was terribly wrong when the chaplain summoned him to his office. He didn't participate in any religious activities, so why did the prison chaplain want to see him? It could only be one reason, death in the family. *Enough is enough already*, he thought to himself. He arrived at the chaplain's office quickly.

"Have a seat, young man," the old Caucasian prison chaplain said. "How are you feeling today, son?"

"I felt good. Dat was, until I heard you wanted to see me. I know this can't be good." Corey took a breath. "Who died?"

The chaplain began, "All things must come to an end. It is an evitable part of life. Just like the changing of the seasons. In spring, flowers bloom and in the fall they wither and die."

Politely Corey listened to the chaplain's long, drawn-out

speech about life and death. He was growing impatient. He wished the chaplain would just skip the preliminaries and tell him who had passed on, now.

"Son, your father suffered a massive heart attack last night, in his sleep. The Lord called him home."

Corey broke down and cried. Long, body-racking sobs went through him.

The chaplain got up from behind his desk and laid a hand on his shoulder. "Don't worry, son, your father is in a better place. Everything is going to be all right."

When Corey's father died, gone with him were all thoughts of reconciliation. Corey wanted to apologize to his parents, his father, in particular, for stressing their marriage. Now that he had time to think and to see things clearly, Corey finally realized all the unnecessary trouble he had caused. Many a day he had put his mother in an awkward position as she tried to conceal her son's devilment. Now that Corey had grown older and a lot wiser, he saw for himself that all his father had ever wanted was the best for him—even if he sometimes went about it the wrong way. Corey really felt that they needed to have a sit-down meeting, face-to-face, man-to-man. But now death had robbed him of that chance. He regretted never having the opportunity to tell his father he loved him, one last time. Now he saw just how frail life could be. Death could touch anyone at any time. No one was immune.

* * *

Slowly, Corey walked back into the hearing room. He scanned each face of the parole board members for any indication of their decision. He found the same steely, expressionless looks painted on their faces. Unlike the first time, he didn't have his hopes up high; his mind-set was whatever happens happens. Soon he'd be approaching his mandatory release date. So no matter what happened here today, soon they'd have to release him whether they liked it or not.

"Mr. Dixon, it is the decision of this board to grant you parole," a member stated.

At first Corey couldn't believe his ears. Did they say what he thought they said? It wasn't until they started briefing him on some of the terms and conditions of his parole that it actually hit him.

The day that Corey had dreamt about from the very moment he was sentenced was here. His hands shook as he signed his release papers; this time tomorrow he would be a free man. His only regret was that he was leaving two of his favorite people behind, Doc and Tate. Before he left, he consulted with each of them.

* * *

Corey entered the prison yard in search of Doc and Tate. This would be his final farewell, his last conversation in prison with either of them. Knowing how packed the yard gets in the summer, Corey dreaded searching the entire yard for them. He didn't have to look far for Doc; he stood waiting for Corey near the prison yard entrance.

"Well, tomorrow's da big day, huh? Bet ya monkey ass can't wait either," Doc joked. Slowly they began to walk the yard. They each knew the finality of the situation. Neither man was in a rush to part company.

"You damn right I can't wait!" Corey stated. "I ain't tell nobody I'm comin' home. I can't wait till I see the look on their faces when they see me. It's a whole new ball game."

"I heard dat!" Doc exclaimed. "Look, don't faget about da old man when you get out there in da world. Send me some packages and money orders when you get on ya feet. Don't hit da bricks and get new on me. Keep ya word! Don't you not know ya word iz bond?"

"I got you, Doc, don't sweat dat! I'ma make sure you don't want fa nuttin'. I promise you. I'ma look out. I'm goin' home ta take over dat block. Dat shit iz minez! I remember whut you usta say, men do whut they want and boyz do whut they can. Doc, I'ma man!" Corey ranted.

"I hear ya. But listen, Scarface, take ya time. Slow motion betta than no motion. Slow money betta than no money. And if ya out there slinging that shit and you ain't savin' no money, you ain't playin' the game. Da game iz playin' you. Don't go jumpin' from da fryin' pan into da fire."

Corey knew Doc spoke from experience. And Corey felt honored to hear his wisdom. Doc allowed Corey to pick his brain for angles, and gave him pointers on how to succeed in the drug game. Doc—and for that matter, Tate—were truly people one met once in a lifetime.

"And anotha thing, don't go out there fuckin' wit those bum-ass bitches. Get yaself a nice, fine young lady wit a job. Whoever you start fuckin' wit, make sure you get an understandin' wit her first. Put all you cards on the table. Be up-front, let her know da deal. Say look dis iz how it iz, like it or leave it. . . . Let her make the choice for herself. Don't lie or game her up. Dat's how shit get fucked up. The reason you gotta do dis iz, females are possessive by nature. And they get superpossessive when you fuck their brains out."

"Yo, Doc, I see Tate over there and I need to get with him a minute. But I'll be right back. I gotta talk ta him 'for I go and time is getting short."

"Man, I don't know what you ever saw in that dude. He too smart fa his own damn good. He's so smart, he's stupid," Doc remarked. "He ain't my cup of tea."

"I know. Here you go wit dat shit again. Leave dat alone. You my man and he my man. And dat's all dat matters. Now, I'll be right back, okay?"

Quickly, Corey stepped up to catch Tate, who was standing with his hands behind his back, waiting on Corey's arrival. He had spotted him as he approached.

"Hey, jitterbug. You outta this rotten muthafucka tomorrow, huh? I'll be happy to see you go too."

"Yeah, Tate, I'm outta here like yesteryear," Corey said. "You need me ta take care of anything out there fa you? Need any money or anything once I hit da bricks?"

"No thanks, lil bro. Do you know how many times I done heard dat from some cat goin' home? Nuttin' against you personally, Corey, but I heard it all before. You can show me betta than you can tell me. The only thing I really want you ta do fa me is . . . Well, two things I want you ta do."

"Whut?" Corey snapped. "Whutever it iz, I got you, Tate!"

"One, don't go slinging dat shit. If you do, jail or the graveyard will be waitin' on you. You got dat? Jail iz fa suckas. It's da biggest form of contraceptive known to the black man. They keepin' us from reproducing our own kind. By locking our dumb ass up. Corey, go home and do the right thing. Be there fa ya mom in her old age. Remember da drug game is dead. Finished! Over! Cats is tellin' like I don't know what. I seen brother tell on brother and son tell on mother. It's every man for himself. This younger generation done changed the game for good. Honor and respect are things of the past. Now it's a dirty game. Drug dealers don't grow old. They don't collect pensions. The game is open to everybody but it's not for everybody. . . . If you do go back out there ta sell drugs, I strongly suggest that you know who you fuckin' wit. Because when the deal goes down, who gonna take the weight? There are many who said that they don't squeal, until they get caught. They'll be the first one to point a finger. Two, don't ever come back! Make this ya first and last bid. Don't you ever let me see you back up in here ever again in ya life."

"I hear you, Tate. You got dat. I ain't neva comin' back ta dis miserable muthafucka again."

Tate stopped dead in his tracks. He looked Corey in his eyes, searching for any sign of sincerity. He found none. He knew Corey was running game on him. He said nothing. Tate still felt it was his duty to warn the young. After that, it was out of his hands.

Tate paused for a moment before continuing, "You gotta good head on ya shoulders. This is your second chance. You know how many inmates in jail, lifers, wish they could get another chance? You know how many inmates wish they could take back that fateful day they committed their crime? Wish they could turn back the hands of time? Too many. Corey, go home and do the right thing, be there fa ya mom. Don't be like me and Doc. We doin' life on the installment plan. Back and forth. In and outta prison. Dat ain't da move."

Together they continued to lap the prison, making small talk. Doc watched Corey give out commissary items to other inmates he was cool with.

"Yo, Dee!" Corey yelled out. "Yo, c'mere! I got these packs fa you."

Quickly, the inmate came jogging in Corey's direction till he reached him. Corey produced two cartons of Newport cigarettes from his waistline, handing them over to him.

"Yo, good lookin' out, kid!" Dee exclaimed. "So you outta here tamorrow, huh? Dat's whut'z up. Yo, be safe out there. You's a good dude."

"Dee, keep holdin' ya head, kid. You be home inna minute," Corey said.

"I know! I ain't gonna sweat it. One day it'll be my turn."

"You already got my info. Write me," Corey told him. "I'm out, nigga!"

The two men quickly embraced, then went their separate ways. Corey continued walking around the yard looking for other inmates he had promised commissary items to.

"Yo, Teddy, c'mere!" he hollered.

"Yo, I already heard. Nigga, you out!" Teddy exclaimed. "You got me?"

"No question. Here go them cards you wanted and two books of stamps. I know how much you like to write, kid."

"Yeah, you know me. I stay tryin' ta get wit some chick out in da world. I ain't gonna do dis time by myself. Fuck dat. I need somebody ta bid wit," Teddy said.

"I hear you. Yo, I'm out! Be safe, kid!"

They slapped each other five and parted ways.

On and on Corey went, seeking out inmates to give them the items he had promised them. Tate accompanied him in silence, while Corey chitchatted. Tate willingly shared Corey's final hours with the others.

The only thing he was taking home with him were letters, pictures, and memories. The time he spent in prison was a truly unforgettable experience, something that would live with him for the rest of his life. In prison, Corey had learned some of life's lessons through hardships. His dilemma was, once he got home, to apply those lessons learned to his life outside prison.

That night he didn't sleep a wink. It was as if he were having an anxiety attack. Corey tossed and turned in bed, thinking about what lay ahead of him. Those thoughts he manifested in his head had to be turned into action. Finally, in the wee hours of the morning, he dosed off. He began to dream of the streets, but his dream quickly turned into a nightmare. He woke up in a cold sweat holding his chest. Corey had dreamt he had just been shot. After realizing it was just a dream, he was relieved. Never in his life had he had a dream like that. What this a premonition? Or was it just a silly dream? Corey didn't want to know, but he would soon find out.

BACK ON THE BLOCK

Chapter 20

On a midsummer's day, a Greyhound bus delivered Corey and a handful of inmates released from Elmira Correctional Facility at New York City's Port Authority Bus Terminal. The way they stared around in amazement at everything gave away to anyone watching that they were newly released from prison.

Corey had remained silent and distant from the other freed inmates on the ride down from upstate, choosing to sit in the back of the bus. He listened to their loud conversation.

"Man, I'm gonna tear some pussy up when I get home," one Hispanic man swore. "My baby momma waitin' at da crib fa me right now! Oh, it'z on."

"I heard dat!" another man agreed. "My sister's friend iz waitin' fa me at her house too. I'm knock sparks outta her fat azz."

"Nigga, you crazy!" yet another man interrupted. "I ain't fuckin' wit no fat chicks. . . . I'll jerk off first. I got too much pride fa dat."

"Shit! Fat girlz need luv too. Don't knock it till you try it. Big girlz take good care of ya, put some meat on ya bones. They can cook."

The man replied, "I'll neva know 'cause I ain't fuckin' wit 'em."

Corey laughed with the rest of them, but knew their mind-set was totally different from his. He was focused on making a dollar, not on a female. He'd gone without sex for this long, he figured a little longer couldn't hurt.

All the way to New York City on the bus, Corey had contemplated calling his mother. He felt guilty about not letting her know he was on the way home. Guilt got the best of him, so he stopped at a pay phone and called her.

"Hello, Ma?" he spoke into the phone.

His mother's curiosity immediately arose. She instantly noticed this was not a collect call.

"Boy, where are you? Why ain't you calling collect?"

"I'm home!" Corey blurted out. "I'm downtown at da bus station."

Corey's mother let out a scream so loud, he had to move his ear away from the phone.

"My baby's home! My baby's home!" she rejoiced.

"Calm down, Ma. Look, I'll be there in about two hours. Aiight?"

"Okay! You want me ta make you something special?"

"Nah! I ain't hungry. I gotta go catch dis train. See you inna few. Bye."

He walked to the lower level of the Port Authority and saw swarms of people going to and fro. He fit right in; following the signs, he headed toward the No. 2 subway. There's nothing like a subway ride to put you back in the rhythm of the city.

He intently looked around the slightly crowded subway car, closely inspecting everyone. He couldn't believe how short and tight some of the females wore their skirts and shorts. He spent the ride to the Bronx letting his eyes roam from girl to girl. Big butts and weaves were the rule for women in New York City these days.

The No. 2 train made its prescribed stop, on Gun Hill Road in the Bronx. This was not the same part of Gun Hill Road he needed to be on, but he was fine with it all the same. He figured he'd just walk home. That way he'd get to see all the changes that had occurred in the entire neighborhood, not just on his block.

On the way home he noticed new homes being built. He also discovered vacant lots where buildings once stood. His neighborhood was undergoing a major face-lift.

After walking through various blocks and avenues, Corey finally arrived at his block.

The block looked a lot different from what Corey remembered. His project seemed to be rotting away like a human corpse. The only thing missing was the horrible odor of death. In various buildings, glass panes were broken and graffiti seemed to be everywhere. It was as if people had stopped caring. He had heard about the changes and had tried to prepare himself, but hearing and seeing are two different things. The crack cocaine plague was in full swing. It had come in and accelerated the gradual decay caused by time.

By keeping his release from prison a secret, Corey came home to no fanfare. For years he had been away and now he was back. He preferred to see people in their natural state; Corey didn't want to give anyone the opportunity to put on a fake front. He wanted to see how they were living while he was away.

Glancing around, Corey spotted no familiar faces. Though the faces had changed, the name of the game on the block remained the same, drugs. Younger kids had now entered the ranks of the game, replacing Corey's generation as the workers. The vicious cycle was repeating itself, producing more soldiers for the drug war.

Before long, Corey was spotted by one of his longtime childhood friends, Lil Marco.

"Yo, Corey?" Marco said, surprised. "When did you come home? Damn, you got diesel, kid. Yo, niggas gonna bug when they find out you home. Oh, my God!"

Exchanging embraces, the two men pulled away to get a better look at each other.

"Lil Marco, you ain't changed, Ya ass still ugly as a muthafucka and short!"

"Fuck you! Da bitches like it," Marco joked.

"Yeah, right! You ain't had pussy since pussy had you!" Corey fired back. "Anyway, yo, whut da fuck iz goin' on round here? Where da fuck everybody at?"

"Where else?" Marco asked rhetorically. "Dead, locked up, or outta town! Da only nigga really eatin' round here iz Lord! Most of these lil niggas you see out here work fa him."

"Word?"

"Word!" Marco replied, sounding dejected. "He got da block on lockdown. Either these lil niggas buyin' weight from him or they takin' packages from him."

"Yo, how dat bitch-ass nigga get in power?"

"Like I said before, niggas started goin' outta town, ta Washington, D.C., Delaware, Baltimore, VA, wherever. And whoever didn't make dat move, da Feds bagged them when they came through wit their drug sweep. Everybody who was somebody gone. Shit wuz wide open, and dat nigga Lord got a crew and took over. It'z him, some nigga from downtown named Homicide, and a gang of lil niggaz. My nigga, I'm so glad you home. Shit iz 'bout to change."

Marco knew Corey's presence alone would trigger some needed changes. In him they now potentially had someone to stand up and challenge Lord's rule of the crack cocaine trade on the block. Corey was someone who could defeat the bully. He was someone the weaklings could rally around, someone with fire, determination, heart, and muscle.

"Yo, whatever happened ta Swift and Head? Whut they doin'?" Corey asked.

"Well, Head usta hustle out on da block. He had it on semi-lockdown fa a minute. Then him and da nigga Lord got into it and Lord had his man Homicide hit him up. Yo, gonna bug when I tell you da rest of da story. Da nigga Head said he 'saw the light' and went and got saved. No more drug game."

"Whut? I ain't neva heard no shit like dat in my life. Whut da fuck got into dat nigga?" Corey said in disbelief.

"Jesus!" Marco joked. "Afta he got shot up, Head did a

one-eighty. He changed. I tried to get 'im to strap up, me and him could go blast them niggaz. But he didn't want no parts of dat shit. I wuz crazy mad too. But whut could I do, it'z his beef. He got represent himself. But if you ask me, I think da nigga wuz scared. He wuzn't built like dat."

After receiving that news flash, Corey shook his head in disbelief. He wondered how his friend could go soft like that. Why didn't he retaliate against a man who tried to take his life? That could never have been him, he mused to himself. He would have at least made an attempt to go back at him.

Marco continued, "Will got two kids. He works fa da city as a toll collector. He lives in a brownstone in Harlem, and Swift, he turned into a real live crackhead. Matterfact, there he go right there. Yo, Swift!"

Marco began yelling and motioning with his right hand for Swift to come over. After they saw what appeared to be a drug transaction, Swift did come over to them. Corey watched in amazement as his once close friend came into closer view. The person before him could easily have been a total stranger. This wasn't the Swift he knew. This guy was dusty in appearance, his hair was unkempt, and he was rail thin.

"You must got somethin' fa me da way you shoutin' me out like dat," Swift stated matter-of-factly. "You must do."

Completely ignoring Corey, Swift turned his full attention to Marco. He was looking for a handout.

"Listen, you ain't got nuttin' comin'. I ain't even gonna lie ta you. Yo, do you remember dis muthafucka." Marco said, pointing to Corey.

Swift looked Corey up and down, from head to toe, before recognizing him.

"Yo, Corey, whut'z up? When you get out? Lemme get five dollars?" Swift asked rapidly.

What amazed Corey was how nonchalant Swift was about his return home. He acted as if he'd seen Corey regularly. He acted as if Corey never went away. Swift's drug addiction had him caring about nothing or no one but himself. All he wanted to do was get high. World be damned.

"Nigga, I ain't got no dollar!" Corey snapped. "Whut da fuck wrong wit you?"

"Aiight, y'all, I'll see y'all later. I gotta take care of sumthin'," Swift announced while walking away.

"Yo, you seen dat shit?" Corey asked. "Dat nigga there gone. He a real live crackhead."

"Yeah, I told you! Scarface wuz right, neva get high on ya own supply."

"Anyway, fuck 'im! Yo, whut'z up wit Monique? She still around, right?" Corey inquired.

"Yeah, she still around. Right up da block! Where da fuck she going? Dat nigga, her baby's father, bounced, before she even had da baby. She ain't had no good luck since she crossed you, Corey. Dat shit wuz real foul. When da cat's away da mice will play. Fuck it! Fuck her! You home now! You bound ta run into her and she gonna be on ya dick too. She gonna want you back, especially now. You all swoll up and shit. Whut bitch wouldn't want you. There's alotta lil chicks dat done grew up since you was gone. Hit one of dose bitches. Get ya nutz out da pawnshop. It'z been a minute since you hit sumthin'. Shit, you might kill a broad if she give you some right now. Might fall in love."

"Neva dat!" Corey remarked quickly. "Love iz fa suckas and I ain't no sucka."

"Good!" Marco said. "I'm tryin' ta stay sucka free. Dat'z why I stay by myself."

"Yo, lemme get ready ta get outta here. Gotta go see Ma-dukes. I know she waitin' on me. She da only one dat did my whole bid wit me."

"Yeah, go see ya momz," Marco agreed. "Yo, where she moved to? Afta ya popz died, she rolled out. I ain't seen her inna minute."

Corey started to reveal his mother's whereabouts. But something seemed to stop him. He remembered something Doc had told him: "Ya best friend can turn into ya worst enemy. Ya enemies will neva become ya friends. But ya friends all have the potential to become enemies."

"Yo, she moved ta New Rochelle," Corey lied.

"Yo, datz cool. At least she safe up there. Shit iz gettin' kinda hectic round here. Corey, how you gonna get all da way up there?"

"I'm about to walk up da block and catch a cab there. Da cab base still up da block? Right?"

"Yeah, itz still there. Dat shit ain't goin' nowhere!" Marco insisted. "Want me to walk you up there?"

"If you want to. If not, it'z aiight! I know my way up there."

Something was eating at Corey's mind. Something that Marco had neglected to mention was still prevalent in

Corey's mind. Even after all these years, he had still remembered it.

Prisoners are frozen in time, so no matter how long ago an incident transpired, to them it is as if it happened yesterday. They will remember it even if it was ten years ago.

"Yo, Marco. Between me and you, who killed O?" Corey asked, looking him in the eyes.

Silence fell between them. Marco returned his longtime friend's gaze before he spoke his mind. He was contemplating his thoughts, as if he didn't want to come up with the wrong answer.

"Yo, keep dis on da down low, don't go no further than here," Marco began. "But, yo, I heard ya man Lord had sumthin' ta do wit dat. You know how O was livin'. It wuz wheneva and whateva wit him. You know he robbed Lord a long time ago. Supposedly, dat happened ta him cuz of dat. Nobody knows fa sure. But dat'z whut da word iz on da block. And I hear homeboy ain't denyin' it. It'z almost like he want muthafuckaz ta believe it, ta fear him."

Marco's last statement once again brought Corey back to another phrase Doc used to say a lot: "Neva make people afraid of you! A scared nigga will kill you!"

"Word?" Corey announced. "He on it like dat?"

"Yep! No doubt!" Marco admitted. "Round here, he da nigga bigger than large. He think he can't be stopped."

* * *

Though Corey had told Marco his mother lived in New Rochelle, she had actually moved a short ways away, to

Co-op City, a middle-class enclave for the working and some retired senior citizens.

Corey had a hard time finding his mother's building. The names of the streets, avenues, and loops were strange to him. When he finally found it, he buzzed his mother's doorbell.

"Who is it?" came a soft woman's voice over the intercom.

"Me, Ma! Buzz me up!" Corey replied.

"My God," she said, pressing a button to unlock the door.

"He's on his way upstairs," his mother said excitedly. "Now cut da lights out! Let's surprise him."

Against Corey's wishes she had put together a last-minute welcome-home party. It consisted strictly of immediate family: Corey's brothers, Chris and Courtney, his sisters, Paula and Felicia, and his various nephews and nieces. His mother gathered them all to share in this special day. Finally the day had come when all her children were together. She was in heaven. When Corey was in prison, it was as if a piece were missing of the family puzzle.

Corey finally reached his mother's apartment door and rang her doorbell. She quickly opened the door to her darkened apartment.

"Surprise! Welcome home!" they all shouted in unison.

The lights were flicked on, revealing to Corey the source of the noise. Like a deer caught in a set of car headlights, Corey stood in the hallway with a bewildered look on his face. His family engulfed him and led him into the apartment.

The place was decorated with colorful balloons and decorating paper. From the kitchen came the strong aroma of some good soul food. Corey saw enough food on the table to feed a small army.

He wished that his father could be there for the celebration. Corey was glad that his mother did this for him. He loved his family. While he was in prison, he realized they were all he had. After a harrowing experience like that, serving time, the word *family* took on a whole new meaning.

Corey's mother smothered her son with hugs and kisses.

"My baby's home! My baby's home!" His mother beamed.

"Dag, Ma, can someone else get a chance to hug him?" Paula questioned. "Let da boy neck loose, he can't breathe!"

"Oh, hush up, girl!" his mother responded. "You'll get your chance when I'm done."

Corey began to feel soft tugs on the legs of his pants. Looking down, he could see the young, smiling faces of his nieces and nephews. He scooped two of them up into his arms. He began to make strange faces at them; in amusement they laughed. After he put them down, he began to go around the room greeting his family.

"God, Corey, you got big," Felicia gushed. "You takin' steroids or somethin'?"

"Girl, stop playin'!" Corey told her. "Dis all me. One hundred percent natural."

"Uncle Corey! Uncle Corey! Pick me up too!" he heard his niece yell.

Accommodating her, Corey scooped her up in his arms. Lovingly, she wrapped her arms around his neck. Corey then walked over to his two brothers.

"Can't call you lil brother no more," Chris joked. "You bigger than the both of us now. Look at 'im, Courtney."

"He may be bigger than us both, but I still can take 'im. I did it before and I can do it again!" Courtney said confidently.

Growing up, Courtney and Corey used to fight like cats and dogs, with Courtney always coming out on top.

"Things done changed now!" Corey boasted. "Don't be like them old boxers who stick around too long and get knocked out. Things change in time. Challengers become champions."

"Oh, yeah? From what I was told, the more things change the more they stay the same. I'm from Missouri, that Show Me State. Make me a believer," Chris stated.

"Dat'z whut ya mouth say, punk! But you don't want that," Corey kidded him. "I'd hate ta spank you in front of ya kids."

That comment caused the brothers to break out into a long, extended laugh. They continued making small talk for a while. Then Courtney asked the question that Corey knew was coming.

"So, Corey, now dat you out the big house, what are ya plans? You gonna get a job, right? I know you not goin' back out to that damn Boston Road and fuckin' wit them knuckleheads out there?"

"Them dudes out there sellin' crack ain't goin' nowhere! Nowhere fast!" Chris added.

Without missing a beat, Corey replied, "Nah! I ain't wit dat no more. I'm goin' out there and try to find a job. I ain't tryin' ta go back to jail."

"Yeah, I hoped you learned ya lesson," Chris added. "Ain't nuttin' out on dat block but trouble. You gotta change people, places, and things. The people you hung wit, the places you hung at, and the things you did, all lead you to prison."

"You ain't gotta tell me dat. I had enough time ta analyze everything. I know where I went wrong," Corey admitted.

"Aiight, now! So you know what you gotta do then. Stay away from dat block," Chris warned him.

Then it was time to eat.

Corey's stomach bubbled with excitement. His mother brought him a large plate, piled high with all the fixings. Corey began to savagely dig into his plate, as if it were his last meal. Prison had subconsciously trained him to eat fast. Inmates were only allotted a limited time to eat, due to the vast numbers of them and the limited seating capacity of the mess hall.

"Boy, slow down, chew ya food!" Chris suggested.

"Dat food ain't goin' nowhere, Corey! Take ya time! Ya not in jail now!" Courtney stated.

Corey ignored all their comments and continued to eat as he pleased. Soon his family members left him alone. They were focused on tending to their respective children. Corey watched in amusement as his siblings disciplined their children.

"Brian, come over here and sit ya behind down and eat. Leave dat damn video game alone," one of his brothers said.

"Tee-Tee, stop playin' with ya food!" a sister shouted.

Corey found the whole scene amusing. He was on the outside looking in. He now saw his brothers as fathers and his sisters as mothers before his eyes. And that blew his mind. These were the same people whom he'd laughed with, fought with, and cried with; to see them now as adults, as parents, was mind-boggling. It was as if Corey thought they'd be children forever. The winds of time had brought about a dramatic change. This was a transition that one day Corey too would make.

The party wound down; soon no one was left in the two-bedroom co-op except Corey and his mother.

"Corey, did you enjoy your party?" his mother asked. "I know you didn't want me to have nothing for you, but you been away for so long, I couldn't resist the opportunity to bring the family together."

"It's aiight, Ma. I ain't mad. Everything turned out all right. It was good seeing everybody in one room at the same time. At least I didn't have to run around to everybody's house."

"Corey, I wish your father could have been here to join us. That would have been nice," she said regretfully. "But I know he's up in heaven looking down on his family."

Corey didn't share his mother's opinion about his father being in heaven. It always bothered Corey that everyone who passed away was presumably sent to heaven. Well, Corey didn't know for sure, and neither did his mother, if his father had done the necessary things to warrant entering heaven. Yet out of respect he remained silent on the subject.

"Corey, I hope you don't come out here and get involved with that devilment again," she advised. "Remember what happened last time? Look how long you were gone. Time is too precious to waste. And for God's sake, please don't go out there trying to avenge that boy's death. I know how you kids think. Promise me you'll leave that alone. Promise me."

Looking in his mother's eyes, he saw a pain so deep that it almost made him cry. It pained Corey a great deal to have to lie to his mother. But there was no way in the world he could go back on his word to O. His mother just couldn't understand.

"Ma," he began, "I promise you I won't do nuttin' ta nobody. I'ma leave it alone. I'll be a good boy. I'm done wit da streetz."

"That's what I wanted to hear. Let God handle that. Whoever did it may have escaped justice on earth, but on the Day of Judgment they will be held accountable for all their sins."

Suddenly, Corey was overcome by a long yawn. His mother said she was going to bed. He kissed her on the cheek and they entered their respective bedrooms.

Just as on his last night in jail, Corey was unable to sleep. He was wide-awake reflecting upon his first day home. For some reason, his old schoolteacher in prison, Mr. Fisher, had popped into his mind. It was a statement he'd made some time ago: "Never go home again." Images from Corey's first day of freedom flashed through his mind: the young drug dealers, the state of the block, and his family. It was almost all too much for him to digest in one day.

Chapter 21

Within the next few days, word of Corey's release had spread throughout the projects like wildfire. Everyone from his past wanted to get a glimpse of him. He was somewhat of a celebrity around the way, like a returning war hero. All this attention was unwanted by him. He preferred to remain a mystery to those who didn't know him.

On one of his foray's to the block, Corey went to visit his deceased friend's mother, Ms. Patterson. It had taken him longer than he had planned to work up the nerve to see her. He knew his sudden appearance would evoke memories of Omar. He realized that she might become overcome with grief, and Corey didn't want to get too emotional in front of her.

Arriving at her apartment door, Corey pressed the buzzer and waited for a response.

"Who?" someone barked from behind door.

Instantly Corey recognized the voice. It belonged to O's little sister, Keisha.

"Me. It'z me, Corey!"

"Corey?" she questioned, before sneaking a peek out the peephole.

From the other side of the door, Corey could see a brief amount of light, followed by darkness. He knew she was verifying his identity.

"Ma!" came the cry from inside the apartment. "Guess who here? Corey! Corey Dixon!"

The locks were quickly undone and the door was flung open. Standing in the doorway was a young, sexy female. Corey gave her the once-over before his mind overruled his manhood. In his mind he said a brief prayer, asking O to forgive him for looking at his little sister like that. Still, he had to admit, Keisha had grown up and filled out a good deal since he had last seen her.

Keisha stood in the doorway posing sexually, until her mother interrupted their private stare-down.

"Girl, if you don't get ya hot tail outta dat door and let dat boy in dis apartment, I'll beat da black off you," she fumed.

"Hey, Corey," Keisha said in a gigglish voice. She then hugged him.

"Ma!" Corey yelled excitedly.

"Corey, look at you. I don't know what you been eating, but you big as a house. Look at these big muscles you have. Jail sure look like it agreed wit you." Ms. Patterson wrapped her arms around Corey. She loved him like a son.

"When you get out? Why you ain't let me know? I coulda at least cooked you a special dinner," she said, bombarding him with questions.

"I been home a few days."

"And you just comin' ta see me now? Afta ya mother, I shoulda been da next stop you made. You probably was too busy chasin' behind them hot-behind girlz runnin' round here."

"Nah, Ms. Patterson, it wasn't like dat. I been chillin' in da house fa a few days, just takin' it easy."

"Yeah, I bet!" she fired back. "Anyway, Corey, it'z good to see you. I'm glad you still remembered me. After Omar got killed, most of these rotten-ass bastards stop comin' by. When he was alive, I couldn't keep 'em outta my damn house. You know what I mean! Now I be lucky ta get a hi or a wave from 'em. Muthafuckas be right in front da building when I come home from work and won't speak."

The incessant ringing of the telephone temporarily broke up their conversation. Ms. Patterson finally went into the kitchen to answer it.

"Excuse me fa a minute, baby," she said.

Seizing the opportunity to get a word in with Corey, Keisha pulled him into the hallway toward what once was O's bedroom. "C'mere, Corey, I gotta show you somethin'."

Reluctantly, Corey allowed himself to be pulled in that direction. Inside the bedroom, everything was still in place, just as Corey had remembered it. To Corey it seemed strange, as if someone expected Omar to be resurrected from the dead.

"Yo, my brother would have wanted you to have dis. You wuz his man, no doubt!" Keisha said, opening the closet door.

Bending over, Keisha's whole upper torso disappeared inside the lower half of the closet. When she reappeared, she dragged out of the closet a green military duffel bag. Pulling it as far as she could, she opened it up, exposing the contents.

"Look!" she commanded.

Corey peeked inside the bag and saw nothing but guns, clips, and ammunition. By his account there had to be at least half a dozen weapons, of various shapes and sizes. Enough weapons were inside the bag to invade a small country.

"Do ya momz know dis shit iz here?"

"No, she never come in here. Every time she do, she start to cry."

"Listen, put dat shit away. I'll come for it when I need it. Until then, leave it right there."

"Corey, you gotta kill dat muthafucka Lord. Dat nigga bodied my brotha. Don't be like these other pussy-ass niggas, all talk, no action."

"Keisha, I'ma take care of dat. Don't worry, I'ma step ta my bizness. Gotta get dis money first though. Afta dat, Lord's ass iz history, him and whoever's runnin' wit him."

Keisha's eyes lit up with joy. Finally she had found someone with enough heart to take Lord off this earth. Everyone else in the projects was too scared to do it. They reasoned "that was between O and Lord" and didn't have anything to do with them.

"Keisha? Corey? Where y'all at?" Ms. Patterson called.

"In da room lookin' at some old pictures. We comin' out now," Keisha yelled.

They quickly stashed away the weapons and went to the kitchen. Ms. Patterson was cutting up some chicken for tonight's dinner.

"Keisha, do me a favor? Go in my pocketbook and take dat five-dollar bill, run ta da corner store, and get me some seasoning salt and a pack of cigarettes."

"Aiight, Ma! I'll be right back, Corey. Don't go nowhere!"

Keisha looked back at them, smiling as she headed out the door. Corey smiled back and nodded his head.

"Girl, g'head and carry ya ass to da store!" Ms. Patterson put her hand on her hip. "And stop flirtin' wit Corey!"

"Ain't nobody flirtin'," Keisha said, her voice fading behind the closing door.

"Bye!" her mom replied. "Go in peace, fa you leave in pieces."

"Omar would have been twenty-two years old next month," Ms. Patterson said, turning to Corey. I'ma go visit his grave on his birthday. Dat's whut I usually do. I miss my baby. She put the chicken in a bowl, sat it to the side, and wiped her hands with a dish towel. "Corey, don't you let none of these niggas out here hurt you! None of them!"

"Don't worry, I won't, Ms. Patterson, I won't!"

She cupped her hands over her face and leaned against the counter. "Them fuckin' bastards killed my baby!" she cried. "They shot 'im down like a dog in the streetz."

Corey walked toward her, reaching his hand out, thinking she might collapse. Seeing the tears and the anguish in his friend's mother's eyes added fuel to the fire. Corey was about to do all the wrong things, for the right reason—friendship.

* * *

Corey ran into Lil Marco again later that evening. The two sat on a parked car, on the block, reminiscing about old times. As they talked, Corey counted in his mind the various drug sales that were taking place around him. He could see how profitable the crack cocaine trade had become since he was away. There were so many customers that at times they had to wait for more product to come out of the stash houses. The demand for crack cocaine was that great. Visions of dollar signs began to dance in Corey's head. He wanted in.

Before long, Corey saw a face he knew all too well, a crackhead named Smokey. They had had a run-in many years ago. He was accompanied by an equally shady-looking character.

"Whut'z up, Smokey?" Corey greeted him. "Look like you up to no-no good."

"Oh, shit, Corey," he said excitedly. "Nigga, when you come home? I ain't seen you inna good long while."

"I just came home a few days ago. But I been on da DL. I see ain't nuttin' changed in ya game, you still beamin' da fuck up. Surprised ya heart ain't stop yet."

"You know me, ain't no shame in my game. I smoke like a Navajo Indian. Nuttin' but the finest crack available. Out here, everybody do somethin'. Sell drugs, do drugs, or drink. What da fuck? You gotta die of somethin', right? I just know what'z gonna kill me. Drugs! Drugs will be da death of me!"

"Nigga, you outta ya fuckin' mind!" Corey stated. "You suicidal!"

Marco said, "Why don't you just take a gun and just blow

ya brains out. It'll be a whole lot quicker." He laughed. "Nigga, you dead anyway, smokin' dat shit."

"Look, young boy, don't worry 'bout me. I got dis," Smokey said.

"Yo, Smokey, remember when you robbed me up in the crack house around da corner, and me and O caught up ta ya azz on the late nite? We wore ya azz out wit them batz," Corey joked.

"Damn, sound like they beat da bullshit outta you, Smokey," his friend commented.

"Shut da fuck up!" Smokey snapped. "Fa I beat da black off ya azz. Dis nigga here family. And families go through changes sometimes. I robbed him and he got me back. Datz da name of da game. What comes around goes back around."

Smokey glared evilly at his get-high partner, furious that he had even opened his mouth.

"Ask Corey. Did I snitch? No! I took my azz whuppin' like a man," Smokey said. "Nigga, I'ma retired gangsta. I took whut I wanted. You niggaz these dayz iz sneak thieves stealin' packs."

Corey and Marco began to laugh hard as the two men bickered amongst themselves. If this continued, they were sure a fight was going to break out.

"Later, Corey!" Smokey exclaimed. "I gotta go beam up ta Scotty. There are no intelligent life-forms down here."

"Wait up!" his friend suggested. "Half dat shit iz minez."

Corey and Marco watched in amusement as the two crack addicts disappeared into a nearby building.

"Them two niggaz there," Marco stated, "got it da fuck bad!"

"You tellin' me?" Corey chimed. "Whut a fuckin' life."

"So, Corey," Marco began, whut we gone do? Whut you 'bout ta get into? You wanna get some of dis money or whut?"

"No question! I jus' wuz peepin' shit out. Tryin' ta see who's who and whut'z whut."

"Good! I'm glad we on da same page. I'm starvin', I need ta make a move soon!"

"Yo, just hold ya horses. We gonna get dis paper, Marco. We just gotta take our time. I ain't goin' back ta jail fa nuttin'. Our time ta shine iz comin'."

Moments later, a brand-new burgundy BMW 535 with matching burgundy eighteen-inch BBS rims rolled upon the block. Lord was in the driver's seat; Homicide was next to him. They were there to check on their workers. Corey's blood began to boil. They were like dogs and cats, natural enemies. There was no way in the world these two could coexist.

Even from this distance, Corey could see Homicide's lazy eye. It made him look as if he were always up to something.

As Lord saw Corey, he seethed. He still harbored resentment from the run-ins they'd had in the past. With a simple nod of his head he acknowledged Corey from across the street. In return, Corey nodded his head and flashed a sly smile.

From across the street, Lord seemed to mask his contempt for Corey well. As he went about his business, Lord glanced over at Corey, taking note of his new bulked and cut-up physique. *That weight don't mean nuttin' out here though*, Lord mused to himself. *I got somethin' for all that. Try that strong-arm shit if you want to.* Lord knew that Corey threatened his position on the block. And if he had his way, Corey would be right where O was now.

When his business was done, Lord summoned Homicide, who was standing guard. Together they walked toward Lord's car.

"Dat'z dat nigga Corey, across da street, I been tellin' you 'bout," Lord whispered.

"Don't worry 'bout him. I'll take care of him if he get outta line," Homicide said.

"Oh, dat nigga ain't no killa. He just usta hang wit some. His strength iz gone. Let'z see whut he gonna do now dat his man ain't around ta protect hiz ass."

Lord had built up a false sense of security, an illusion of invincibility. But now his stronghold was about to be challenged.

From across the street, Marco stared at Lord and Homicide until they were out of sight.

"Don't sweat dat, kid!" Corey told him. "Their day iz comin'. Sooner than they think too."

Corey knew the block was a place where everything had to be earned or taken. That's exactly what he planned to do, take over.

Chapter 22

Marco set Corey up with a girl from his former project complex. She had peeped Corey and was asking a lot of questions about him that let Marco know that she'd be down with whatever he wanted to do.

Chavon was her name. She was a younger female who had had a crush on Corey while they were growing up. He, on the other hand, never knew she existed, even though she lived directly across the street from Omar.

When Chavon had hit her adolescent years, she had begun to run with the wrong crowd and hung on the block at all times of the night. She was strictly attracted to the bad boy drug-dealer type.

Corey and Marco stood in front of the pizza shop on the ave. They were there no longer than ten minutes when Chavon strolled around the corner. She had on a pair of skintight Daisy Duke blue-jean shorts that left little to the imagination, and a white, cutoff tank that revealed her sexy, flat stomach. Her hair was pulled back into a ponytail.

Chavon had a nasty walk that had Corey's eyes riveted to her midsection.

"Yo, Chavon, dis my man Corey," Marco announced. "Corey dis Chavon. I'm gone! Y'all take it from here."

* * *

"Ummmm, hummmm!" Chavon purred. "Keep it right there."

They began this romp in the missionary position. Then Corey pushed her legs up over her head to drive his manhood deep inside her. Working at a feverish pace, Corey seemed to be in a zone. He had Chavon right where he wanted her. Whenever he had sex, it was like an actor taking to the stage, he wanted to give a great performance. This was something Chavon would be talking about to her girlfriends for months to come. Corey knew that younger guys were selfish lovers. He had been one too. But now he knew better. Make a female climax and she'll keep coming back.

Sweat dripped off his body as he continued to pound away. Corey looked down at Chavon as she began to make cute "fuck" faces. He knew she had climaxed two or three times. Glancing at the clock on the wall, Corey knew his mother would be home soon. Now it was time to bring the sexcapade to an end. He began to hump faster and faster, until he could feel a surge run through his scrotum, shooting to the head of his penis, swelling it. Without warning, he climaxed inside the condom, inside Chavon. Releasing his grip on Chavon legs, he fell onto her. As the two sweaty bodies merged, they both breathed heavily. As Corey's heart pounded against his chest, he thought to himself, *This was a workout.*

"Yo, get up," he said, coming to his senses. "My momz will be home soon. We gotta jet. Go get in da shower. Wash up or do whuteva it iz dat you do. Da towels and washcloths are beneath da bathroom sink."

Corey knew he was dead wrong for having sex in his mother's house. That was something teenagers did, and here he was a grown man. If his mother walked through the door right now, she'd raise hell. She didn't allow fornication in her home. His father must be turning over in his grave, Corey mused. He definitely didn't tolerate this kind of behavior. But Corey was on a budget; a motel was out of the question for now.

While initially, Corey had had his sexual urges under control, now he was on. He was determined to sample some of the best vagina the block had to offer.

The look on Chavon's face let him know that she was upset. He didn't know if it was because of his rushing her out the door, or maybe she wanted to lie up and cuddle. Whatever the case, Corey didn't have time for it. He didn't bring her to his house to make love, he brought her up here to have sex.

* * *

He washed off, got dressed, and got them out of the door and into a cab. Corey paid the driver and he and Chavon got out on the block. Chavon was still stewing. She gave him little or no conversation.

"Yo, shorty, whut'z da problem? You buggin'! Why you even actin' like dat?"

She rolled her eyes and stomped off.

"Fuck you then! Stupid bitch!" he cursed.

"Wuzn't sayin' dat when you wuz eatin' my pussy, nigga!" she said, loud enough for everyone to hear.

"Ay, yo, Chavon stop fuckin' playin' like dat!"

A safe distance away, she imitated him, "Yo, Chavon stop fuckin' playin'."

"You think I'm playin' wit ya azz? Huh?"

Quickly he took a step in her direction and she took off running. Corey didn't bother to give chase. He just wanted to scare her. He actually thought it was cute. It had been quite some time since a female had caused this much fuss about him.

"Don't let me catch you," he warned her. "I'ma slap da shit outta you."

On the other side of the street, Keisha looked on. She had a smirk plastered on her face. She began to cross the street.

"Soon that'll be ya baby mama, huh?" she stated. "Boy, you need ta slow ya roll. Don't be runnin' round here slingin' dick like you fuckin' Jesse James or sumthin'. Don't you know dat shit out here? It ain't 'bout gettin' burnt no more. It'z bout losin' ya life, AIDS."

"Yo, Keisha, do you think I'm stupid? I ain't runnin' up in none of these broads raw. I strapped every fuckin' time."

Secretly, Keisha was more than a little jealous of Corey's sexual relationship. She wished he was showering her with love and affection.

"Corey, I'm just sayin'," she began. "Yo, you wuz on some chill-out shit wit these bitches at first. So, now you go fuckin' crazy. You, you start hittin' everythin' movin'? Corey, you can't make up for all da pussy you missed while you wuz in jail. No matter how hard you try. Dat'z impossible! Don't spread yaself too thin. You chasin'."

He stood up and gave her a good look in her eyes, wondering exactly where she was coming from with this.

"Whut you worried 'bout dat for?" Corey asked. "Lemme do dis. Aiight?"

"Aiight, Corey, I wuz just tryin' ta look out fa you. Anyway, ya man Marco wuz lookin' fa you."

Corey was clearly irritated. He didn't like anyone up in his business, especially another female he wasn't dealing with.

Corey replied, "How long ago? Where he at now? Huh?"

"It wuz about twenty minutes ago. He said he was goin' up to da park."

"Yo, I'll see you later," Corey said as he headed toward the park. "I'm out!"

* * *

Entering the park brought back a flood of memories for Corey. On the basketball court, he was legendary. He had spent much of his childhood here. Hanging out here was as much a social event as it was a time to play, and from the looks of things nothing had changed.

"Ay, yo, Corey!" Marco called out. "I'm right here."

Corey looked around until he spotted his friend over by the monkey bars. He walked over and they gave each other five.

"Yo, where da fuck you been? We wuz suppose ta meet up a hour ago," Marco said.

"I wuz fuckin', nigga!" Corey snapped.

"Lemme guess who. Chavon? Right? Nigga, you open off dat lil broad. She got ya azz whipped."

"Yeah, right!" Corey joked. "Picture dat! If anything, she open off me. My dick game iz somethin' serious."

"Yeah, dat's too much information for me. Listen, though, I found out da prices on dat yayo, sixteen dollars a gram. I got da mean connection, up on Broadway too. Da coke iz favor too. Da crackheads will love it."

"Aiight, datz whut'z up! Tamorrow, I'll have da paper ready. I got like twenty-five hundred."

"Dat's cool! We can get a big eighth wit dat," Marco explained. "Dat'll be more than enough ta get us started."

"Yo, we gotta get a crew together before we do anything. You been working on dat, right?"

Corey knew the key to this drug-dealing operation was absolute control over the young boys. They were pivotal to his plans. This could mean the difference between feasting or famine on the block.

"I got three or four lil niggaz that'z down for da get-down," Marco said. "All we gotta do iz get da work and we can get busy."

They continued to toss ideas back and forth on how things should run. Without their mentioning it, it was clear that Marco was to be Corey's lieutenant, his second-in-command. They mapped out their strategy.

"Ay, yo, look who just walked into da park," Marco commented.

Turning his head, Corey looked toward the park's entrance. His old girlfriend, Monique, was pushing a baby stroller. She hadn't changed a bit. Having a baby had agreed with her; she had put on weight in all the right places. Corey had to admit, Monique still looked good.

Taking her toddler out of the baby stroller, Monique sat on a wooden bench, watching closely as her son played with the other children.

"Yo, you gonna go say somethin' to her or whut?" Marco asked. "Don't go over there and do nuttin' crazy, like smack the shit out of her."

"Man, I don't hit girlz. Dat ain't my style. Of course I'm gonna go say sumthin' to her. It'z only right."

"Well, don't lemme hold you up! Ain't nuttin' between y'all accept air . . . and ya fear!" Marco remarked playfully.

Ignoring him, Corey walked over to Monique. She had her back turned and never saw him approaching. Upon reaching her, Corey placed both his hands over her eyes.

"Guess who?" he asked in a deep voice.

Almost immediately Monique felt something was wrong. She wasn't up for playing this game. Instinctively she pulled at his hands.

"Corey?" she gasped. "When you get out? I mean—"

She started to shake inside. She bit her lip. She thought he might get physically violent at any moment. Sensing this, Corey made a joke to ease her fears.

"How ya like me now?" he asked while striking a pose.

"Lookin' good, Corey." She put the child in the stroller and pulled it closer to her. She kicked the ground beneath her feet, not knowing what to do. "How long you been home?" she asked again. He told her and studied her shoes as she shuffled her feet; he raised his eyes to take her all in, her body, her face. She insisted, "How many girlfriends you got now? I know these chicks round here all over you."

"Nah, not really. I ain't claimin' none of them," he said. "Da only girl I got iz my momz. She's da only female worthy enough ta wear dat title. She wuz the only one there fa me throughout my whole bid."

Corey was trying to make her feel bad for leaving him. He couldn't, nor would he ever, forget how she had crossed him. The little boy was reaching out of the stroller, down to the ground.

"Travon, put da rock down!" she shouted to her child.

"Dat'z ya lil man, huh? Yo, he looks just like you, Monique. Word! Yo, dat'z suppose ta be me and you right there."

Monique never regretted having her child, but she did regret not having the child with Corey. True, she loved her child's father, just because. But she wasn't in love with him, not the way she had been with Corey. When she'd come to that realization, it had caused a strain in their relationship. Monique found herself unhappy, somewhat depressed. She found herself trying to make the relationship work for the sake of her son. One day she woke up and decided to be happy, and ended it.

Luckily for her, the boy's father still maintained a relationship with him, despite what had transpired between him and the child's mother.

"Corey, dis may be too much, too little, too late. But, I'm sorry dat things turned out da way they did between us. I didn't mean for it ta go down like dat. You wuz too good ta me. I loved you."

The mention of her betrayal brought back bad memories for Corey, memories that he'd tried to leave behind locked in that cell. Whether he wanted to or not, Corey became emotional.

"Monique, whut I can't understand iz, if you loved me da way you say you loved me, then why didn't you tell me yaself dat you wuz pregnant? Why I had ta find out from someone else? If you really loved me as much as you say, you could have at least told me. You owed me dat much."

"Corey, I wuz scared ta tell you. I didn't know whut ta say or where ta start. How do you tell someone dat you love dat you havin' da next man's baby! How?"

Staring her straight in the eye, Corey could see she was about to cry. She held her child's hand.

"You find a way, dat'z how! We wuz bigger than dat. You wuzn't suppose ta go out like dat. Monique, you know whut? Nobody will ever love you da way I do! Nobody!"

"I know, Corey. I know. So I guess you hate me now, huh?"

"Why you say dat? *Hate* iz such a strong word. I could never hate you, I once loved you; I can't take back my feelings no matter how hard I try. They are whut they are. They not dependent upon whut you do ta me or fa me, how good you make me feel or how bad you make me feel. My love's unconditional. I'll always love you. I just know now I can't fuck wit you while I'm out here doin' dirt. You hurt me. You hurt me ta my heart."

"I'm sorry, Corey! Tell me what I can do ta make it up ta you."

"I don't know, Monique. I just don't know."

Without knowing, Monique had fallen right into Corey's trap. He had her right where he wanted her, feeling guilty. After expressing himself, Corey toned the conversation down. They chitchatted about each other's family and what was new in their lives.

* * *

When Corey arrived at her apartment later that night, his heart started to race. She opened the door wearing a red-lace negligee. Her parents were away on vacation, so the house was empty, besides her and her child.

"Corey, gimme a minute. I'm in da middle of puttin' my son ta sleep. Go sit down in da livin' room. I'll turn the TV on."

Flopping down on the couch, Corey grabbed the remote control and turned to ESPN. He wanted to see some sports highlights and scores. In prison it was sport seasons that helped through the years. When one sport's season ended, another began.

Soon instead of watching television, the television began to watch Corey. He fell fast asleep. The next thing he knew it was morning, the crack of dawn. The loud chirping of the birds had awakened him. He couldn't remember a thing from that night. Slowly he opened his eyes to see if he was naked and in bed with Monique.

Much to his surprise, he wasn't. He looked down at his

fully wardrobed body and cursed himself. When reality set in, he walked through the apartment to find Monique. After finding her, he sat on the edge of the bed, watching Monique sleep. She seemed so peaceful, he dared not disturb her. Quickly he noticed her son, asleep in the crib, in the corner. With all his might, Corey fought the temptation of undressing and joining her in the bed. He deliberated for about an hour, his body telling him yes and his mind saying no. It was a respect thing in Corey's eyes. Though he didn't have a kid, he reasoned that if he did, he wouldn't want anyone to have sex with his child's mother while the child was in the room, whether or not the child was too young to comprehend what was going on. Right was right and wrong was wrong. At all times Corey tried to show respect for the next man, because one day the next man might be him.

Frustrated, Corey decided to head home. But before he did, he gently shook Monique awake.

"Git up. Git up! Monique, I'm out!" he whispered.

"Whut?" she asked groggily. "Huh? You leavin'? Whut time iz it?"

"Yeah, I'm out! Dat'z aiight. You ain't have ta wake me up last night. You know whut we wuz suppose ta do."

"Corey, I tried ta wake you up, but you didn't move. I kept tryin'."

"I don't believe you. You shoulda tried harder. Dat'z dat bullshit. Whut kinda gamez you playin'? I wuz suppose ta tap dat."

"We still can do it. We can go in da—"

"Nah, dat'z aiight. I gotta make some moves taday. Thanks fa nuttin'."

"Come back later."

"Bitch, get da fuck outta here!" he cursed. "Dat wuz a one-shot deal."

Giggling to himself, Corey left the apartment. *Payback was a bitch*, he thought to himself.

Chapter 23

The money that O had sent him over the years became Corey's start-up capital to finance his drug ring. After withdrawing close to twenty-five hundred from the bank, Corey and Marco went to Manhattan to cop some powder cocaine from the Dominicans on Broadway.

There they met Marco's connection, who gave them 125 grams of cocaine for their money. After the purchase, the duo hailed a cab and traveled back to the Bronx. They proceeded to a crackhead's house, and Corey watched in amazement as Marco cooked up the powder cocaine, transforming it to crack cocaine.

"Yo, nigga, where you learn how ta cook up from?" Corey asked. "You turned into a smoker while I wuz away?"

"Stop fuckin' playin'!" Marco fired back. "Mostly everybody round da way know how ta cook up coke. Niggas got tireda of da crackheads beatin' us outta grams. You might not see it at first, but dat shit adds up. We ain't have no choice but ta learn on our own. Or keep gettin' robbed."

As they talked, Marco continued to stir the large batch of crack in the clear, nonstick Corning Ware pot. Corey looked into the pot and saw beigelike gel moving around at the flip of his friend's wrist. Suddenly, Marco reached over and turned on the cold water. Grabbing the pot handle, he placed the pot beneath the cold water. The cold water overflowed inside the pot, cooling the crack cocaine, turning it into one hard, beige substance.

"Chef Boyardee ain't got nuttin' on me," Marco exclaimed. "I cooks dis shit up ta perfection and bring it back every fuckin' last gram. We ain't never hear a complaint about dis. Dis home-cooked."

Corey watched as Marco placed the crack cocaine on a napkin, which absorbed all the excess water. Then he aimed a small fan on it to speed up the drying.

They began spreading out all the drug paraphernalia, single-edge razor blades and the tiny, clear baggies. When that was done there came the hard part—packaging the drugs for street distribution and sale. Paying close attention, Corey looked on while Marco began chopping and slicing the hard, beige mound in front of him. Cutting the crack cocaine into the smallest pieces possible, Marco shoved them to the side and let Corey place them inside the tiny baggies. By any means necessary, Corey forced the crack cocaine inside the baggies, using the razor blade, his pinkie, or a ink-pen top. For hours they sat at the kitchen table bagging up crack cocaine. They opened so many, Corey's thumb and forefinger hurt.

"I hate dis shit!" Marco stated. "It take too fuckin' long."

"I see whut you mean," Corey replied. "We already been in here fa two fuckin' hours."

The incessant sound of razor blades slicing through the crack cocaine, hitting the plate, could be heard throughout the apartment.

Soon the impatient crackhead appeared in the kitchen vestibule, looking for his payment for use of his home for packaging the drug.

"Nigga, why don't you sit ya ass down some fuckin' where?" Marco cursed. "Ain't nobody leavin' witout fuckin' takin' care of ya monkey ass."

"Nah, I say nuttin'. I wuz just comin' in here ta get a glass of cold water. I'm thirsty!" he lied.

Marco snapped, "Yeah, right, muthafucka! I wuz born in da day, not yesterday."

One thing Marco hated was an impatient crackhead pressing him for some get-high. The people could be just like children when they were chasing a high.

"Here, muthafucka!" Marco said. "Take dis shit and get da fuck outta my face!" Marco then handed him a plateful of crack cocaine crumbs. The man greedily snatched the plate and took off to his room. He was about to get high.

"Hope ya heart bust! Ya crackhead muthafucka!" Marco added.

"Why you treat dat nigga like dat?" Corey questioned. "You talk ta him like he ain't shit!"

"He ain't! I gotta talk ta them fuckin' crackheads like dat 'cause they take ya kindness fa ya weakness. Give 'em an inch, they'll take a mile. You hear me? I ain't out here ta make friends wit no fuckin' crackhead!"

Corey understood his reason, though he didn't agree with it. *To each his own,* Corey mused. Corey felt that any person in a position of power should be careful not to misuse it. There was a fine line between use and abuse of power. In the game that they were in, Corey thought it wise to go out of your way to be nice to customers; the people's livelihood depended upon it. Repeat customers were the name of the game.

Corey resisted the urge to debate the pros and cons of niceness with Marco, though. One thing he knew, and that was you could never change what's in a man's heart. So there was no sense in even trying.

"Yo, I'ma 'bout ta call up our workers. Tell 'em ta be on point. We about to drop da bomb on da block," Marco revealed.

"Yo, call 'em up here. I wanna meet 'em," Corey said. "I gotta drill sum shit in they headz. Make sure we all on da same page."

* * *

About a half hour later, all Corey's workers began to arrive one at a time, Mikey, Ron-Ron, and Stevie. The boys ranged in age from thirteen to seventeen. No one out of the bunch was new to the drug game, this was a way of life to them. Corey was careful in selecting only those who were already involved with the game; he didn't want to corrupt anybody who wasn't already. He'd rather they have been turned on by someone else. He had sinned enough already without adding this to his list of bad deeds.

"Listen, all of us here are family. No, more like a team. Da reason I picked da word *team* iz because it means sumthin' very special ta me. It meanz, Together Everyone Achieves More. Dat'z sum real shit right there. If we all move as one, think as one, we all gonna prosper. We all gonna get money," Corey preached.

As he looked around the room, Corey saw the hunger in each boy's eyes. There was a desperate desire to make money, a drive that only comes from having the lack of necessities. They were hanging on his every word. They were beginning to buy into his sales pitch. Another thing Corey had working in his favor was that all these kids came from broken homes. They wanted to belong to something stable, like a team, crime family, or drug crew. Corey would be looked up to by them as a big brother or even father figure.

The meeting was held inside a tiny bedroom. The crew sat bunched together on a dingy mattress that lay on the floor. Numerous dirt stains were on the once off-white walls. Also on the walls were numerous posters of rappers, cut out of *Right On* magazine.

Corey continued, "No man iz an island. I can't do dis alone. There ain't no big I's and little U's on dis team. Everybody iz important. Everybody has a part ta play. None more or less important than the others. Da lights iz on. Da stage iz set. All we need iz fa everyone ta play their position.

"We on our grind," he said, meaning he was taking all the profits that were going to be made and putting them back into the pot. This was known on the street as flipping money. Corey promised his workers, "It'll get greater later." He talked them into waiting a few weeks, "to let the pot grow" before they got paid.

When they were alone, Marco gushed over Corey's communication skills.

"Yo, kid, you got game. Dem lil niggaz ate dat shit up!"

"Marco, I ain't got no game. Dem niggaz just know a real nigga when dey see one. Real rep real! Understand?"

* * *

Taking the road of least resistance, Corey, Marco, and their team of workers began to move their narcotics on the late night. This was when all the loose cannons, crackheads, stickup kids, lone drug dealers, and the police came out. Corey knew he didn't have the quantity of drugs to even begin to compete with Lord and his crew for control of the block. But if he played his cards right, it would only be a matter of time before he was moving "weight" on the block. His customers began to come in droves, since it was tough to get quality cocaine late at night. He was one of the few options that crack addicts had then, as customers "rolled the dice" and took their chances, buying drugs from whoever appeared to be a legitimate drug dealer. With Corey and company, they got good product, quality and quantity. Corey and company quickly became kings of the night. When other drug dealers abandoned the block, to party, to eat, to reap the fruits of their labor, they came out, their work was just beginning. With workmenlike precision, they sold crack. One was actually responsible for selling the crack cocaine, another was assigned to look out for the police and suspicious-looking characters. Yet another boy's job was to stash the money and drugs in his house.

Word spread that the "late-night crew" had it going on. Crack addicts from the surrounding areas began to frequent the block.

With the new influx of business, rivals began to spring up. But Corey and company beat back every challenger. They were just too well organized, too focused. They ran away everything and everybody that was bad for business. They had shoot-outs with stickup kids and chased away anyone selling fake drugs.

From Chavon's house Corey oversaw the entire drug operation. Chavon lived in a single-parent household and her mother was on crack. All Corey had to do was supply her habit and he had full run of the house. And that's just what he did.

* * *

Mrs. Dixon sat in her housecoat at the kitchen table sipping a steaming hot cup of tea while she read the daily newspaper. As she read the articles about drugs, guns, and murder, her thoughts shifted to her son Corey. Her mother's intuition told her that something was wrong with him. That he didn't work the night shift for a security firm, as he had claimed. Her instincts told her that her son was back dealing drugs again, and though she had no concrete evidence of that, she believed it in her heart.

Mrs. Dixon began to ponder her son's future and what troubles lay in wait for him. The two ever-present ones jumped out at her: imprisonment and death. She couldn't bear the thought of seeing her son, her baby, facing either.

Like any good parent with a troublesome child, she began to wonder where she had gone wrong. Was Corey raised right? Was he given the proper guidance? Could she and her late husband have done more? She wrestled with question after question in her head until she began to doubt herself as a nurturer, a provider, and a mother.

In the midst of her thoughts, she heard the sound of keys jingling and her locks unbolting. It was Corey, fresh from putting in a shift on the block. He was physically drained, but the ill-gotten gains in his pockets seemed to invigorate him.

"Ma, it'z me!" he called out.

His voice broke her out of her deep thoughts. "I'm sitting in the kitchen, Corey."

Corey walked over and kissed his mother. He couldn't help but notice by the expression on her face that something was wrong.

"Good morning, Ma. Somethin' wrong? Why you look so serious?"

Mrs. Dixon started to broach the subject of his illegal street activities, but decided against it. She knew her child too well. She knew that whenever Corey was confronted with something he couldn't explain, he'd lie. So instead of dealing with that nonsense, she decided to wait till she had more proof. She knew what was done in the dark must one day come to light.

"Nothing's wrong, Corey," she said. "I wuz just sitting reading the newspaper and it's so damn depressing. Who needs to go to the movies these days? You got killings, rape, and drug dealing. A lifetime full of drama for fifty cent. Sometimes I don't know what this world is coming to. We all going to hell in a handbasket. Listen, Son, you hungry?" She went over to the refrigerator and looked in. "I can make you something."

"Ma, I'm all right. I'll take some juice." He was too keyed up to eat. "Times have changed. New York City iz not South Carolina. Things happen up here. And it's gettin' bad everywhere. Not just here. Just dat there's more people here, so there's more crime. Dat's all! Besides dat, you ain't goin' ta hell. You too nice."

"Corey, niceness don't get you into heaven. Your faith and your deeds do. You can't think about living righteous, you have to live righteous. You have to live like the world is coming to an end tomorrow. On the day of judgment you shall be judged on your deeds. You better pray that your good deeds outweigh your bad. You ever heard the sayin' 'the road to hell is paved with good intentions'? Well, it's true." She handed him a glass of orange juice.

Corey understood her concern, though he thought it was misplaced. He wondered to himself, *Why did I even get her started?* Though he never expressed thoughts like this out loud, out of respect for his mother. Before he'd ever disrespect his mother, he hoped to die. Corey hated to see people be disrespectful to their mothers. He didn't care if his mother was a lying, conniving crackhead, he'd never disrespect her, because of the lone fact that she was the woman who'd birthed him.

"Ma, whut you tryin' ta say? Where dat come from? I

know I'm not as spiritual as you are. I'm not even close ta dat spiritual plane. But, Ma, whose to say I won't ever be? Dat's between God and me. I don't got time ta go ta church and pray right now. My time iz best spent tryin' ta feed myself."

"Son, you're wrong. Your time is best spent serving your God. Doing the things that are pleasing to him. You say you don't have time for God? When will you have time for God? When you do have time for God, will he have time for you? Boy, something got to give! You can't keep runnin' 'round here sinning like you ain't never gonna meet your maker."

"Ma, just because I did bad things, do you think that makes me a bad person?"

"No! Son, you did things out of ignorance. You didn't know any better. But now you older, you know better. One day your gonna be held accountable for your acts."

Corey wished he had kept his mouth closed. His mother sure knew how to get to him. Her words were more than words, they were food for thought. They left everlasting impressions on his mind.

"Corey, you know what? Out of all my children, my nieces and nephews, I thought you'd be the one who'd make it. After all, you had the best opportunity of them all. You had two working parents, plus you were the baby of the family. The baby always has it good. But you wasted your opportunities. Are you ever gonna live up to your potential? They say the worst thing in the world is wasted potential."

Corey was speechless. How could he respond to that? He let his mother talk on without interrupting her. It was obvious to him she had something on her mind. An old saying came to his mind, "Moms know best."

"Look, boy, your past is your past. You can't change that. You made a few mistakes, we all do. Some to a greater or lesser degree. But your life is by no means over. On the contrary, Corey, it's just beginning. Now is the time to move on. Don't make no excuses about how hard it is out there. It's hard for everybody. Many people have done more with less. You just got to give the right way a chance. Corey, don't come to my funeral in handcuffs." Corey sat up in his chair and looked her closely in the eyes. "I already told your brothers and sisters, if and when I die and you're in jail, don't tell you till after I'm buried. I don't want you there wit them sheriffs surrounding you looking over my casket, like you was at your father's."

Up until this point, he had never known that his incarceration was a source of pain and embarrassment for his mother. He had never known how ashamed she was to see him handcuffed, shackled, and escorted by the sheriff's department to his father's wake. Now he knew.

For days, weeks, and months after, Corey thought about their conversation. It sank into the inner crevices of his mind. But he continued doing what he was doing.

Chapter 24

Corey's drug operation was making money hand over fist. He kept his promise to his workers. He rewarded them handsomely. With their newfound riches, they purchased motorized dirt bikes, big gold chains, designer clothes, and sneakers. They were satisfied. They had never had it so good.

Corey rewarded himself by buying a brand-new four-door Acura Legend. He decided not to go the flashy route and put spoilers, aerodynamic kits, and rims on his car. He didn't want his car to look like a drug dealer's car. Nor did he want to depreciate the value of his automobile. It was bad enough that happened as soon as the car rolled off the lot.

His lieutenant, Marco, purchased a new black Mazda MPV van. He did the opposite of Corey. He equipped it with a loud-booming stereo system, tinted windows, and black BBS rims. He was making money for the first time in his life, and he wanted everyone to know it. His car screamed drug dealer and he didn't care.

In the meantime Marco and Corey decided to move to greener pastures, more profitable hours. They decided to expand their business hours to the day shift, while maintaining their late-night crew. They hired another team of daytime workers, luring them away from competitors by paying better wages. Corey took it even further, placing everyone on salary. He promised to share some of the profits with them if they reached their weekly quota.

Corey knew that the honeymoon was over though; now it was time to make his move.

* * *

"Yo, why iz dis money short? Where da fuck iz da rest of my paper?" Lord barked.

He had just got back in town. He and Homicide had been tricking with two chicks down in Virginia Beach. He didn't know about Corey's power move, which had cut into his profits.

"Yo, dat nigga Corey stopped our flow," a worker explained.

"Whut?" Homicide snapped.

"Whut da fuck you mean, he stopped my flow?" Lord added.

"Da nigga got boulders as big as ya shoulders. He got jumbos! His bottles iz bigger and fatter than ours. Crackheads iz runnin' ta dem niggas. They got all our customers."

"Oh, yeah?" Lord exclaimed. "How long dis been fuckin' goin' on? Huh? You fuckin' idiot!"

"Like a week or two," the workers replied weakly.

"See whut happens when you leave his dumb ass in charge?" Homicide asked. "Shit getz all fucked up! He can't even hold the fort down."

Lord fumed, he couldn't believe that Corey had the heart to step on his toes. This was serious now, Corey was taking food out of his mouth.

"Look, muthafucka!" Lord began. "You tell da rest of dem lil muthafuckas to get they ass ready ta do some work. Y'all niggas gonna get my paper right."

When the worker left to inform the others of Lord's comments, Lord and Homicide were free to talk amongst themselves.

"Yo, whut you want me ta do?" Homicide questioned. "I'll kill 'im. Just gimme da word and his ass iz out!"

"Nah, not yet. Why make da block all hot? Not now anyway! I'ma put him out of business. We gonna do dis my way. I'ma flood dis whole muthafuckin' block wit coke. He ain't gonna be able to eat no more."

Besides control of the crack trade on the block, something else was at stake here, pride. And when it was wounded, it could be a dangerous thing. Lord wasn't going to relinquish his stranglehold on the block, not without a fight.

* * *

Over the next few weeks, Corey and Lord waged a small-scale crack war, with each trying to outdo the other. First, Lord increased the size of his crack vials while keeping the prices the same. Smaller, less-organized drug dealers who didn't have the weight to compete were crippled.

In response to that move, Corey came up with the gimmick of selling two for ten dollars. This caught the crackheads' attention. They thought they were getting over or getting something for free. The move went so well that Corey had to hire more workers. He began putting out teams of three workers around the clock. And every hour on the hour, Marco would come by and collect the money. Corey understood that even though he was losing money over the long haul, he could make money by getting rid of his crack cocaine. His products began to turn over quickly.

Though Lord could match Corey in quantity, he couldn't match him in the quality department. Corey's crack cocaine was unmatched on the block. The crackheads were craving his product. Corey was the new king of the block.

Corey now had everything a drug dealer could want—money, power, and respect. He was making real money on the block and everything was better. The water was colder and the girls were easier. Yet, he still felt empty. He thought maybe it was because his good friend O wasn't there to share it with him. He was beginning to feel that it was time, time to take care of his real business and kill Lord. But before he could act on that, something happened.

* * *

"Yo, dis my customer, back da fuck up!" Ron-Ron yelled.

"Nigga, dis wuz my custy before he wuz yourz!" the boy shouted back.

"Nigga, nobody fuckin' wit dat trash y'all got. Ya work iz garbage! He don't want dat! Ask him."

"Yo, Harold, man, who you out here to see?" the boy demanded.

Harold was caught between a rock and a hard place; he hated being in the middle of this private tug-of-war. But a decision had to be made. Neither of the drug dealers was going anywhere till he got the word from the horse's mouth.

"Ron-Ron thing iz better than yourz," Harold admitted. "I gotta copdat thang from him. Sorry!"

"Whut?" the boy uttered before swinging at the man, striking him in the face.

Before long the two boys began to scuffle in the middle of the street. Quickly Ron-Ron overpowered the boy, sending him away defeated.

Around the corner, Homicide stood in front of the pizza shop when the boy walked up to him with a swollen eye.

"Yo, whut da fuck happened ta you, kid?" Homicide asked. "Who beat you down like dat?"

The kid was so mad, he wanted to see somebody really get hurt. So instead of telling the truth, he decided to tell a lie: "Da niggas jumped me around the corner."

"Who fuckin' jumped you? Who? Where they at?" Homicide fumed.

"Dem niggaz dat work for Corey!" he barked. "They jumped me over a custy!"

Quickly, Homicide walked over to his car, a money-green Mercedes-Benz 300E coupe, opened the glove compartment, and retrieved a small, gunmetal-colored .380 caliber semiautomatic. Tucking the gun into his waistband, he marched back around the corner with his worker in tow.

Normally he would not have handled the situation like this; he would have let the younger boys handle it amongst themselves. But since the situation involved Corey's crew, he wanted to send a message.

Corey's crew were going about their business, making drug sales. They didn't notice that their competition was easing back on the block. Until they were upon them.

"Point 'im out! Which one a dem did it?" Homicide asked. "Who had sumthin' ta do wit it?"

"Him, right there!" the boy shouted.

Instinctively, Homicide reached into his waistband and drew his gun. He began to fire.

Ron-Ron attempted to run, but it was too late. Homicide already had his gun trained on him. He squeezed the trigger.

The first shot caught Ron-Ron in the left shoulder blade. He ran toward a building. Wounded, he crashed against the door, still courageously trying to enter the building and get his gun. But it was not to be; Homicide caught up with him, put a gun to the back of his head, and squeezed the trigger.

Blood splattered against the door as Ron-Ron's lifeless body slumped to the ground. Homicide then turned his attention to the rest of Corey's workers, but they had disappeared. Homicide vanished around the corner, speeding away from the scene of the crime.

Keisha watched from her window in shock. She phoned Corey.

* * *

"Whut?" Corey shouted into the phone. "He's dead?"

"Yeah, I think so. I don't know how he could still be alive,"

Keisha cried. "Homicide started wildin' out. He hit him up in the doorway of da building."

"Word? Look, grab them guns and get in a cab ta my house. Now!"

Slamming down the phone, Corey quickly picked it back up and called Marco. He told him everything. Corey made clear what had to be done in no uncertain terms. Things had gone too far to turn back. Now Corey regretted not taking care of this problem, Lord and Homicide, sooner.

Chapter 25

Police presence was heavy on the block. Which meant business was bad for all parties involved. Everyone suffered, some more than others. All, if any, drugs were sold out of sight, away from the watchful eyes of the law.

Weeks had passed since the murder. The wait was killing Corey. He knew he had to take either Lord or Homicide off this earth, because the streets were watching and waiting for his response. It was as if the entire block were anticipating another murder. They were waiting to see who would die next.

The police were unable to come up with any leads. Many people weren't surprised, believing that in the black community, cops were as much the problem instead of the solution. With no intelligence to work with, they were forced to withdraw and focus on other heavy crime areas in the neighborhood.

Corey picked up the phone. It was Keisha. "Yo, dat nigga Homicide back out here! I just saw him and Lord talkin' to some bitches in front of da park."

"How long ago wuz dat? Huh?" Corey asked.

"A few minutes ago. I came upstairs and called you soon as I saw 'em."

"Aiight! Keep an eye on 'em! Lemme know if they go somewhere."

"You got dat! Just hurry up!"

After hanging up with Keisha, Corey placed a phone call to Marco. "Yo, they out there. Grab ya gun and meet me on da block."

"Aiight! Bet!" Marco replied.

* * *

Wearing black hoodies, Corey and Marco casually approached from two different directions, sneaking up on their intended victims, who were too preoccupied with a pair of pretty young girls to notice them. Before long Corey and Marco were within a few feet of them.

"I'm sayin' whut'z up with tonite? Y'all tryin' ta go ta Sammy's on City Island? Get sumthin' ta eat and whut not? Then, you know, we go swing an episode at da mo," Lord spoke sweetly.

Corey hadn't taken into account two innocent bystanders. This was just supposed to be a seek-and-destroy mission, point and shoot. But the two young girls had put a monkey wrench in his plans. He had to do something to remove them from his line of fire, but what?

Thinking quickly, Corey removed his nine-millimeter Glock semiautomatic from his groin area and held it high over his head.

"Ay, yo, Lord!" he called out before he fired a warning shot in the air.

The shot had the desired effect, causing the girls to scatter. But it also enabled Lord and Homicide to duck behind a car.

Simultaneously, Marco began letting off numerous shots from his military-issue .45-caliber automatic. Corey followed suit, letting off a barrage of bullets. Lord and Homicide were carrying guns too, and a vicious gunfight ensued. Bullets were flying everywhere. Corey could hear the bullets as they cut through the air and whizzed by his head.

Unbeknownst to the shooters, at the corner a pregnant woman began to cross the street. She was unsure of what all the crackling noises were. The Fourth of July was just a few days ago; she didn't know if the sounds were leftover firecrackers being detonated or what. She was getting into her car when a slug found its way into the back of her head, killing her instantly.

Pure pandemonium broke out on the block as everyone in the vicinity ran for cover. Marco had expended all his ammunition, and by the time he realized it, he was an open target. Horror registered across his face as Homicide popped up from a crouching position and began unloading his clip into his face. Corey watched as Marco dropped dead onto the concrete. In response, Corey turned his pistol on Homicide, spraying him with bullets in his side. The slugs did internal damage, wreaking havoc on Homicide's large intestine, liver, and kidney. All the while he was shooting, Corey kept thinking to himself, *Is this how I'm gonna die? Is this how I'm gonna go out? Just like my man Omar!*

"God help me!" Homicide begged as he lay curled up in a fetal position on the ground. "Yo, I'm fucked-up, kid. I don't know if I'ma make it."

Hiding behind the car, Lord glanced over at his fallen comrade and saw that his life was indeed slipping from his body; he lay in a pool of blood. Lord realized there was nothing he could do for him. His energy was best spent trying to save his own life. He looked away as Homicide writhed in pain.

For a brief moment, Corey and Lord exchanged shots at each other. Then in the distance they heard the faint wails of a police siren. That signaled the momentary end of this war. Corey turned and ran through the project maze, while Lord jumped in his car and sped off in the opposite direction.

* * *

When the smoke cleared, the block was abuzz with gossip, about who'd seen what and who'd done what. Local politicians began to place pressure on the police department to bring the perpetrators to justice. Arrest warrants were issued for Lord and Corey.

The warrant squad raided both their mothers' homes, searching for them. They were on the city's Most Wanted list.

Out in Brooklyn, Corey stayed in one fleabag motel after another. One day after walking around the corner to the store, he came back and noticed a patrol car parked alongside his car, in the hotel parking lot. One officer appeared to be peering through Corey's dark-tinted windows trying to look inside, while the other talked to the motel clerk. Corey took notice of them before they saw him and kept on going. But for both him and Lord, the nooses around their necks were tightening, the walls were closing in.

* * *

Corey's fugitive status was wearing on his soul. He was living out of the trunk of his car like a vagabond. Life on the run wasn't agreeing with him. He hadn't spoken to any member of his family for fear their phones might be tapped by the police. Corey didn't want to go back to prison. He knew he would be there for a long time, possibly life. With all the media attention surrounding the case, there was a good likelihood of just that.

Corey spent his days and nights in and out of various seedy motels. Chavon was often with him and vowed to stay with him no matter what. Her presence was a welcomed relief from the madness currently surrounding him. The murder of an innocent pregnant woman weighed on his mind deeply. The cops raiding his mother's house only added to his burden and distress.

Lying naked in the bed of a motel room in Queens, Corey and Chavon listened to each other's heartbeat.

"Corey, I know dis iz a bad time ta ask dis, but whut you gonna do? Da police iz lookin' fa you. You can't keep livin' like dis," she announced.

"Think I don't know? You don't gotta remind me," he said sharply. "I'ma 'bout ta go down South, move down there. Come back and get a good-paid lawyer. I think I can beat dis case. I know my bullet ain't the one dat killed dat pregnant lady. And I don't think Lord will tell on me fa killin' his man. I don't know fa sure though."

Corey stared off into space as he contemplated what he had just said. He thought to himself, *If only things were that simple.* He knew that even with a good lawyer the legal system was unpredictable.

"Before I do all dat," he continued, "I got some unfinished business to take care of wit Lord. Dat nigga gotta die! He done too much dirt to live."

"You lookin' fa Lord?" Chavon questioned.

"Yeah, you muthafuckin' right!" Corey snapped. "Why?"

"I know where he be! He gotta baby wit dis girl I know. She live right in back of Eastchester projects."

"Word? Where? Why you ain't neva tell me dis shit before?"

"You neva asked!"

* * *

Lord woke up to the sound of his car alarm going berserk for the second time. Looking out of his child's mother's bedroom window, he stared at his car. Reluctantly, he decided to go outside to see who or what was setting it off. Lord left the house dressed only in a white tank top and basketball shorts, car remote in hand.

From a few feet away, Corey watched closely, hidden in the shadows, behind a parked car.

As soon as Lord was near, he sprang from his hiding space.

"Whut'z up now, nigga?" Corey said strongly as he approached Lord, gun in hand. "Let'z see how tough you are now. You a killer, right? You a killer who 'bout ta get killed!"

Boooooommmmm! The gun roared as the slug hit Lord in the stomach, sending him to the ground. Pain raced through his body, a burning sensation like he had never felt before.

"Don't kill me! Puhleazzze don't!" he begged like a coward.

Lord had mercilessly sent many men to their death. Now that he was knocking on death's door, he wanted a reprieve. But Corey would have none of it.

As Corey stood over him, he paused for a moment. He loved the look of fear in Lord's eye. He thought it poetic justice. What comes around, goes around.

Suddenly, Corey heard a scream. Lord's girlfriend yelled out the window, "Get away from him. Da police are on their way."

Coolly, Corey ignored her and went about finishing the job he'd started.

"Nigga, you gotta second ta make peace wit your maker. 'Cauze you 'bout ta meet him," Corey snapped.

"Yo, Core, I known you most ya life. Don't do dis, kid!" Lord pleaded.

Corey fired back, "Yeah, you knew Omar too. Dat ain't stop you from killin' him, muthafucka."

"I ain't kill Omar!" Lord cried. "It wuzn't me!"

Those were his last words, as the roar from the gun blast drowned him out. Corey pumped shot after shot into Lord's face and chest, killing him, while his child's mother looked on in horror. For good measure Corey spit on the corpse.

An unmarked police car, responding to the call, arrived on the scene. The officers exited the unmarked car, guns drawn. "Police! Drop your weapon!"

Corey knew he wasn't going back to prison. He couldn't stand to do all that time. This time the resolution would be different. He spun around, clutching his gun, pointing it in the direction of the police officers. They began firing instantly, thinking that they were going to be shot. Corey wasn't going to shoot them though. He knew what he was doing. Five gunshots riddled Corey's body. The police did him a favor.

* * *

Mrs. Dixon's phone rang incessantly; she looked up at the clock and wondered who could be calling at this hour. Her mother's intuition told her this was bad news.

"Is this the Dixon residence?" a formal-speaking man asked.

"Yes, it is. Who may I ask is calling?"

"Are you Mrs. Dixon? Corey Dixon's mother?"

Her heart began to pound at the mere mention of her son's name. She wondered what he had done now.

"Yes, sir, that is me. Now, would you please tell me who you are?"

"This is Detective James Bradley from the homicide divison. Your son, your son has been shot and killed tonight. We need someone in the immediate family to identify the body."

Mrs. Dixon dropped the phone.

* * *

Doc was standing in the middle of the grass at Elmira prison, conversing with another younger inmate, when he looked up and noticed Tate headed in his direction. *What the hell is he coming over here for?* he thought.

When Tate reached him, he went into his back pocket and produced a newspaper, then handed it over.

"You haven't heard?" Tate asked.

"Whut you talkin' about? Heard about whut?" Doc responded.

"Read it!" Tate insisted.

Doc opened the paper; his eyes were quickly drawn to the highlighted article. "Two Bx Men Dead."

> Responding to an emergency call, two Bronx detectives arrived on the scene allegedly just in time to see suspect Corey Dixon firing a fatal shot into victim Lord Freeman. The alleged suspect turned, pointing his weapon at the detectives, who, fearing for their lives, responded with deadly force. Numerous shots were fired, five striking the alleged suspect, killing him on the scene.

Doc shook his head in disbelief. He felt a tiny tinge of guilt. He started to say something but Tate just walked away. He had nothing more to say.

* * *

Game Over

Epilogue

"Truth, justice, and the American way only work for Superman. They don't work for the black man." I don't know where I've read that or heard it, but from my experiences with the judicial system, it appears to be true. Personally I can't say I have been railroaded by the system. I was never mad about being in jail, because I did whatever it was they said I did. I was mad I was caught. But if you look at the figures (they say numbers don't lie), it's evident that something is very wrong with a picture that shows so many young black men in jail, that shows so many violent scenes—such as the one between Lord and Corey—taking place in the black community. Why is that?

African Americans make up 12 percent of the population of the United States, but over 50 percent of its prison population. Now you have to ask yourself, how can that be? Do you really think that African Americans commit more crimes than the other races? I don't. How can so few do so much?

Before you go there and say, "He's playing the race

card"—I'm not. I'm just calling it the way I've seen it. I've been in prisons and witnessed the warehousing of inmates. Due to budget cuts and policy changes, I've seen rehabilitative programs canceled. I've seen illiterate men sign plea agreements for life imprisonment. I've seen all kinds of travesties and miscarriages of justice, committed in the name of the law.

The legal system, particularly the corrections department, is the biggest-growing industry in America. Every year some politician bases his or her campaign on crime. And those engaging in this "get tough on crime" campaign, those playing on the public's fear, usually win.

I say to you, something is not right in the halls of justice. But you don't have to take my word for it, do your own research. All I know is, numbers tell the story, you do the math.

COMING SOON . . .

B-More Careful 2: The Saga Continues
Code of the Streets